I WAS ONL

"HH&H gives a s........................who have been there ten years," I told the detective. "Fred had one, and he always wore it. But he didn't have it on him when I saw him dead."

"We know about the ring," Greenhouse said. There went my great contribution toward solving the mystery. But I pushed on.

"I'll bet you anything that ring has something to do with the killing," I said. I wanted the murder relegated to the "Finished and Over With" file.

"I wouldn't say that if I were you," he said.

"Why? Aren't you going to look for it?"

"We have found it." His voice was flat, no expression. The sound of it made me look at him closely. He did not have a happy face.

"What is it?" I asked.

"Fred Critelli's signet ring was found hidden in a Kleenex box, in the second drawer on the lefthand side of a desk. Your desk."

A SIMONA GRIFFO MYSTERY

THE TROUBLE WITH A SMALL RAISE
TRELLA CRESPI

ZEBRA BOOKS
KENSINGTON PUBLISHING CORP.

In Memory of Paul

This book is a work of fiction. Names, characters, places and incidents are either the product of the author's imagination or are used fictitiously. Any resemblance to actual events, locales or persons, living or dead, is entirely coincidental.

ZEBRA BOOKS

are published by

Kensington Publishing Corp.
475 Park Avenue South
New York, NY 10016

Copyright © 1991 by Camilla Trinchieri

First printing: January 1991

Printed in the United States of America

Cast of Characters
in order of appearance

Simona Griffo	Italian art buyer at HH&H, and narrator of this story.
Luis Mendoza	Hispanic concierge, who does more than guard the entrance.
Giovanna Esposito	Another import from Italy. She works at HH&H as cook to an elite few.
Frederick Critelli	Creative Director and partner at HH&H. His charm is his strongest asset and most dangerous liability.
Jenny Fenton	Fred's small and bouncy secretary, who thinks a cloud automatically comes with a silver lining.
Mattie Washington	A big woman in charge of the mailroom and the receptionist's desk, whose heart gets her into trouble.
Geoffrey Price	In-house illustrator and good friend of Simona's.
Bertrand Monroe	Number One Art Director with special talents that clash directly with Fred's.
Harold Harland	Founder of HH&H, who loves to travel to faraway places.
'Moneybags' Heffer	The second H of HH&H and dour guardian of the agency coffers.

Rafael Garcia	Muscular detective with the 13th precinct who turns out to be very helpful.
Stanley Greenhouse	Garcia's crime-solving partner. There's something about his eyes that gets to Simona.
Evelyn Dietz	Traffic Coordinator, who likes to sneeze away her problems.
Dana Lehrman	Number Two Art Director, whose loud voice is often heard, but not often appreciated.
Ann Lester	Efficient Account Supervisor of Janick, Inc., who loves to cover her ex-model's body with American designer clothes and international perfumes.
Wally Burgh	Copywriter for the Janick account, born and raised in Brooklyn.
Jean Janick	Elegant owner of Janick, Inc., a cosmetic firm trying to compete with the giants.
Julia Monsanto	Vague head of the TV department. She knows Fred from way back when.
Paul Langston	Handsome photographer, who has trouble fitting into the picture.
Ellen	A beautiful young woman kept secret by her father, who is the answer to Simona's prayers.
Scriba	The Janick, Inc. photographer, who thinks he's the Fellini of print.
Johnny	Scriba's agent and fastidious factotum.
Mrs. Edwin Monroe	Bertrand's mother and formidable Connecticut dowager, formerly of Boston.

Plus an assortment of models, male and female and related entourage.

Chapter One

It wasn't going to be the usual manic Monday some-one on the radio was singing about. It was going to be much worse. I had finally decided I was going to face Fred in person. My notes, even letters, got me nowhere with him. I had flirted, cajoled, pleaded, threatened, but my boss remained elusive. He had even had the gall to apologize to me when I cornered him by the coffee machine, and I stupidly said I understood, I realized he was a very busy man with important decisions to make. Only afterward, as I stared at my bland decaffeinated coffee turning cold, did I realize what I had done. One gallant apology and I was tripping over myself to please him. Admittedly a little dumb, but it wasn't all my fault. The man had a way about him. The first time I met Fred, at my job interview, his stern, strong-jawed face stared at me just long enough to completely unsettle my stomach. Then he came toward me, wrapped one arm lightly around my shoulders and walked me to the long window that covered an entire wall. Before us was a startingly bright January day and the southern Manhattan skyline.

"It's a very jagged city," Fred said quietly. "Very different from your soft Roman skyline." He turned toward me, the stern look beginning to wilt in the sunlight. "Are you sure you want to live here?"

"Yes," I answered.

After a moment of silence, he let go of my shoulders

and reached for both my hands. "Then welcome to HH&H Advertising." And Fred smiled, a smile that covered his broad face with genuine happiness, a smile that included me. For the first time since I had come to New York, I felt welcome; I felt someone cared. That's the knack he had, to spotlight you just long enough to make you feel the warmth and win you over. It didn't end with that first meeting. At odd moments, when I least expected it, he'd repeat the performance: a touch on the shoulder as he hurried by me in the corridor, his tall frame filling the opening to my office just long enough to ask, "Are you happy in New York, Simona?", never waiting for an answer; a chance meeting in the elevator with Fred saying, "I wonder about you sometimes," just as the elevator door opened to let him escape.

My loneliness fed on those moments, but eighteen months had passed since Fred Critelli, creative director of HH&H Advertising, Inc., had hired me so abruptly as art buyer at starvation wages, and I could no longer wait for a raise. I simply wasn't making a New York living. Fred came to work very early on Mondays, "to start the week with the right attitude," he liked to say, and I was starting with the right attitude too. That morning I was going to corner him.

I got to the office at eight o'clock. That's very early for the creative department of an advertising agency, and Luis, the concierge, a tall Latino sporting what he considers a very sexy mustache, greeted me with sleepy eyes and raised eyebrows.

"Ehi, what happened? He kick you out of bed?" Luis did a small, sleek sideways tango step to let me pass. Barely. "Now, if it was me . . ."

I interrupted him with a deaf smile and a brisk "good morning" and walked by quickly.

The elevator sighed to a stop on the seventeenth floor, quivered slightly, and then reluctantly opened its doors. The only sound that greeted me was the low hum of the air-conditioning system. It was strangely cold for a Monday morning, and I hugged myself for warmth and courage.

I stood perfectly still, listening. No one was about. I had come at the right time; Fred would be alone. Slowly I started to work my way around the modular maze of cubicles that separated me from his office, and just as slowly relived the scene that I had imagined throughout the night:

As usual Fred would be sipping his morning espresso in his palatial corner office at the far end of the floor. I approach the wide door, flung open for all to know that the monarch is in residence. His carpet is soft and thick as I step into his domain, and I resist the urge to take my heels off. The breathtaking view he showed me that first time is still there, the same except for the July sun hidden behind clouds. He is sitting behind his kidney-shaped, ebony desk with the Twin Towers of the World Trade Center directly behind him, somehow confirming his power. I haven't rehearsed a speech. The sight of Fred's smile would make me forget everything, so I'm going to "wing it," more or less. I see myself sitting down, pretending assurance, not waiting for his invitation. I'm going to play WOMAN. Not Sophia Loren, more Catherine Deneuve.

Crossing my legs discreetly, I simply state that I'm dying of starvation. I don't look at his summer-sky blue eyes. I know I couldn't do that without my voice softening into mush. I don't know if I'm hoping for a raise or for him to kiss me.

The daydream vanished when I saw Fred's closed door. That was not part of the plan. That door was supposed to be open, making it easy for me to enter Fred's lair. I began trembling, whether from the air conditioner or the disappointment, I don't know. I cursed my "genteel" Italian upbringing, an upbringing that taught me a man would take care of me for the rest of my life, that money matters do not concern a lady, that a woman's life was easy. "Liars!" I wanted to scream at that door. I took a deep breath instead and let reason settle in my lungs.

9

Oh, God, at least let him be there. I'll never have the courage to do this again.

I knocked and waited. No answer. I knocked louder. Nothing. Grabbing the door handle, I started to turn it and then stopped. Barging in rudely was certainly not going to get me a raise. I listened, trying to catch any sound, the rustle of paper, the scratch of a pen. Nothing. No raise for me that morning, no blue eyes, just frustration and a tremendous sense of defeat. How did Fred always manage to sidestep me and where was he anyway? His secretary's desk stood just a few feet away from his door, right in front of me. I looked at Jenny's calendar open to that day. A doctor's name was neatly printed next to the 8:30 A.M. slot. The mystery was solved; my boss had decided to get an update on his health the very morning I was going to badger him for a raise. How very clever of him.

Forlorn, I walked to the opposite corner of the floor for some coffee. Next to the coffee machine stood a little refrigerator which held our daily allotment of one quart of milk. There was room for little else. Obviously, the higher powers felt they paid us so handsomely we could afford to eat out every day. There was no milk in the "ice bucket," as someone had lovingly christened the refrigerator, which didn't help my mood very much. Giovanna, a fellow Italian immigrant and the HH&H cook, brought the milk up every morning along with coffee freshly brewed for Fred in the downstairs kitchen. Even for milk I have to wait for His Highness, I thought as I slammed the refrigerator door. The singer on the radio had definitely got it all wrong. Instead of manic, that Monday was turning out to be plain depressive.

Back in my little cubicle, I started sorting through the files on my desk to see what task I was going to tackle first. None of the work appealed to me, so I quickly decided that the milk situation didn't matter: I'd drink coffee and smoke cigarettes for the first half hour or at least until someone sociable walked by to tell me all about his or her weekend.

A woman shrieked. A long, shattering shriek that sent me running back toward the far end of the office, stumbling in my high heels and gasping in fear. Fred's door was wide open and Giovanna, trembling, stood on the threshold. An empty tray dangled from one of her hands; cups and silver coffeepot had fallen to the floor. Coffee slowly trickled into the thick carpet in a black velvety ribbon, but the cups hadn't shattered. It's the only detail I noticed at first — those fragile china cups sitting up like proud survivors.

Giovanna's shriek turned into a howl, a low, hollow sound of horror that forced me to look beyond her shoulder. Fred was in the room. He had been there all the time, in front of the window where he stood that first time holding my shoulder, pointing to the jagged New York skyline. Except he wasn't standing that Monday morning. Fred lay motionless on the floor, his arm stretched out toward us, as if waving good-bye. He looked quite dead. What made me sure were his eyes, those summer-sky blue eyes I had dreamt about the night before. The blue had turned stone gray. Fred had slipped away once again. Forever.

I don't know how long Giovanna and I stood there looking at him. She wailed her Sicilian mourning, I concentrated on the coffee cups, thinking only how lucky that they hadn't broken. Anything not to think of Fred lying there, as if reaching out for the help. At some point I blanked out.

When I came to, I was still with Giovanna, both of us sitting in a small room. Tall, comforting Mattie, a black woman who ran the mail room and the receptionist's desk, was handing us each a glass of brandy and urging us to drink. Giovanna sat on a cot, and I sat, rigid, in a metal folding chair, the only other seating accommodation in the room. A big white medicine chest hung above a small sink.

"What am I doing in the first aid room?" I asked Mat-

11

tie. "There's nothing wrong with me."

"You better drink that stuff. You're as white as a sheet, and I don't want you fainting on me again."

Dead. Fred was dead. "Why?" I wanted to scream. "How?"

Mattie towered over me, pushing the glass to my mouth. I drank, and my insides exploded. "See, the color's back," she said, very happy with herself. "Now this lady here," she pointed to a very unsteady Giovanna, "has got God's Walkman stuck in her ear and from the smile on her face, it sure isn't playin' a funeral march." Mattie took the glass away from her and eased her down on the cot. "I guess three drinks are about her limit."

"Where did you get this wonderful brandy?" I wanted to talk, to chitchat about stupid things, ordinary everyday things. I didn't want to think about Fred's eyes and what they had become.

"I just went up to the nineteenth floor and got it from Mr. Harland's office. He's got tons of this stuff. Why let it go to waste? He's never around to drink it."

"How clever of you," I said. "How did you know it was there?" Mattie's territory was down on the first floor. Eighteen floors separated her from the penthouse.

"Honey, Mattie can smell liquor from here to Coney Island. I got myself a great sense of smell and my eyesight's even better. Don't let these thick glasses fool you." She must have seen the doubt on my face. "My hearin' ain't so bad either. And with all these three things put together, I'm tellin' you he got what he deserved. I heard and I saw what he was up to, and I could smell he was rotten all the way down here. God does punish the wicked. I always said He did and He does. So don't go askin' yourself what killed him." The woman could read minds. "Mattie can tell you that. God's will, that's what it was. That's what got him. God's will." And with that Mattie poured a hefty dose of brandy in my glass and drank it down in one gulp.

"I don't know what you are talking about, and I do think you should take that bottle back. Giovanna and I won't need it anymore." Giovanna was fast asleep on her back, snoring lightly, and I was suddenly feeling very righteous. "And unless you intend to celebrate, I don't think you need it either."

"Honey," Mattie said, her voice soft as butter on a pancake, "with the help of God I do my own decidin' on what I need or don't need. No use gettin' huffed up about it 'cause you know exactly what I am talking about. That man got you hooked too. I could tell. The way you dressed up so pretty to go to the office. And when he was out of town for a couple of days, there you were lookin' just like any tired, overworked woman. I just hope you had enough sense not to get too near him."

I felt myself turning red, and tears started to smart my eyes. "It wasn't sense that kept me away. He was just too busy elsewhere." With that confession, rare for me, I walked out and took the elevator back to my floor.

As I arrived, I saw the paramedics taking Fred away in the service elevator, and I thought how he wouldn't have liked that. He wasn't going out in style and style had always been so important to him. He had made style his whole life, from the clothes he wore to the ads he had created and supervised. Style, flair, and always a touch of the enigmatic in his person and his ads. Well, I thought, he may not have left in style, but the enigmatic touch was still there. Dying without any warning; his outstretched arm seemingly calling for help; the palm of his hand open like a beggar's. If only I had got to work earlier or had opened the door, maybe, just maybe . . .

I went back to my office, avoiding the crowd of employees that was now huddled outside of Fred's closed door trying to get answers from two policemen standing guard. Another policeman followed me, asking "routine questions" as he put it. He seemed strangely afraid I would get hysterical. I was in perfect control.

Everything quieted down after a while. I don't know how long it took. I just sat and smoked. The phones had stopped ringing, and the floor was eerily silent. Mattie, forever efficient, had probably directed all calls to reception where her army of girls would keep the demands of the outside world at bay. As logical as that explanation was, I couldn't help thinking that the phones had stopped ringing because Fred had stopped breathing. The door to his office was closed, the King of the Creative Department was gone, and we were surrounded by silence. He had died. July 14th. Bastille Day. "Death to the aristocracy," they had cried as they stormed the walls of that prison. "Long live the people." I burst into tears.

I was sent home in a taxi like a sick schoolgirl, and I rode the ten blocks to Greenwich Village with eyes and ears closed to the restless city. Once inside my building on Ninth Street it was quiet, but I still faced four flights of steep, unlit stairs before reaching my studio apartment. Taking my shoes off, I started the climb like a zombie returning to its tomb.

Silently in my bare feet, I reached my door. I saw the splintered wood of the doorjamb and dropped my keys on the bare floor. That's when he heard me. My door was jerked open before I got a chance to touch it and a man loomed in front of me for an instant before pushing me against the wall. I threw my arms up to protect my face and leather brushed against my open palms. He ran past, in too much of a hurry to harm me, and hurtled down the narrow stairs. All I could really see in that dark tunnel were his high-top sneakers, so new they practically shone. Those white shoes flashed repeatedly in my head, like a strobe light gone berserk.

The front door slammed, followed by silence that brought a sense of safety. Slowly I turned my head toward the open door of my apartment and forced myself to look into the room. The place was a mess. The mattress of my loft bed had been overturned, the sheets thrown on the rungs of the bed's ladder; my clothes were strewn on the floor; my trunk was open and all its contents scattered; my letters had been opened; books searched. Still in a daze, I walked over to the bathroom and looked for my jewelry. It was gone, of course. I didn't have much, a few antique pins and earrings carefully wrapped in toilet paper and stuffed in my curler bag. He hadn't touched the fake stuff. With the apartment door still open behind me, I looked down at the floor covered with the material symbols of my life. It sure wasn't much, I remember thinking. I didn't turn around.

I sat on the floor and fingered the scattered sheets of my letters. Was it anger that had led him to trash the room? Was my jewelry not going to buy enough crack, the rejected black and white TV not salable? Maybe he didn't believe I possessed so little, had gone through my books and letters looking for hidden cash to feed his habit. Well, he hadn't found money or secrets, just memories. That's what made me turn around—the thought of my past. I looked toward the door and my heart almost stopped.

The first thing I had done when I moved into that studio apartment was to cover the wall surrounding my door with blown-up photographs of Rome. I cherished those photographs taken from the terrace of my old apartment much more than jewelry or pretty clothes. They were my windows with a view; the Tiber, escorted by the long rows of sycamore trees above each bank, meandered toward the Mediterranean; the cupola of St. Peter's commanded attention in the background; friends sat around a table on the terrace with mounds of pasta and liters of wine waiting to be downed. The four seasons were represented in those photographs: from the messy clutter of lobed sycamore leaves obliterating everything except the summer sky to the uninterrupted view of the river in winter. One photograph showed a rare Roman snowfall with branches drooping or broken by the unexpected weight.

That Monday in July, my heart almost stopped for the second time because the thief hadn't liked my photo-

15

graphs. He had sprayed them with black slashes of hate; the wall looked like a Seventh Avenue subway car. I turned toward the destruction and slow, uncomprehending tears wet my cheeks. "Why?" I asked out loud. "Why did he have to take this away from me? I have nothing left." In that moment of total desolation, I wanted everything back, my jewelry, my photographs, my large Roman apartment, my crazy, wonderful job dubbing films, the man I had fallen in love with and married, the best friend I had lost to him. And I wanted Fred back because he, too, had become part of that past.

A police siren in a nearby street screeched to wake me up and face the facts. Keeping the apartment door closed with a chair, I took the photographs down one by one. I thought of calling the police to report the theft but then, *"Basta. Basta, basta basta,"* I repeated. Enough was enough was enough. I didn't want to deal with it. I was just going to wipe it away; maybe spray the whole memory a blinding black, as the thief had done. Besides, the city was too big and busy to worry about me. Still barefoot, I took the photographs downstairs to join the rest of the garbage of the building. When I came back up, I hung up my clothes, changed the sheets on the bed, put away my books, placed my letters back in their envelopes and into the trunk, then got out the Ajax can and scrubbed every crevice and corner of that twelve-by-fourteen-foot apartment to get rid of the bastard's presence. Except for the wall. I didn't touch the black sprayed lines that had spilled beyond the photographs. Nor did I throw out the empty Krylon spray can he had left behind.

Chapter Two

"How are you feeling?"

I looked up from my desk as Gregory handed me a cup of espresso. I wanted to hug him. Actually I always want to hug Gregory, not just that Wednesday, my first day back at work, because he is one of the kindest, gentlest men I have ever met. He has transparent blue eyes, a baby's rosy complexion, and hair so fair you can't see any beard growing. It's thinning and turning gray, but he still looks like a child to me. When his mouth breaks into a shy smile, he awakens any woman's mother-instinct. He never seems to stop eating but, infuriatingly, Gregory stays thin and taut, a small man with the body of a jockey. He always brings some fabulous piece of cake to the office or some paté that he's made the night before. We both love to cook and we often sit in my office munching and exchanging recipes. Whenever he has time in the morning, Gregory makes me espresso with the little machine he has stored behind all the Magic Markers on his long desk. Gregory is the in-house illustrator. The art directors come up with the idea for the ad, and then they bring it to Gregory and he draws it up so the client can see what we are talking about. The entire creative department depends on his wonderful talent. I depend on his friendship.

"Thanks, Gregory, I'm all right," I lied, discovering that I couldn't bring myself to talk about what had happened in my apartment. The proffered coffee smelled wonderful and I drank it down in one gulp. There wasn't much of it to begin with, which is just as well since the strength of it bores a hole through your stomach.

"What did Fred die of?" I asked through the protective haze of a freshly lit cigarette.

"Let me get you another cup of coffee." Gregory offered. I shook my head. "How about some chocolate mousse cake? I made it last night. You'll love it."

"How did Fred die?" I demanded, almost screaming.

Gregory gulped in my smoke-filled air, straightened himself up and announced, "Mr. Harland has called a meeting of the entire staff in thirty minutes. For once he's around when he's needed."

Mr. Harland is the founder, chairman, and the first H of HH&H Advertising. Usually we see very little of him because he spends most of his time enticing foreign companies and governments to use HH&H as their ad agency in the New World.

"Some kind of memorial service, I suppose," I said, inhaling air and smoke deeply. "That's to be expected, although I don't think I'm quite ready for it."

Gregory just looked at me. Nothing showed behind his transparent eyes.

"You still haven't told me what Fred died of," I said. "What was it? Stroke, heart attack, cerebral hemorrhage?"

"I think Mr. Harland wants to be the one to tell us." Gregory stood up and removed the empty coffee cup from my desk. "I'll save you a seat downstairs in the conference room."

That's Gregory. Always kind.

"The medical examiner has determined that Fred Critelli died of cyanide poisoning."

The whole room gasped. I reached for Gregory's hand, next to me. It was as cold as mine.

"It is with deep regret that I say this," Mr. Harland continued, raising his voice to quiet the crowded confer-

18

ence room. His face, designed in sleek lines, had no un-
even edges. All feeling had been canceled long ago by
some magical eraser. I envied him that.

"HH&H has suffered a great loss. As you all know,
Fred has guided the creative talents of this agency for the
past eleven years."

Someone in back of me started crying softly.

"I realize the horror of his death, but unfortunately I
have spoken the truth. I wish it were not so." Mr.
Harland paused and looked at his captive audience. His
hair, white and smooth as mother of pearl, glistened
under the lights.

"The police believe the cyanide had been placed in
some capsules . . ." His hands went up, palms open to
fend off any questions. "There is no need to worry. All
medicines in the building have been confiscated, and no
traces of cyanide have been found." An open palm, like
Fred's as he lay dead. Why did that palm bother me so
much?

"We do not know exactly how his death came about,
but the police do not believe . . ." Mr. Harland was interrupted by Bertrand Monroe's entrance. They smiled
at each other in greeting. Bertrand, the number one art
director of the agency, looked around the room noncha-
lantly, as if he were at a boring cocktail party. Someone
in the front row offered him a chair. Bertrand just shook
his head, waved to a few people across the room and
stood facing us, with his arms crossed, next to Mr.
Harland and the second H of HH&H, "Moneybags"
Heffer. I realized I was seeing the new triumvirate
standing before me. The empty space left by Fred had
already been filled, even before his funeral.

"The police are being cautious in their statements
until they have investigated further," Mr. Harland continued, "but I assure you there is no need to panic."

"Could it have been suicide?" I found myself asking
out loud.

"Of course, suicide has not been ruled out." Mr.
Harland said sternly.

There was a collective sigh of relief, and people began to move in their chairs again. A solitary act of self-destruction was preferable to the idea of a possible murderer lurking in the corridors of the agency.

"However, the police will investigate further," Mr. Harland continued. "I have to ask for your full cooperation in this delicate investigation. The more we help the police, the more quickly they will leave us to continue our work. And now, I would like to introduce the detectives who will conduct the investigation."

The door opened on cue and two detectives stepped in slowly, proud of their importance. Their entrance seemed so well staged that I almost applauded. The only thing missing was a drum roll.

"Detective Rafael Garcia of the Thirteenth Precinct." Mr. Harland paused to let the man step into the limelight. He was a man of average height, five ten or so, with a heavy frame bulging in muscles. A walking Jack LaLanne ad. He nodded to us silently and quickly stepped back when Mr. Harland introduced the other partner, Stanley Greenhouse.

This one was attractive. Very attractive. It wasn't anything special, like a gorgeous profile or a great build. He wasn't even very tall. But he had a serious face with brown eyes that twinkled despite the solemn occasion. Above all, they were kind.

"As Mr. Harland said, there is no reason to panic." Greenhouse's voice was calm and confident, soothing us. "We have the situation in hand, but we would appreciate your cooperation. We will have many questions to ask you, we will probably try your patience. We must get to the bottom of this and we will."

Good, sound Hollywood lines. He certainly knew what he wanted. No messing around.

"We intend to discover all the circumstances that led to Fred Critelli's death."

My body suddenly felt hollowed out, like an empty coffin, and Fred Critelli's death stared at me in the face. There was no running away.

Gregory poked me on the shoulder. Mr. Harland was calling my name.

"Simona, I would like you to act as hostess to the detectives. Set up the interviews they want, see that everyone cooperates. If you have problems with anyone, please let me know." He started to leave.

"I don't know . . . my work . . ." I was trying to find words to object. Why me, what had I done? I hadn't even discovered the body.

"The only other person you will work for is Bertrand," Mr. Harland ordered. "It seems," he added doubtfully, "that he cannot do without you in his new perfume campaign. And now," he raised his hands in a papal salute, "it's time to go to work." He walked away with Bertrand and "Moneybags" a respectful step behind him.

Greenhouse stood by the door and watched impassively as everyone filed out . . . Detective Garcia stood immobile by his side, a friendly grin pasted to his face, reminding me of an overstuffed teddy bear. Some employees went up to the detectives and introduced themselves. They were mostly the account group who worked under Mr. Harland. They consider themselves the nononsense business people who carry the agency and don't get hysterics like the creative department. Mr. Harland had trained them well, and surely they believed they had nothing to fear from the police.

"Don't look so unhappy, Simona," Jenny whispered to me as I was about to leave.

"Oh, Jenny . . ." I started, then the sight of her face shut my throat. For the first time since I had known her, Fred's secretary had lost her buoyant look. To see Jenny's face creased with pain was hard to take on top of everything else.

"I'm so sorry this happened to you," Jenny said and bobbed her curls to add conviction to her words. She always seemed to think an apology would make the world one big happy place again. "It must have been awful for you and Giovanna."

At that moment, Greenhouse turned to look at me

and I stiffened with unexplained fear. Jenny noticed him, too, and whispered. "Don't worry. Everything is going to be all right." Her small hand patted my arm. "If you want to talk about it, remember you're a friend, and you can always count on me." With that she gave me a wink, turned on her three-inch heels and pranced off.

I definitely didn't want to talk about it to her or anyone else, but I was both glad and surprised she had called me a friend. I was going to need the support.

Chapter Three

I went back to my office and found Dana Lehrman, number two art director and general ball-breaker, standing in front of my desk.

"Oh, Simone," she wailed in her unmistakable, loud voice and getting my name wrong as usual. "You just have to help me." Her voice was swaddled in a bad summer cold which helped to mute some of her crystal-shattering tones, but I still could have done without her just then.

"What is it, Dana? Those two detectives are coming up here any moment."

"Well, if you're too busy to do your job . . ." She walked out of my office.

"No, Dana, come back," I yelled out. If I didn't cater to her greedy ego right away, she'd make me carry her damned heavy portfolios up and down the steps of hell. She came back to the room reluctantly. In a starkly white face, her black-lined eyes shone suspiciously.

"Sit down, Dana. Let me help you. If you explain carefully what you need, I might manage it." And I smiled like a perfect hypocrite.

"Yesterday I told a photographer I wanted him to shoot my next ad."

"The one for Merry Shirts with three women on a bridge waving at a man in a rowboat wearing a tuxedo?"

"Yes," she said and didn't continue. She just stared at me, the red smear of her mouth twitching slightly.

Either she didn't want to acknowledge her problem, or her cold had put her brain in parentheses.

"You told this photographer you wanted him . . .," I prodded gently.

"He said he'd love to do it, but I can't use him." She cried, the tears finally coming easily.

I reached out and touched her hand, blinking back my own tears. Tears always start a chain reaction in me, like yawning or vomiting.

At my touch, she hastily placed both her hands in her hair and pulled at her long, gelled, black bangs. "This morning I found out our client can't stand him. I don't know the reason, but I'm in no condition to handle this." She swallowed and produced an unpleasant face. "You have to understand that I'm running at a really high stress level right now."

"Why don't I call him up for you, and say the client has asked for a change in layout, and we'll let him know in the near future whether he would still be appropriate? Would you like that?"

"Yes, yes," Dana said, finally showing some enthusiasm. "His name is Paul Langston. Call him. Call him right away. No, no, wait 'till I'm back in my office. I don't want to talk to him. I have to go now. I can't tell you how busy I am. And now without Fred's help, you just don't know what it's like." She got up quickly as if the chair had pinched her. "Make sure you call him." she reminded me. I nearly threw the phone at her.

When she reached the doorway she hesitated. "Are those two men really coming up here?" I nodded.

She looked down the corridor, turning her head right and left as if she didn't know which way to go. "They're going to make me waste so much time."

"They may not want to see you at all," I reassured her.

For a moment she looked disappointed. "I sure hope not," she said, quickly recovering. "Besides, I don't know anything about Fred's life, and I wasn't even here on Friday." She quickly walked out on any more questions, and I watched her ample body sway in her Armani linen suit

24

with shell to match. No matter what Dana wore, she didn't make much of a fashion statement, I thought, but her ads were very successful. They were not targeted for the sophisticated Big City market. Her clients made clothes for the average working woman who lived in a medium-size city or even a small town, and who needed to dream, who didn't want to think that Romance was lost. Dana gave them the fairy tale. Soft blurred visions of long-haired blondes looking off into the distance waiting for HIM, or girls together having fun and giggling, also waiting for HIM. Sometimes she advertised a man's shirt and the male model would be the strong silent type, softly caressing the locks of his one and only love, her face conveniently off screen so that whoever looked at the ad could envision her own face belonging to that luxuriant hair being gently touched. All her ads were a variation on one theme — The Quest for Love — and the clients lapped it up because the ads worked. They sold the product.

I had just finished my phone call to the photographer when I heard Greenhouse's voice in the corridor. "Inhale through the nose, exhale through the mouth," I told myself. Relax.

"My son has a pet mouse —" He appeared in the doorway . . . "and the mouse goes in and out of a maze all day long. That's what these offices remind me of."

So he was married.

"Modular furniture, not inexpensive, but practical," said I in my nasal what's-it-to-me voice. "You can shift the walls around, you can take them with you, and you can hear what everybody else is doing."

"No privacy?"

"No privacy," I reiterated. Greenhouse smiled. I had obviously scored a point. Detective Garcia also looked pleased, but with some private thought of his own — perhaps that it was lunchtime. I, for one, was starved.

"Hello, hostess," Greenhouse said amiably and

25

stretched out his hand.

I took it. "Simona Griffo. I'm sorry about the hostess bit, but Mr. Harland likes to be fancy. He insists we call Luis a concierge instead of doorman."

"We'll play along for the moment. No sense putting unnecessary wrinkles in that thousand-dollar suit of his."

I lit a cigarette and looked at the detective in front of me. His eyes looked even kinder closeup. And fun. There was no reason to be nervous. Wipe out the memories. "All right, how can I help?" I asked.

"That's not good for you," Garcia's voice surprised me. It was very gentle and barely audible, as if he didn't use it much.

"I'm sorry," I replied, taking a last drag, "it's a European disability I'm having a hard time getting rid of." I put out the cigarette and blew the smoke above my head. Garcia watched it disperse across the ceiling, but he didn't look relieved.

"You really should turn up the air-conditioning in here," he said. "It gets rid of the smell." I put the ashtray in my drawer.

"Why gray?" asked Greenhouse, aiming those eyes at me.

"Gray what?"

"Everything in this place is gray. Walls, carpet, stainless steel ashtrays, steel chairs, an arrangement of pussy willows on the reception desk. That's a bit much, isn't it?"

"You should see the private bathrooms that Mr. Harland and Fred have. The toilet paper is gray. They bring it in from Milan. Not just plain gray. Light gray with a thin steel gray stripe. Quite a switch from the American tourist who packs twelve rolls of soft, domestic toilet paper before leaving this country."

Greenhouse laughed and the room suddenly seemed to explode with festive firecrackers. Married or not, I had to sit down. "What about Mr. Heffer?"

"Mr. Heffer is the vice president of finance," I answered staring at that happy mouth, "and he refuses to

26

have a private bathroom. He says it's undemocratic, which is his way of protesting the expense."

"I'm glad someone in this agency is doing something to protect the bottom line. So why gray?"

"It was Fred, Mr. Critelli, who wanted gray. He thought it was a cool, modern color, the color of power. So everything became gray."

Greenhouse picked up my notepad with the company logo in the corner. "HH&H, Harland, Heffer. Who's the third H?"

"Actually it was Fred," I answered. "He replaced the original third partner and creative director; a Mr. Higgins who died twelve years ago, I think."

Garcia edged toward the doorway. "Not too lucky being creative director in this place, huh?"

"Mr. Higgins died of a heart attack," I explained.

"Dead is dead," Garcia said evenly, then in a stronger, impatient voice, "Come on, Stan, we got to get going. We're just winding up an important case." He looked at me and snapped his fingers. "I bet you read about it in the papers." Snap again.

Greenhouse didn't let him go any further. "Before we go I want to talk to Mattie Washington. I was told she's in charge of the first aid room."

"That's right." I stood up and reached for my purse behind the filing cabinet. "Mattie's on the first floor. I'll take you down." I was anxious to get out and settle my head and stomach with food.

"We really appreciate the time you're taking," Greenhouse said. "Just a few minutes more."

"Lady, don't depend on it. Me, I don't trust the guy," Garcia said, then added with a wink, "and I'm not the only one." He took out a chocolate bar from his breast pocket and offered me half. Food was going to be our common denominator.

I gratefully took a bite. "Well, I hope at least his wife trusts him."

"I wouldn't depend on that either, lady. They're divorced."

27

"Raf, in the future I'll do the talking about my private life."

"Oh, shit, I'm sorry." Garcia was completely crestfallen, and I could have hugged the big bear.

Mattie was lucky enough to have gone out to lunch already. She was due back any minute and Greenhouse decided to wait. Garcia gave his colleague a dirty look and ambled down the corridor.

"Mr. Harland said you're Italian," Greenhouse said.

"That's right. I came to this country almost two years ago."

"You barely have an accent."

"Oh, I've lived here before," I gurgled, happy with all the attention. "I studied here and when my parents . . ." I was all set to recite my résumé but a loud whistle stopped me.

"Hey, Stan," Garcia called from the end of the corridor. He was very audible now. "You should see this."

Greenhouse and I quickly walked down to find Garcia staring at the agency kitchen as if he'd found another corpse. It was a large, expensively tiled room with all the amenities necessary to cook a full-fledged meal for thirty people.

"Whatta place! I could get used to this." Garcia began opening all the cabinets and peering inside. "Is this where you guys cook your lunch?"

"Oh, no." I had to laugh at the thought. "Giovanna is the only employee who's allowed to use the kitchen."

"What do you know about her?" Greenhouse asked.

"I'm sure she's around somewhere. Shall I get her for you?"

"She's not. She had to be sent home after this morning's meeting."

"Yeah, she threw up like she was pregnant or something. All over that neat gray carpet," Garcia added with gusto.

I shut my stomach up tight.

"She's Italian, like I am. Fred brought her over about eight years ago. She's worked at HH&H ever since. She takes care of the meals for Mr. Harland and Fred. They often lunch in the conference room. Once or twice a month we have an important luncheon, either for a client and his management staff or for prospective clients, but that usually involves too many guests for Giovanna to handle alone, so Jenny calls in some caterers. Giovanna is also in charge of Mr. Harland's and Fred's breakfast. That's why she found him."

"And Mr. Heffer doesn't get any because it's undemocratic," Greenhouse said. He was catching on.

Garcia stuck his head in the refrigerator.

"Are you looking for something?" I asked him. Was the kitchen harboring mysterious clues?

"Naw, I love kitchens. I love to cook."

I knew food was going to make us friends. "I love to cook too," I said, my voice betraying my enthusiasm.

"That's great, lady."

"Please call me Simona."

"Good name. Sounds Spanish." Then getting back to our favorite subject, "I'm the best paella maker in the five boroughs. What about you?"

"Oh, anything Italian, really. A lot of pasta." I led them out toward the switchboard room.

"Hey, we could trade recipes," Garcia said enthusiastically. "You know something, Stan? I'm beginning to like this assignment." I got the special Garcia grin as confirmation.

Chapter Four

Mattie was back and seated in the switchboard room going over a telephone bill as thick as the NYNEX Yellow Pages. I quickly made the introductions and was ready to slip away.

"Where you goin', honey?" asked Mattie as she saw me shift my feet. "I ain't talkin' to no cops without a witness." I pointed to the two switchboard operators sitting behind her.

"A white witness."

I looked at Greenhouse, and he smiled gently at Mattie. "If it makes you more comfortable, but I should remind you that we will be asking you questions you might consider private."

"I ain't got nothin' to hide," Mattie said and unfolded slowly from her chair as if wanting to show both policemen the strength of her large, tall body.

"Where's the first aid room?" Greenhouse asked, seemingly unperturbed by having to lift his chin slightly to look at her.

Mattie didn't answer, but walked us down the corridor that led back to the kitchen. She took out a set of keys that were attached to the belt of her dress and opened the door. There was barely room for the four of us, and once she closed the door behind us, I felt like I was in a cell. There was no window, and the only air came from a small vent in the middle of the ceiling. I sniffed and thought I smelled Monday's brandy. Detective Garcia and I sat on the cot. Mattie refused to sit and insisted Greenhouse use the only chair in the room. She leaned against the small sink, crossed her arms and glowered at all of us.

"Now what can I do for the New York City Police Department?"

"We just have a few questions to try and clear up Mr. Critelli's death," Greenhouse answered.

Garcia took out his small pad and a two-inch-long pencil. The point had been carved with a knife. I stared and remembered the Roman greengrocers, spare stubs safely secured behind their ears, adding up the bill on rough, wheat-yellow paper. Prices summed up on a torn piece of paper always seemed less exorbitant than when they appeared on the cold printout of a cash register.

Garcia lifted his elbows and flexed his powerful arms. He was ready to write.

"He got what was comin' to him," Mattie said. "I even told Simone here. That man was no good, and God punished him, amen. The very mornin' she found him I said that, didn't I, honey? It's God that killed him, I said."

"According to the autopsy report, Mr. Critelli was killed by potassium cyanide poisoning." Greenhouse leaned back with his metal folding chair in a futile attempt to distance himself from Mattie. "We found an empty bottle of an antihistamine called Nozphree under his body and no antihistamine in his stomach." He paused and jutted his chin out from under his collar. "We believe he was murdered."

"Couldn't he have put cyanide in the capsules himself?" I asked. "I mean, who would want to swallow that stuff loose?" Please don't let it be murder. "I can't even swallow an aspirin," I added lamely.

"Listen, lady, the guy left no note," Garcia explained. "And only his fingerprints were found on the bottle. Now why would he wipe . . ."

Still keeping his eyes on Mattie, Greenhouse shifted in his chair, causing Garcia to stop as if he had suddenly

31

forgotten his lines. Greenhouse reached in his side pocket and brought out a small, empty plastic bottle. Only half the label was left. "Have you seen this bottle before?" he asked her.

Mattie shook her head in disbelief. "I was wonderin' what had happened to it."

"Could you please explain?" Greenhouse's face registered no surprise.

"Tuesday mornin', Dana came down with a real bad cold. She wasn't feelin' good at all."

"Who's Dana?"

Mattie snorted. "You better do a little homework before you come in here askin' foolish questions." She pointed to the ceiling. "Dana's real important upstairs."

"Dana Lehrman," I quickly explained, "is the art director in charge of all the fashion ads. She has a corner office on the sixteenth floor."

"Now I keep a handy supply of pills," Mattie continued, ignoring the interruption, "for all kinds of ailments — muscle ache, backache, headache — you name it, and Mattie's got the thing for you. I keep them all locked up in this medicine chest here."

She selected a key from her bunch, held it up to us as if to show she had no tricks up her sleeve, and then proceeded to unlock the medicine cabinet.

"Of course I had to buy a whole new supply since some rude New York City cop wiped me out Tuesday mornin'. And I can tell you that Mr. Heffer wasn't any too pleased about it, neither. Well, here they are." And she stepped aside to let us see her rows of neatly stacked medicines. Judging by the amount of pink Pepto Bismol bottles I saw, working at HH&H meant having a constant upset stomach.

"They ain't dangerous pills; I wouldn't fool with that; I know better. But still I buy them with agency money, and Mr. Heffer would skin me alive if I left them out loose for anyone to grab. The way he figures it, you have to be in real pain to come all the way to the first floor to get your pill. He's hopin' most people end up buyin' their own. Let me tell you, that man's got his bags of money sealed up tight."

"Why do you think the bottle we found in Mr. Critelli's office came from your supply?" Greenhouse asked with the hard edge of impatience in his voice.

"Hold your horses, Mr. Detective, and maybe I'll tell you." Mattie locked up the cabinet, put her keys in her pocket, leaned against the sagging sink, crossed her arms again, and gave Greenhouse a nice long stare. Mattie was the only employee in the agency who had the courage to stand up to "Moneybags" Heller. In fact she had given him his nickname. Greenhouse was no match for her.

"As I said, Dana had this real bad cold. Half the agency got a cold after Monday mornin'. It was freezin' in this place when I got here at nine o'clock. I don't mind it cold 'cause I'm at that time of life, well, never mind, but the girls in reception complained all mornin' long."

Greenhouse started tapping his foot loudly.

"You hearin' some music we ain't hearin'?" Mattie asked him. I would have laughed if my stomach hadn't growled instead. "She asked for some Nozphree and I went to get it, but it was gone. And it shoulda been there. That messy bottle's been sittin' there for ages just irritatin' me. I don't know who tore at that label, but it was a real act of vandalism. It made my medicine chest look sloppy and I can't stand that."

"Didn't you give Dana the medicine?" Greenhouse asked easily, as if the answer didn't matter.

"It would have been bad for her," Mattie said turning her back to us to lock the cabinet again. "Tylenol's much better for a cold anyway. Caplets. I buy caplets now. That's what I gave her. Caplets." She turned to face us and her eyes went blank, as if the light had been turned off.

There was an awkward silence that was broken only by the rhythmic tapping of Greenhouse's left foot. Garcia had stopped writing, as if he knew something important was going to come up. Maybe Greenhouse's foot

33

warned him.

"Speaking of dangerous medicine, is it true that Mr. Critelli had your nephew arrested?"

Mattie stood up for a second and then let out a long silent breath, her large body slowly deflating.

"You know the answer, why bother askin'?" Mattie whispered, her lips barely moving, as though the pain came from a wound in her mouth.

"Is it also true that at the time you threatened to get even?"

Mattie nodded her head up and down slowly. "I didn't kill him, if that's what you're after. And I'll tell you why. God wouldn't let me. He just wouldn't let me." She put her hand to her mouth, holding back more words. Her hand was so large it covered most of her face, even tilting her glasses up on her forehead. All I could see were her dark eyes floating in tears.

"Did Mr. Critelli ever come to you for pills?"

Before answering, Mattie shut her eyes and puckered up her face, all her wrinkles deepening into grooves. I thought of a wet towel being wrung dry. When she straightened out her face, the tears had disappeared.

"No, he didn't dare look at me after what he did to Buddy."

"Would he have sent his secretary?"

"Jenny never came to me for pills, for herself or anyone else. I guess she bought her own."

"Do you always keep the keys to this room and the medicine cabinet with you?"

"Except when I go on vacation, then I hand them over to Luis, our concierge."

"When did you last go on vacation?" The small room had gotten unbearably hot.

"Last two weeks of May." She waited for another question.

Greenhouse was busy looking at his left foot, Garcia was busy writing. He was taking down every word.

"Since you got no more questions," she said after a few seconds of silence, "I'm goin' to get myself some cleaner

34

air."

Greenhouse nodded and stood up. We waited for her to lock the door behind us, then watched her walk ahead. I smiled at her back, hoping that warmth would reach her. Despite the hurt she must have been feeling, she still managed to fill that long corridor with her presence.

Chapter Five

"I knew he had been murdered all along," Bertrand said, after I had dramatically made the announcement.

I nearly dropped my lasagne to the floor. "What do you mean, you knew?!"

"It was obvious. Suicide is the drastic result of self-loathing; Fred Critelli was only capable of self-love, ergo, he was murdered."

Bertrand Monroe is the art director in charge of our main client, Janick, Inc., a French cosmetic firm which spends enormous amounts in advertising trying to compete with Esteé Lauder and the big rivals from its own shores: Lancôme, Chanel, and Christian Dior.

At that moment, Bertrand was kneeling on the floor of his office and I was sitting at a little round side table that he kept in one corner. I had a partial view of Fifth Avenue reaching north. It wasn't the sweeping southern view that Fred had in his room, but for someone who worked surrounded by gray-felt partitions lighted only by fluorescent tubes, eating my lunch in Bertrand's office felt like feasting at the Windows on the World.

He was busy looking over his scrap material. Mr. Janick, Jean Janick to be precise, insisted that any idea Bertrand came up with for an ad had to be illustrated, not by the use of imagination or Gregory's deft strokes of magic marker, but by "scrap": pre-existing photographs taken from magazines, books, whatever. He had no ability to visualize, which was odd for a Frenchman, and he was very distrusting, which was not odd for a Frenchman. These traits combined made him insist on seeing a photograph that closely resembled the ad Bertrand was trying to come up with. Shooting the photograph ourselves on speculation was, of course, too expensive, so we relied heavily on "scrap." "Who could have killed him?" I asked. The thought of having a murderer around was more frightening than I liked to admit, even to myself.

"I don't know and I don't care," Bertrand admitted as he frenetically leafed through old issues of *Vogue* and *Harper's Bazaar.* "Let the police worry about that one." He stopped to lick his dry index finger.

"What are you looking for?" I asked as I got up to throw my untouched lasagne away. I had lost my appetite.

"Don't you dare throw that wonderful ethnic food away. Please feed a starving artist." I handed him the tinfoil container and watched His Elegance eat. Like Gregory, Bertrand can eat anything and still look like a Giacometti statue. He has the height to carry it off, too. He ate with one hand and leafed with the other.

"A face, a face, my acres of lawn for a face," he said between bites, riffling the magazine pages with his free hand.

Though he was sitting on the floor, he had not taken off his custom-tailored, beige linen jacket. His shirt (white background with dark brown pencil-thin stripes) and tie (the color of bitter chocolate) were subdued Turnbull and Asser, shoes — Ferragamo loafers. Upon my arrival in New York, I discovered the game of "Success by Apparel." Gucci meant Pass Go and Collect; jeans sans designer label was Off to Jail and Miss Three Turns. Working in an ad agency that specializes in fashion had quickly taught me all the rules and regulations, and even though I didn't have the chips to play, I loved to watch. Bertrand was always a winner. Matching the constant elegance of his clothing is Bertrand's well-sculpted face, a small nose, high cheekbones, and a perfectly chiseled jaw that looks handsome even as he spreads it wide open to hungrily eat lasagne. I don't think his mother would approve of the way he devours his food, but that is the only thing he does with visible feeling. Otherwise, Bertrand is always controlled; even his curly brown hair is kept in order by a hair dryer. When it's very humid his hair will curl naughtily, ignoring his attempts to smooth it down with the palm of his hand. By most standards, he should be very good looking. All his single features are, but put together they surprisingly lack substance and you could easily pass him by. Only his height, at least six feet four inches, and the ambling grace of his walk make you stop and look again, and then you convince yourself that he is indeed a handsome man. But it always takes a second glance.

"Jean has finally chosen the name 'Free' for the new perfume," he said. "We are all set to go. Look." He showed me the prototype sitting next to him on the floor. It was a shiny white package, around seven inches high and four inches wide. On the front panel the name "Free" burst from a barely discernible bottle rim in a spray of multicolored drops that spilled onto the other panels of the package.

"So Stinko finally has a name." I smiled as I watched Bertrand stop chewing an enormous morsel and stare at me coldly. I loved to tease him. Stinko was the name Fred had coined for the new Janick perfume. Actually, the perfume's code name had been "Essence," which in French can also mean gas for the car. Fred had read Bertrand's memo regarding the code name and had burst out laughing. "Gas?" he had yelled for the whole floor to hear, "Smells like a stinko to me." By the following morning all of HH&H referred to the perfume by Fred's name, not the client's. Bertrand had not been amused, to say the least.

"The packaging is very pretty and gay," I said, "but the name 'Free' makes me think of a perfume to be worn on those special days, along with your MaxiThins."

Bertrand gave me a look of horror Stephen King

would have envied. "I suppose your Catholic upbringing makes you go for the 'sin' perfumes like 'Passion,' 'Obsession,' 'Opium,' or 'Poison.' "

Poison was the one word I wish he hadn't brought up. "I was only joking, Bertrand. But, seriously, isn't the name a little vague? Free what?"

He rose from a cross-legged position with one movement. He must have trained with Fred Astaire to be able to get up that way. "Free to be happy, free to be anything you want. I think Lauder had a great idea when they went into names that are states of being, like 'Beautiful' and 'Knowing,' but what's the point of being beautiful and knowing if you're not free?"

"What's the bottle going to look like?"

"A streamlined champagne bottle."

"Oh, I get it. Free to drink."

"Let's not have any of your Italian put-downs," Bertrand wagged a long finger at me. "Do you have any cigarettes?" As rich as he must have been on his salary, not to mention the family coffers, Bertrand made it a point not to buy cigarettes, just to bum them. He said it cut down on his smoking. "I want to make the perfume stand for a mixture of *Gaieté Parisienne* and our Fourth of July."

I handed him a cigarette. "This perfume campaign has hardly been festive," I said, referring to the fact that we had almost lost the account. Thanks to Fred's exaggerated need to have the last say, especially when dealing with the haughty Frenchman, Mr. Janick had started reviewing other agencies. General panic had ensued since most believed the agency wouldn't survive without Janick, Inc. Bertrand had been brought in as a last resort and the H's discovered that he knew how to parry with Jean Janick very well. The latter belonged to a very old Parisian family; the former, although recently transferred to verdant Connecticut, was a Bostonian descendant of an early English settler. Mayflower decorum and French snobbery had married well. Mr. Janick was properly mollified, Fred for once receded in the background, and the agency started smiling again.

"Those days are gone now," Bertrand said, smiling. "Dead and gone."

"Why did you dislike Fred so much?" I asked, wondering if Fred's enlarged ego was the only reason.

Bertrand looked at me in mild surprise. "I thought I'd made that clear. He only believed in his own talent, didn't recognize anyone else's."

"You got to be senior vice president."

"I have Janick and Harland to thank for that."

"Fred promoted Dana," I countered.

"Dana is a woman, and Fred was never threatened by a woman, no matter how good she was." He leaned over and squeezed my foot. "Besides, it seems she has something he couldn't do without, which reminds me that we have to find a model quickly for this 'Free' campaign." He pointed to the pile of magazines on the floor. "I'm desperately looking for an interesting face. The lovely French actress the TV department found has backed out on us. She's been offered a movie part she's convinced will make her a big star. I'm afraid it's up to you to bail me out." He smiled at me encouragingly.

I was totally dismayed. Not at the thought of having to look for a model at the last minute; I hadn't even gotten there yet. I was dismayed at what Bertrand had implied. Was it possible that Dana and Fred had . . . I tried to stop myself from going any further. Unattractive Dana, every intense feature from glossed red lips to gelled black mane screaming for attention, was impossible to imagine in Fred's arms. I thought of Dana's ad showing a man caressing hair belonging to a hidden face. Maybe it had been her face she left out of the picture. All those romantic ads reflecting a hidden love . . . It was hard to think of Dana being loved. After all, no one was loving me. But it did explain her sudden rise to fame. Screwing the creative director, I thought bitchily, was bound to do great things for any woman's career.

"I want a spunky brunette. Short hair, not too short. We've got to be able to work with it." Bertrand was en-

40

grossed in his problem, and it was time I paid attention. "It has to be a relatively new face and young. Not so young that you can't imagine her in a sexy situation. What I mean by young is . . ." I didn't let him finish.

"No wrinkles, that's what you mean." At thirty-five, I was feeling very sorry for myself.

"Of course no wrinkles; advertising detests wrinkles."

"Older women wear perfume, too," I argued uselessly. "Older women are also 'Free'. In fact, they are freer. Most of them have gotten rid of the 'follow the herd' instinct."

"But it's that very instinct we want," Bertrand said quietly, as he put both hands in his pocket and shook one leg at a time so that his trousers would fall carefully over each loafer. That instantly reminded me of Fred and depressed me even further. Both of them so vain. No wonder they had disliked each other.

"If one buys the perfume, they all buy the perfume," said Bertrand. "Look, Simona, I know demographics are changing. I know this country is getting older, but no one wants to look reality in the face, so we give them pretty, young faces. Older women will buy the perfume, too, because a young face is a happy thing to look at. And stop feeling so down and out. This whole business will be over before we know it." Bertrand stroked my cheek lightly with one finger. Fred wouldn't come back, I thought. Neither would my pictures. My ex-husband had kept the negatives. What the hell . . . I smiled back. He really was being very patient and kind.

"Where was I with the description?" he asked.

"Young," I answered with feigned cheer.

"Yes, young, and with a slight bit of sophistication. A brunette, I see her as a brunette."

"Why don't I just start looking for some interesting faces without limiting ourselves so much. If you find the face that's right, the hair color can always be changed. Is TV going to help me by looking for actresses, or am I alone on this?"

"No, they're looking," Bertrand said, "but I'm counting on you. I'm sure Detective Greenhouse isn't going to need you." I had a feeling he was right, at least not for fun.

"I want that face yesterday, Simona. I start shooting print in two weeks, and then I follow up with commercials."

"Does she have to talk, act?" I asked. Some of the models had just come here from Czechoslovakia, Finland or wherever, and they hardly spoke English.

"No, she just has to be beautiful."

I knew from experience that Bertrand's "beautiful" meant more than sheer good looks. Beauty wasn't going to be enough for a campaign of this importance. Once the model was picked, they wanted her to stay with the product a long, long time, for economic reasons as well as image consolidation. She might stay until the wrinkles on her face could no longer be removed by retouching. Just like the Esteé Lauder model, Karen Graham, the face that launched a thousand creams. She had represented the Lauder products for nearly twenty years. They had taken shots of her even when she was pregnant, the camera staying close to her face. As she aged, the camera had moved away and a new "young" face, Willow Bay's, had started to take her place slowly, advertising only a few products at first. Karen held on to an expensive perfume the longest, "Private Collection," its target audience being the older woman, but then one too many wrinkles had appeared and Karen disappeared. Then Lauder sought a new sophisticated image and the bland-looking Willow Bay was replaced. No, simple beauty wasn't enough anymore. They were going to want a "little something special," to quote Fred. Oddly enough he had said that about women in general. He felt they all had "a little something special."

As I walked out of the office after work, I saw Jenny rushing down the street in her stiletto heels. I called out to her. Without breaking stride she yelled, " 'Bye, Simona," and waved a small arm in the air.

"Hey, wait a minute!" I ran to catch up.

She looked at me in surprise. "What's the matter? I didn't get your name wrong, did I? It is with an "a," isn't it?"

I forced a smile. "You're the only one who always gets it right," I assured her.

She looked a lot better that evening. Her face was freshly made-up in bright colors and some of her innate optimism was showing behind the swollen eyes. Jenny is only five-foot-one, with no fat on her and bones that look no thicker than my little finger. Despite her small size, there's something very resilient about her. Maybe it's the incongruity of her beaklike nose in the middle of a happy, round face, or the surprising fullness of her breasts perched on top of a gracile rib cage. Then maybe that something is her never-ending bounciness. When Jenny walks she looks like she's warming up for a jog around the park. I don't know how she manages to get that motion going on three-inch heels and forty-five years of life, but everyone stops to look when she charges by, which is just the way I think she likes it.

"I thought I'd walk you to the subway. Do you mind?" I asked her, glad for a chance to postpone going home. She shook her bleached, permed curls at me, and we started walking toward Union Square, just a few blocks away.

"You know what I've been thinking all day?" Jenny said. "Fred's got no one to mourn him. Isn't that awful? I mean, no wife, no family. The man lived for his work and now that he's dead, the two H's probably won't even miss him."

"They'll miss his work," I ventured.

Jenny raised her meticulously plucked eyebrows. "Of course they will. He came up with some great campaigns, and he got the agency lots of new clients." She didn't mention that he had almost lost us the Janick account. She was too loyal.

"You know what else I've been thinking?" she went

43

on. "I've been thinking I'd like to get hold of the guy who killed him and, and, and—" she trembled in anger—"and squash him like a roach." She stomped a size five shoe on the asphalt, then friskily moved on. If she hadn't been so serious I would have burst out laughing at the absurdity of the image.

"Do you have any idea who it is?" I asked her, taking a long stride to catch up with her.

"A thief, who else?" Could the tall man in my apartment have murdered me: sprayed me with black paint, and knifed me to death? Had a thief killed Fred?

Jenny kept talking. "I know nothing was taken, but Fred could have caught him in the act. He had a knack for catching people doing something wrong. I mean, it can't be anyone we know. Not in the office. I know there's a lot of jealousy, a lot of stuffed shirts getting in each other's way, but I'm not going to believe there's a murderer around." Jenny looked at me defiantly, a feisty sparrow ready to peck at me if I disagreed.

"I don't know any more than you do," I said in my defense.

She seemed momentarily appeased. "Last Friday, Fred said that HH&H really stood for Hate, Hate, and Hate. He was so mad." She scrunched up her face as if she were angry too.

"What about?" We had reached Union Square and I stopped to take in the small oasis of green. The stalls of that morning's Green Grocer's Market had been dismantled, but a few crushed flower petals and lettuce leaves had not yet been swept away. The renovated park looked surprisingly clean. A man shuffled close to me and I jumped back in alarm. Jenny gave him her token and pointed a sharp nose at me. "He's only poor. He's not going to do anything to you."

I hadn't told Jenny about the thief. I hadn't told anyone. It was too mortifying, too much like a rape. "I'm just a little jumpy."

She was instantly contrite. "Oh, I'm sorry. I forgot about you seeing Fred. They had covered him up by the time I got to the office. Was it very bad?" Instead of answering her, I started walking toward the subway on Fourteenth Street, at the southern end of the square. "Why was Fred angry on Friday?"

"He got a call on his direct line," Jenny answered, "and after that it was awful. It had something to do with work, something about 'still being in control.' That's what he yelled to whoever it was." She raised her whole body up in one giant shrug. "Egos. Big, fat egos always getting in the way." She looked east at the Con Edison clock, peeking between the Zeckendorf Towers a block away, and gasped. "I didn't realize it was so late. I'm sorry, but I've got to fight my way through that subway crowd. I've got to go; I'm a long way from home." People were pouring into the stairwell of the subway station clutching briefcases and shopping bags of all shapes and sizes. They looked like ants returning home from a foray.

"I know it's going to be all right," Jenny said. "It's no one we know." Before her broad smile could reassure me, she turned around and left. Her short, permed curls bobbed up and down, and her breasts, pointing home, tried to keep up with the rhythm. I watched her energetic walk and her determined face. She was still smiling. She was going to hold on to her silver lining no matter what.

Chapter Six

The next morning, Detective Garcia appeared in the opening to my office just as I was putting my purse away for the day behind the filing cabinet.

"That's a funny place to keep a bag," he said as he sat down without being asked. After one day he felt at home.

"I'm being prudent. We had a theft recently."

"Oh, yeah?" I could almost see his ears perk up. "What was taken?"

"My small tape recorder, money from my wallet, some clothes from the prop closet."

"Prop closet?"

"That's where we keep clothes and props we need for a shoot. Usually a stylist will bring what's needed the day before, the client will send over the merchandise, and I lock everything up in the prop closet until it's time to send it over to the photographer's studio."

"That theft's been taken care of, right?" Garcia asked. "I don't have to worry?"

"It's been taken care of." The theft had taken place on June tenth. I remembered because we were shooting an ad for a new client the next day, The Charme-eze Company, makers of "comfort clothing." The thief hadn't wanted their shapeless junk, had only taken a Burberry raincoat and a leather jacket.

"That's good. We got more important things, right?" He handed me a list of people that Greenhouse wanted to see that afternoon.

Oh, God, I thought. "This isn't going to be easy. Today is Friday, and we close at one o'clock." The one o'clock summer closing, a habit that all the major agencies of the Big Apple had adopted years back, was a new and very welcome one for HH&H. No one was going to give it up willingly, especially for a murder investigation. I was also knee-deep in models' portfolios looking for the perfect face to advertise Stinko, and I just had a few hours to get through them in one day. Portfolios are very much in demand, and the model agencies never let you keep them long.

Garcia snapped his fingers and dropped the list on my desk. Looking at the names I realized that all of them were tied to the Janick account in one way or other, with the exception of Jenny and Dana. I topped the list and was scheduled to see the police exactly at one in Fred's office.

"Hello, Miss Griffo, thank you for coming," Greenhouse smiled.

"I didn't think I had a choice," I answered somewhat rudely.

The vast, plush room had lost all its warmth, despite the sun that was streaming in from the southern window. Three long, pale gray walls still held Fred's career—Clio awards, proofs of the best ads, letters of thanks from clients, all neatly hung like works of art in a museum—works of a dead artist. Fred's kidney-shaped, ebony desk still dominated the room by its sheer size and darkness, but it was bare. There was no mass of white, long-stemmed tulips waiting to greet him; the black Olivetti Praxis on which he typed all his personal notes was gone; the usual stack of storyboards, waiting for Fred's approval before being shot into commercials, were not leaning against the walls; the gray leather sofa was cleared of magazines and books. Even the large ficus to one side of the window drooped thirstily. It had

47

become an awful room. A room of death and hate.

Greenhouse was sitting in Fred's chair, swinging from side to side. His somber reflection crossed the top of Fred's desk back and forth, back and forth.

"Why did you come to the office so early on Monday?" The chair stopped swinging, and Greenhouse looked straight at me.

"I came to ask for a raise."

"Why Monday morning?"

"Fred always came in early on Mondays, and I hoped to catch him before anyone else did."

"You had asked for a raise before?"

"Only in writing."

"A lot of writing." With that comment, he put a small stack of sheets on the desk. I didn't remember having sent so many notes.

"Toward the end, you were very angry." He picked up the top note. "Or desperate." To my great shame, he starting reading out loud, " 'Fred, I simply cannot go on this way. You have to do something!!!' You punctuated that with three exclamation points."

"I wasn't angry enough to kill him, if that's what you're implying. Just terribly frustrated." Frustrated because I liked my new job, but could barely pay the rent, angry because I had walked out on my husband without asking for anything, desperate because I was too proud to ask my parents for help. I couldn't tell policemen that. It wasn't any of their business, it had nothing to do with Fred's murder.

"Did he die that morning?" I asked. "What I mean is, if I had come in earlier, perhaps it wouldn't have happened?"

"No, you can relax about that. He died on Sunday, sometime between five and seven in the evening. You couldn't have saved him."

"I've been feeling so guilty . . ." I stopped. Greenhouse turned away to face the window. Garcia sat in the corner nearest the door, bent over his notebook. I couldn't tell whether they believed me or not.

48

"Why was he here last Sunday?" I asked.

"Miss Griffo, you're in this office because I have questions to ask. Now I find I'm answering yours."

"Please," was all I could say to him. Why did I care? Why was I beginning to feel I had to know everything about Fred's death?

"We don't know why he stayed here Sunday night. Perhaps he had work to do, perhaps he was going to meet his murderer, who knows? All we know is that a great many people were here during the day on Sunday, and we want to know about it. Were you here on Sunday?"

"No, but you'll know who was here by asking Mr. Heffer for a copy of the I.D. numbers that came in that day. On weekends and after six o'clock on weekdays," I explained, "the door to the building will only open if you press your employee I.D. card against a sensor that's located by the entrance door. The number gets registered and the door opens. It's the only way to enter and leave the building. 'Moneybags' had it installed for security reasons and also to keep tabs on people's overtime hours."

Greenhouse turned to Garcia, who shrugged and said, "Not my fault we don't have it yet. That 'Moneybags' guy told me the system is set up on a weekly basis, from a Friday to a Friday. We're supposed to get last Sunday's sensor readings this coming Monday. That's what he said." Garcia didn't sound very convinced.

"Then you'll have proof I wasn't here on Sunday."

"You could have come in with someone else." Greenhouse had a good point there.

"Where were you on Sunday?" he asked. We had come to alibi time and Greenhouse's face looked harder than a bronze death mask.

"I was mostly home. I went to the eight o'clock movie at the Waverly and laughed myself silly. When I came out I was in such a good mood that I pigged out on Steve's ice cream, and then I went to bed. I was alone for all of the preceding."

"What's your favorite?" my food friend asked.

"Cookeo with Reese's pieces."

"Too much chocolate. I get Razzamatazz Berry with Chips Ahoy and mixed nuts. Now that's what I call an ice cream. Fruit and nuts, healthy," Garcia boasted and flexed his right arm.

I don't know if he had done it on purpose, but that grinning, muscle-bound bear had just managed to make Greenhouse and me smile. Mine was a wide grin, his was just a hint, barely there. I gave Garcia a mental pat of approval on his iron triceps.

"How do the elevators operate on weekends?" Greenhouse had gone back to playing serious detective.

"The elevator will only take you to your floor and back down. If, for example, I want to go from the seventeenth to the sixteenth floor, I need a special key that only the bigwigs have. This is true after six o'clock on weekdays too."

"What about the stairs?"

"They get locked at six o'clock, and they stay locked during the weekend."

"Who has this special elevator key?"

"The three H's, of course. The third H was Fred," I reminded him. "Bertrand Monroe, number one art director, has one. Dana Lehrman, number two art director, has one. So does Ann Lester, account supervisor for Janick, Inc. Jenny as a secretary doesn't rate one, but she could always borrow Fred's. Julia Monsanto, the head of the TV department, has one. Luis must have one. That's all I know about."

"Raf tells me you've had some thefts."

I was surprised Garcia had even mentioned it. "Yes, but nothing important was taken." A leather jacket. Black leather. The thief had run past me, and I had felt leather against my hand. There's no mistaking the smoothness of leather.

"The theft wasn't reported at our precinct."

Why had the thief of my apartment worn leather in the heat of July? Unless he had stolen it and couldn't

50

wait to show it off. Like a woman showing off a new fur coat at the mere hint of fall.

"Why do you think it wasn't reported?" Greenhouse insisted.

No, I was imagining things. "I guess Fred wanted it kept quiet. What's the use anyway? As Detective Garcia said, the police have more important things to worry about." I hadn't reported my theft. "Besides, nothing of great value was taken; the clothes were used, the speaker inexpensive. Fred reimbursed me for the money."

"How did it happen?"

"It was around six-thirty. Everyone on the seventeenth floor had gone home except Fred. I was downstairs with Dana helping a model try on some clothes we were going to shoot the following week. I guess I hadn't closed the prop closet well because when I went to put the dresses back, I immediately noticed the raincoat and the jacket missing." At the time, Fred had hinted I might get into trouble for having left the prop closet door open. Just another way of putting me off about the raise.

"There's no connection with Fred's death, is there?" I asked.

"It's best to look into everything," He swiveled the chair to face the skyline. The sun made him squint.

There's no connection anywhere, I thought. There were thousands of leather jackets out there. Thousands of thieves.

Greenhouse kept silent, so thinking I had been dismissed, I got up from the soft armchair and started toward the door. He didn't speak until I grasped the door knob. "Were you in love with Fred Critelli?"

I stopped and waited a long minute before answering him. I looked at the carpet, at the spot where Fred's outstretched arm had been.

"No, I wasn't," I said finally.

"He sure wasn't a nice guy," Garcia volunteered.

No, he wasn't, I thought to myself, but that's what got to me. I was fascinated by the way he had drawn me in, had made me feel beautiful without the aid of compliments. He had committed no improprieties. He had just given me his seemingly devoted attention for a few brief moments; that had been all. But it had been enough to bring back the memory of the husband who had charmed me into believing I was his heaven and earth. That fairy tale had also been brief, but I held on to the marriage for six years. When it had become too painful I fled to America, and by chance found Fred to remind me, to pour salt on the wound, to pierce the numbness.

"Somehow he made me feel alive," I said, turning around to look at Greenhouse's nice face. "It all has to do with a memory." I thought I saw a flicker of comprehension in those brown eyes.

"I don't think it was a memory that killed him," Greenhouse said.

When I reached for the door handle, I heard him add, "Thank you, Simona." I didn't turn to look at him again before closing the door behind me.

Jenny was sitting in her cubicle facing Fred's door. She greeted me with her standard smile, then went back to work. She was filing her nails, three bottles of polish placed neatly in front of her, ready for use. I watched Ann Lester, draped in a long white gauze affair, walk into Fred's office before sitting down. I was glad to have someone to talk to.

"Isn't she beautiful when she walks in those flat shoes of hers?" Jenny asked. "The air just opens up and lets her glide by, all five feet eight inches of her."

"Why don't you try dropping your feet down to ground level?" I suggested.

"I'd disappear in the crowd." Jenny continued to stare at the open space Ann had briefly crossed. "For my mother's fiftieth birthday I took her to see those Russian folk dancers at the Met. The old Met. That must have been twenty-five years ago. It was just before they tore the place down and we moved to Chicago. At one point they did a dance with these tiny little steps." She rapidly tapped her fingers on the desk to demonstrate. "You couldn't see their feet because of their long skirts. It looked like they were on a conveyor belt or something." She laughed at the memory. "That's how Ann moves. Without any effort."

"I bet if you'd put three-inch heels on her, she'd fall flat on her face," I said.

"Oh, Simona, you know that's not true."

Jenny was right. Ann is so graceful, she would glide even on stilts. She's an ex-model, still beautiful and unmarried, whose years are artfully disguised by layers of expensive clothes, a mask of make-up, and perhaps a tuck or two. Ann is as hard as her acrylic nails, and she's climbed the advertising ladder by sheer determination. Mr. Harland likes to boast that she knows more about the American cosmetics market than the most famous self-proclaimed expert of them all, Estée Lauder.

"I'm sorry, but that was not pleasant," I said and pointed a finger at Fred's door.

"What happened?" Jenny widened her eyes expectantly.

"Nothing, really. It was just awkward."

"Oh, I'm sorry," Jenny said, apologizing for what was not her fault. A wry smile appeared on her lips just as she bent down to apply her base coat. "But I wouldn't mind being shut up in a room with that guy. He's awfully cute. I wouldn't let him slip by, if I were you."

"Jenny!"

She didn't look up from her nails. "It's nothing to be ashamed of. Go for it, Griffo." She waved an imaginary pom-pom in the air and dried her nails at the same time.

"What was happening here on Sunday?" I wasn't just changing the subject, I told myself. I really did want to know.

"Julia, Fred, Bertrand, Wally, Ann, and Mr. Janick himself had a big meeting in Fred's office about the Stinko campaign."

"I thought Fred was no longer involved."

"Fred called the meeting on Friday."

"After he got that bad phone call?"

Jenny looked up. "Yes, come to think of it, it was. Do you think that's important?"

"I'm just wondering why he called the meeting," I said. "Do you know?"

"He didn't tell me anything." Jenny busied herself applying a first coat of *Eté d'Amour*, Janick, Inc.'s fashion shade of the summer, to her left pinky, but the nail was so small, she was having a hard time keeping the polish within its boundaries. After the third try, she had a perfect hot pink dot.

"I miss him, you know," she said without looking up. "He was fun to work for."

"Were you in love with him?"

She looked at me in complete surprise. "With Fred? Oh, no, how could I? I mean, he loved himself so much there wasn't room for anyone else. It wouldn't have made any sense at all." How healthy of her, I thought. And how intelligent. I got up swiftly, suddenly wanting to get out of there. As I moved I brushed my hand against the open bottle of nail polish, and *Eté d'Amour* slowly spread on Jenny's perfectly neat desk.

"I'm sorry," I gasped.

"It's okay," Jenny said and quickly reached in her file drawer for the paper towels. "It'll be gone in a sec." She started wiping with the aid of her nail polish remover, not caring about ruining her newly polished fingernails.

"I wonder why Fred took those Nozphree capsules. Did he have a cold on Friday?" I asked, joining in the cleanup.

"No, I don't think so." She didn't stop cleaning. "He always complained a lot when he wasn't feeling well. He wanted to be treated like a baby. Giovanna would always bring him some awful Italian tea and check his temperature." Jenny started placing her knickknacks back on her cleaned desk, a pink mug that held her pencils and pens, a large stapler, a three-hole punch, Scotch Tape, a tiny teddy bear in a red sweater that she propped against the mug, and finally her desk calendar. She removed that Friday's page and smiled with satisfaction. She had restored her desk to its usual impeccable state.

"The doctor!" I remembered. "Fred had a doctor's appointment Monday morning. I saw it written in your calendar. Maybe he was sick."

"Noooo, that wasn't Fred's doctor." She was laughing. "At least I sure hope not. That was for me. You know, women's things. Sorry, Simona, I don't think Fred was sick at all." She gave her desk another wipe before walking to the service elevator with her full wastepaper basket held at arm's length, as if it were a naughty puppy who had just wet the rug. I wanted to laugh, but found myself sneezing instead. The smell of acetone was overpowering.

"Did you know if Fred had any allergies?"

"Well, I worked for the man almost ten years so I guess I would have known if he had." Jenny settled back into her chair and patiently began to repaint her nails. "He had corns, though." She smiled, seemingly happy she was able to contribute some information of Fred's state of health. "He was always taking his shoes off."

Fred's office door opened, and a calm Ann Lester walked out. She pretended not to see us and slid past holding her head up very high, which was easy for her since she was so tall. Her long white dress floated behind her, and a strong scent wafted our way.

"I guess it's my turn now," Jenny said, blowing on the nail she had managed to repaint. "I think I'm going to tell him how great you are." She bounced through Fred's door before I got a chance to throttle her.

I laughed and walked toward my office, filling my nostrils with Ann's pervasive scent. It was far more appealing than acetone. Sexy too. I made a mental note to ask her what it was.

For the next two hours I looked at beautiful, smiling faces. Many I rejected easily because their faces were too well known. The Czechoslovakian Paulina would have been perfect for Stinko, but Lauder had already grabbed her. Besides, she had been immortalized by the leading photographers, from Avedon, David Bailey, on down the alphabet to Albert Watson, and she was beginning to wear thin. What I needed to find was an unknown Paulina, someone just ripe for discovery, and I only had a few days. I discarded most of the books and kept only four to show Bertrand.

"How can you smile while waiting for the police to question you?" I asked him when I saw him sitting back in his chair staring at a double spread torn from some magazine. "I thought you'd be furious about having to face the five o'clock traffic to Long Island." He had a beautiful gray wooden home buried in the woods of East Hampton.

"No, Jean Janick's in town, so it's off to Nell's tonight. I'll drive out tomorrow. What I'm smiling about is this." He turned the double spread toward me. "What do you think of it?"

It showed a man and a woman jogging along a perfectly flat white beach at sunset.

"Have you ever tried jogging on a beach?" I asked. "Your feet sink in, the sand is never flat so you run lopsided, and your hip aches for a week. It's horrible! Besides, who wants to sweat jogging with a man? I can think of more pleasant circumstances."

"Thanks for the positive thinking," Bertrand said, not minding me at all. "The man isn't meant to be in the ad. This is the only scrap I could find that came close to the idea. She's alone. She's indulging herself, running naked in the sand, her arms spread out to catch the wind. I think I prefer dawn to sunset. Pale colors turning into brightness, the start of a new day, the promise of a new life." Bertrand stared at the double spread, lost in his own clichés. He looked surprisingly sad.

"What happened to the hot dog and champagne happiness idea?" I asked.

"I don't know. I think I'm tired of frivolity. I want to make more of a statement." He tossed the spread down on his desk and got up. "Anyway, I have to see what Jean thinks about it." He stretched his arms out toward the window and contemplated his long, thin hands with fingernails bitten to the quick. "Freedom seen as a never-ending ocean," he said, in a surprisingly sad voice.

Standing in the middle of the room, Bertrand made a handsome picture in his slate gray linen slacks with front pleats, a brown crocodile belt with loafers to match, and an oversized, pearl gray, collarless linen shirt with thin white stripes. He reminded me of Bruce Weber's sepia-colored ads for Ralph Lauren — the rich Hampton look with intense face to match. I watched him admiringly and wondered why he bit his nails or worried about freedom. His color, ethnic background, religion, job title, and money were just right. He had it all as far as I could see.

"Your shirt matches Fred's toilet paper." I said. "When's the big move?"

He dropped his arms and laughed, the reverie broken. "Any day now," he said. "You really love to needle, don't you?" He pointed to the portfolios I was holding in my arms. "Are those for me?"

Mio dio, I was going to walk out of here without showing them to you. These four are the best I could come up with today. Most of the good models are in Paris for the full couture shows and won't be back until the end of July."

"It's the usual terrible timing," Bertrand said and stretched out his arms for the books. "Let's see." He studied each photograph in the portfolios carefully.

"They have possibilities. Of course most of these ads are badly photographed, so it's hard to tell."

"These are new models. They haven't had a chance of being photographed by the top people," I said defensively. "Once a Scavullo snaps them, they're no longer unknowns."

"Let's see them Monday morning." He looked at his watch. "I have to face those two detectives in a few minutes."

Which reminded me. "Did you see or talk to Fred the

57

Friday before he died?"

"I always tried to avoid him."

"Jenny said he was very upset about a phone call."

"Fred throwing a temper tantrum was nothing new," Bertrand said calmly. "You'd better hurry and get on the phone yourself. I want to make sure we have models to look at Monday morning."

I gave him a stiff-armed Mussolini salute and got out of there fast.

Back in my cubicle, I made my phone calls and thought of the weekend ahead. I wasn't going to have anyone to confirm an alibi this weekend either. No date, no friends around, the women I knew were busy with family or boyfriends. I thought of the one person who would welcome me without fail, and I reached for the phone to call Gregory.

Chapter Seven

Gregory had invited me to spend the weekend at his home in Edgewater, New Jersey. Although he had invited me before, I had always felt awkward about accepting. I didn't have any doubts about our relationship. There was no romantic interest on either side, but I did hate to play the orphan role. I wanted everyone to think I was terribly busy on weekends. This time, loneliness had got the better of my pride.

I had taken the bus from Penn Station, and Gregory and his mutt, Patch, were waiting for me at the bus stop. It was only a five-minute walk to his house, but the day was muggy, and by the time we reached the shade of his garden, I was ready for a shower. Gregory didn't take me inside right away. He wanted me to admire his twenty-four-square foot garden which he had crammed with as many flowers and bushes as possible. I counted twelve rose bushes and two pink climbers against the wall of the house. Some of the bushes had buds too closed to give an idea of color, others had given up flowering for the moment, but the climbers had three cauliflower roses in full display, their color reminding me of Jenny's nail polish. To my left, against a raw wood fence that faced the street, Gregory had planted big clumps of dahlias of all colors and had bordered them with red New Guinea impatiens. At the end of the garden was a neatly planted vegetable garden. Bright red tomatoes ready to be eaten and the orange flowers of the zucchini plant told me I was going to be well fed. The right side of the garden bordered on another property, and the neighbour's box hedge had overgrown and reached into Gregory's garden. Behind me, next to the climbers, two large terra-cotta geranium pots marked the doorway that led to the kitchen.

It was a messy, homey, welcoming place, and I sat down on a rickety wooden chair that had seen better days and began to enjoy myself. Thoughts of a shower fled as I sipped the iced tea Gregory brought me, along with four kittens a stray Mamma Cat had left at his door for safekeeping. He had taken the whole family in, much to Patch's chagrin, and after some initial sulking they now all licked and scratched each other in happy abandon. That's how I was beginning to feel, happy and at home, basking in Gregory's attentions. A tray of freshly baked cookies came out next, and Gregory joined me under the shade of an elm.

"I was surprised the police interrogation went as smoothly as it did." Gregory said. "No embarrassments, just obvious questions with obvious answers."

"I was uncomfortable at first. All those questions make you feel guilty even if you're not, but I guess Greenhouse means well."

"The other one played the silent partner with you too?" Gregory picked up a ginger ball of fur and started petting it. The kitten immediately stretched and flattened itself out on Gregory's lap.

"He's the writer in the family. He takes down everything very quickly in some kind of steno." I reached over to touch the kitten. "His ability surprised me."

"You don't think very highly of the Rambos of the world."

"God, no, but Raf's no Rambo. Despite those muscles, I bet he's a gentle man and a great deal more intelligent than he appears."

"Raf?" Gregory asked in a mocking tone.

"Short for Rafael. That's what Greenhouse calls him."

"Then why not Stan, instead of Greenhouse?"

"Raf's a friend," I said.

"So Greenhouse is the one you like, huh?" Gregory said. He dropped the ginger kitten and picked up a little black and gray. Gregory always liked to be fair, distributing caresses to one and all.

"Don't be silly, he's a policeman," I retorted. I noticed that Patch was anxiously waiting to be the next in line, so I pulled him over by the collar and started scratching his back. He settled happily against my leg, oblivious to the warmth he generated.

"Nothing wrong with finding a policeman attractive and showing it. Sure beats finding someone like Fred attractive."

Apparently I had walked through the agency hiding my feelings behind a sparkingly clear glass wall.

"Why do you dislike him so much?" I asked.

"Did, did, Fred is now very dead." Gregory got up abruptly, and the kitten fell to the ground. It quickly proceeded to wash itself carefully. I wished I could hide the humiliation of a fall so well.

"Let's go inside, it's too hot to sit here," Gregory said impatiently.

It had been perfectly comfortable in the shade. A nice breeze had even risen in the last few minutes from the Hudson nearby, but I followed him in silence.

The kitchen was large, almost as big as the garden. Gregory had knocked down one wall and had incorporated the dining room with the old kitchen to make it one large room. I loved it the instant I saw it. In my studio, the kitchen fit into a little closet.

The corner of the wall that led into the living room was mostly covered by cookbooks from all parts of the world. It turned out that Gregory collected cookbooks in all languages, even though he couldn't understand most of them.

I was happy to see that Italy was well represented. "If you want I can translate some of these for you," I offered.

"No, thanks, I like the guesswork."

Next to the bookshelves stood a round wooden table

that could seat eight. In the other corner Gregory had placed a large freezer, the kind you could hide a body in, which he had covered with a bright green cotton blanket from Mexico. On the walls hung copper pots, baskets of different shapes, American Indian artifacts, and cascading plants. The kitchen held an eclectic collection of objects from various parts of America. Gregory had never been to Europe. He had limited his travel to North America, firmly believing "you have to sniff around your own neighborhood first." The fact that exploring such a vast neighborhood would probably use up all the vacations of his lifetime did not disconcert him.

The rest of the house reflected the style of the kitchen, crammed coziness without too much worry about aesthetics. The downstairs was made up of the large kitchen, a smaller living room, and a tiny entrance way. Gregory said he always entered his home from the back door, to be hit by the best part first. The living room was dull in comparison to the kitchen, and it was obvious that most of Gregory's life at home was not spent in that almost empty room. There were two rooms upstairs. Gregory's room was closed, so I couldn't see it, but it was directly above the kitchen, overlooking the garden. The guest room, which faced his room, was small and, like the kitchen, crowded with books and native bric-a-brac.

"We don't have to share a bathroom, which is one of the reasons I bought this house," Gregory said as he showed a bathroom covered in yellowed white tile. "Unpack, wash up, do whatever you have to. I'll be downstairs in the kitchen. It's almost supper time. I'll defrost some gazpacho in the microwave. Then we'll have some cold cuts with garlic toast. We'll keep it light tonight. Save our appetites for tomorrow night."

"What's tomorrow night?" I asked. I didn't think Gregory saved his appetite for anything.

"Evelyn heard you were spending the weekend and invited herself over for dinner. She lives near here. Wally's coming too. I expect you to cook some pasta, so think up something good. There'll be no freeloading at my house." He smiled. "See you downstairs."

I was surprised that Evelyn Dietz was coming to dinner. I hadn't known she and Gregory were friends or even neighbors. Except for the wild sneezes she happily imparted to the whole seventeenth floor, I knew very little about her. The few times we had spoken she had been blunt to the point of rudeness and I had hastily retreated. Besides, she was Fred's traffic coordinator and our jobs were not directly connected, so there wasn't much contact between us. It was different with Wally. He worked with Bertrand, and he was also always slipping into Gregory's welcoming office.

Wally Burgh is a sometimes simpatico and sometimes insufferable roly-poly man with a face still covered with adolescent pimples. He was born and raised in Brooklyn, something he immediately tells you as he introduces himself. "Wally Burgh, born and raised in Brooklyn," he'll say smiling through his pimples, as if he were saying "Wally Burgh, Duke of Gloucester." Then he numbs you with a never-ending flow of words. Wally likes to tell the tale of how he became copywriter for the Janick account. He maintains that his flair for words developed in his family's grocery shop on Twelfth Avenue. Weary, overworked women would enter to buy some essential, and Wally would pounce on them, his words flattering them into buying an extra cucumber to wash their face with and "wipe away the oil of worry," or convincing them their "life would float more easily" if they poured a generous amount of baking soda in their bath water to smooth away the fatigue. Soon, as Wally tells it, cucumbers were replaced by astringents and baking soda by bath oil, and the grocery shop turned into a drugstore. Wally's stories should be taken with a large grain of salt, but he can be fun to listen to, and I have to admit his copy does entice me to buy. He makes everything seem so indispensable.

I took a quick shower, applied some make-up and

vainly ran my hands through my hair hoping to give it some fascinating blown-by-the-wind look, like what I had seen in the models' portfolios. Instead my hair slipped through my fingers and fell around my face like overcooked whole wheat fettuccine. There was no way I was going to look like one of those models. Just a decent face beginning to soften around the edges. Turning my back to the depressing mirror, I struggled into continually shrinking slacks and left the room. On top of the stairs the smell of garlic hooked me by the nose and led me back to the kitchen.

Dinner was wonderful and comfortable. After I helped Gregory wash up and clear the table, we took our decaf espressos out into the garden. The animal family followed. Patch settled himself on both my bare feet as if to protect the guest from the chill of a hot July night. The cats surrounded Gregory. They had not yet decided if I was going to be of any use to them or not.

I wanted to ask Gregory about himself—I knew nothing of his past or why he lived alone—but earlier, when I had asked how he felt about Fred, he had been very abrupt, and I didn't want a repeat performance. Instead I volunteered anecdotes from my past, my travels with my diplomat father, my work in Italy dubbing films. Nothing was said to spoil the evening, no mention of theft or murder. The crickets and I chirped on together, and after a while I didn't know if he was even listening. It had gotten too dark to see his face.

"Gregory, are you sleeping?" I asked softly.

"No, just drawing pictures in my head. I'm not much of a talker, you now."

"What pictures?"

"Of all the places you were talking about. I guess I'm going to have to go over there some day."

"Oh, yes, Gregory," I cried out. "You'll love it, I promise. Why don't you go this September? You haven't taken your vacation yet, and that's the best month for

Italy."

"No, there are parts of Washington State I haven't seen yet. I'll have to wait a couple of years, Simona." He pronounced my name "Sighmona" instead of "Seemona," and I didn't mind at all. It was as if he had a special name for me.

"And it's no use making faces. I can sense you're making one even though I can't see it."

I laughed and gave him a kiss on the forehead. He stood up quickly and declared it was time to go to bed. I think I had embarrassed him.

Once inside he counted the kittens to make sure they were all there, gave a pat to Mamma Cat and Patch and led the way upstairs. Patch watched us go up the stairs mournfully. He wanted desperately to follow. Later, in my sleep, I thought I heard Gregory's door open, and Patch's eager nails dig into the wood of the stairs.

Chapter Eight

Saturday was spent in laziness. A scrumptious breakfast in the garden with freshly baked blueberry muffins made from scratch, a stroll along the streets in the vicinity to admire beautifully kept gardens with an eager Patch anxious to introduce me to all the neighborhood dogs, a lunch hour spent watching Gregory eat leftover muffins and gazpacho, followed by a nap to the hum of the air conditioner in the guest room. Gregory's bedroom door remained closed to my curiosity.

Five o'clock came and I sauntered into the kitchen to start my pasta dish for that evening's meal. Evelyn and Wally were expected at seven. I reached the kitchen just as Gregory was coming in carrying the best of his garden crop in a basket. We had three eggplants, two zucchini, four wonderfully big white spring onions, two green peppers, eight plum tomatoes, and an enormous bunch of basil that invaded the kitchen with its happy smell. I chose to work with two of the onions and all of the eggplant and left the other vegetables for Gregory. I set to work while he went to find some Solarcaine to soothe his mosquito bites, the price he had to pay for gathering his vegetables at that hour.

"The joys of country living," I yelled at his back. I was busy peeling the eggplant. "I have no mosquitoes in my spacious Manhattan home."

"You don't have those vegetables, either." Gregory reappeared surrounded by the pungent odor of moth balls. The basil almost wilted at the insult. Gregory, in contrast, looked relieved.

"Even though I live a block away from Balducci's, the best food shop in the city of New York, I will admit you can't beat the Gregory Price New Jersey Vegetable."

Water was rolling to a boil on the stove, and Gregory dropped the tomatoes in for two or three minutes to make peeling them easier. Meanwhile I sliced the eggplants very thin, laid them out on a double thickness of paper towels, and poured salt on them to get rid of their bitterness. Rock salt is too expensive a substitute to the kitchen salt we use in Italy so I normally use Kosher salt, but Gregory didn't have any and I made do with good old "When it rains it pours." It had taken me days to figure out that ad, and I had a lurking suspicion that was the real reason I preferred Kosher salt. I covered the slices with paper towels, placed a wooden cutting board on top of them and weighted them down with Gregory's *Larousse Gastronomique.* Gregory ignored my preparations and went about his work making a meat loaf he was going to serve at room temperature with an olive and tomato relish. Outside the afternoon sun had not yet tired of giving off heat, and the humidity had risen so much that even Cat and Co. had moved inside.

I sliced three garlic cloves and the onions and sautéed them in about seven tablespoons of oil. When the onions started to color I turned the stove off and since I had at least forty-five minutes to wait for the eggplants to give up their water, I watched Gregory put the kitchen sink into his meat loaf. Minced sautéd onions, pureed zucchini, a beaten egg, tons of parmigiano, and two slices of crustless white bread previously soaked in milk were mixed with equal amounts of twice ground veal, pork, and beef. The mass was patted into a smooth oval shape by fast-moving, expert hands and disappeared into the oven.

"*Evviva!*" I shouted, clapping my hands. Gregory smiled in spite of himself, washed his hands, and slipped his HH&H ring back on on his little finger. I hadn't seen him taking it off, hadn't noticed his left hand without it, and somehow I was annoyed. I didn't have one, of course. I hadn't been with the agency long enough. The ring was another of Mr. Harland's pretensions. After working for the agency ten years, an employee's loyalty and perseverance was rewarded with a dinner and a black onyx signet ring engraved with the agency logo. It was intended to make you feel one of the initiated, make you work harder, just when burn-out was about to settle in. Perhaps it was also meant to compensate for bad pay.

"What happened with Mattie and her nephew?" I asked. She had been with the company more than ten years, but I had never seen her with the HH&H ring.

Gregory turned to me and looked as if he didn't consider Mattie's problems any of my business.

"The police questioned her about him," I said to justify my curiosity. "I'm afraid they consider her a suspect."

"That's ridiculous," Gregory said. He was stripping the thin skin of the still hot tomatoes with deft, quick strokes. "Mattie wouldn't do anything to harm the agency. She loves the place too much."

"She never wears her ring."

"Not on her finger. Mattie thinks hands are made to work, not to look pretty. She's got it around her neck all the time. It's her proudest possession."

"Well, she sure hated Fred. She told me so herself."

"For good reason," Gregory said as he chopped the tomatoes with angry vigor. They were quickly turning into mush. I reached out my hand and touched his arm. He stopped and scooped the tomatoes into a sieve to let them drain.

"What did Fred do to her?"

Gregory looked at my hand still resting on his arm. Perhaps trust came with that touch, I don't know, but he told me her story.

"Mattie's the only one in her family who has made good, so to speak. I don't mean to say that her family is full of bums. It's that they struggle, hold down menial jobs. Her husband is an invalid, one of her brothers is on welfare, the other one gets odd jobs when they come up. She's the only one who works in the white world of business and she's very proud of it. She's also got a heart so she tries to help where she can. She got her nephew, Buddy, a job in the mailroom." As he talked he chopped the cleaned peppers and two cups of pitted black olives in the Cuisinart, raising his voice each time he pushed down the lever. It gave the story rhythm. "The fairy tale came to an end when Fred caught Buddy with some coke. He fired him on the spot. Never even gave him a chance to explain. And what's worse, he reported it to the police. He saw to it that Buddy got arrested." The Cuisinart stopped its churning, and Gregory just stood still looking into the blackened bowl.

"Selling coke is pretty awful," I ventured.

"I'm not saying it isn't, but someone in the agency was buying the stuff from Buddy. Someone who wasn't black and only sixteen. Someone who had a college education or the equivalent, someone who had advantages, who was earning a big salary. You know damn well it wasn't the guys in the mailroom who were doing the snorting. I'll bet you anything it was someone in a plush corner office. Fred didn't bother to look into that. No, all he could do is pick on a scared young black kid." Gregory scooped the sauce into a ceramic bowl. "The funny thing was that Buddy kept his mouth shut about his client. Didn't try to defend himself."

"Gregory, the boy was selling coke."

"He was selling it because someone asked him to get it for him."

"Come on, be fair. You have no way of knowing that. What if he was the one who was doing the tempting?"

"I am being fair. Fred wasn't. Buddy deserved a second chance. Mattie swears up and down the kid had never been involved in anything like that before. Do you know what chances he has now that he's got drug pushing on his record? Who's going to hire him? And what about Mattie, doesn't she mean anything to the agency?

69

Sure, fire the kid if you have to, but don't call in the police. God, she was so upset she swore she'd get Fred for what he'd done to Buddy." Gregory said the sentence simply, evenly. He seemed unaware of the importance of his words.

"Did she kill Fred?"

"He ruined that kid's life."

"Maybe Buddy ruined his own life."

"What did he know about life?" Gregory picked up the Cuisinart bowl and poured the olive and pepper mixture into a big ceramic bowl the color of sunflowers.

"Did she kill Fred?" I asked again.

"With a little capsule? It would just get lost in her huge hand. If she wanted to kill him, she'd have the guts to kill him with a sledgehammer. With her, he would have gone out with a bang."

We resumed our cooking tasks in silence; Gregory chopped the basil and added it to the bowl along with the drained tomatoes; I dried the eggplants, then removed the garlic and onions from the skillet, heated the oil and sautéed the eggplants for twenty minutes, adding torn basil, hot pepper flakes, salt and pepper at the last minute. After that I mixed onions, garlic, and eggplant together in a bowl and put the mixture aside. When Wally and Evelyn came, all I had to do was cook the spaghetti, mix it with grated parmigiano and the cooled sauce, and serve. Gregory had moved on to preparing the salad while I set the table with rough terra-cotta dishes on blue handwoven placemats. I clipped the two pink roses from the climbers and placed them in a small vase in the middle. It was nice to be in a home, a real home, even if it wasn't mine, with guests coming to dinner. Home was something I had left behind and hadn't found again, and Gregory's was a nostalgic substitute.

"Hey, Simona, it's funny seeing you outside the office. You look so nice," Evelyn said with undisguised surprise as she walked in from the garden and let the screen door bang shut. With that rude gesture she took possession of the house.

"Office furniture come to life, that's me," I said. "And by the way, it's Simona, with an 'a' as in Liza with a 'z'."

Evelyn batted her long eyelashes at me. For a moment I wondered why she was wasting the energy, but then she lifted an eyelid and with a swift movement removed her contact lens and held it to the light. "These things are a pain in the neck," she said and then added a smiling, "Zimone."

I was going to like her.

"What's with the cops! Got any interesting tidbits?" Evelyn sat down on one of chairs around the table. She searched into something that looked like an army duffel bag that had seen all the wars and retrieved a flowered plastic pouch. She removed a small mirror and propped it up against a glass. Once the irritating lens was popped back on her eye, Evelyn proceeded to make up her face — eyeshadow, lipstick, the whole thing. I watched fascinated as flecks of purple dust fell on the plate in front of her.

"I tried this in the car, but Wally's a lousy driver," Evelyn said covering her blotchy complexion with short brushstrokes of red blusher. "Bathrooms depress me," she added as an excuse.

"Why?" I personally find bathrooms reassuring, warm places.

"Ev considers the painting of her face an art form, and art cannot be executed where the body defecates," Wally answered as he maneuvered the screen door open with his elbow. His hands were filled with two Fontana Candida magnums. "Besides, the mirrors in bathrooms are much larger. She prefers to digest herself in small morsels."

Evelyn answered Wally's appalling remarks with a smile almost hidden by the stretched lips being painted. Wally blew her a noisy kiss and I knew they were lovers. The idea of plump, pimply Wally, a good many years Evelyn's junior, enjoying Evelyn's sloppy favors put me in a very good mood. There was hope yet.

"Evelyn wanted to know about the police, Wally," I said as I helped him inside by taking one bottle from him. "Is that why you both came over?"

"Hi," Wally said to Gregory, who had just appeared from the basement where he had been feeding his pets. "No, my suspicious *Italiana*," he quickly went on. "I've had enough of the police after yesterday's fun afternoon answering that arrogant cop's stupid questions. We came because Gregory told us he would be entertaining a lady this weekend, and we wanted to give him moral support. Gregory is not used to having women in his house. He is very much the loner, aren't you, Greg?" Wally opened one of the bottles and filled the glasses on the table. I picked up two full glasses and handed one to Gregory. He had turned the color of beets. I had never considered Gregory's sexual inclinations, but Wally had just put some doubts in my mind. "And do remove that perpetual look of need from your countenance, Simona. It makes men reach for their jogging shoes instantly."

"What kind of stupid questions?" I asked as I peeked under the lid to recompose my face and see if the water was boiling.

"Boring, obvious, stupid. Such as 'had I noticed anything unusual on Sunday.' That's moronic. The whole advertising industry thrives on being unusual. And what's more offensive, he sounded exactly like my therapist. Whenever I asked him a question, he'd come up with, 'And what do you think the answer might be.' Absolutely infuriating. Thank God I played dutiful son Sunday evening. I have the perfect alibi." He rolled his eyes to heaven as if to thank God.

"Was there anything unusual?" I didn't think the question was moronic. I thought Greenhouse very intelligent. At least he didn't overwhelm you with words.

"So, what's for dinner?" Evelyn asked before I could get my answer.

"I have shared the kitchen with Simona this time," Gregory said to explain my proprietary interest in the large red enamel pot sitting on the stove.

"Is that the only thing you've shared?" Wally asked, as he wagged a pudgy finger at both of us. I looked at his pointing finger momentarily confused. As Wally started to refill my wineglass, the whole hand reached toward me, pinky ring flashing. I almost cried out as I saw Fred's arm reaching toward me. The open palm had been bare. There had been no ring on his dead finger. I started to tremble.

Wally nudged my hand with the glass of wine. "What's the matter, Simona? See a ghost?"

Fred had always worn the agency ring; that flash of gold had been my point of focus when he waved his hands through the space surrounding him. Why had his hand been bare?

"Yes, I think I have," I finally answered and emptied the glass.

Wally looked momentarily contrite. "I apologize and I'll stop being nasty. By way of distraction, may I tell you, Simona-of-the-now-glazed-eyes, what a great honor has been bestowed upon you? Gregory is very jealous of his kitchen and the attentions he gets from his superb cooking, so try to look pleased."

"I shall look pleased, not needy or glazed." I forced a smile and asked, "Better?" The wine was beginning to make me feel warm and woozy.

"Pure Marcel Marceau" was Wally's answer. He stuck a finger into the tomato relish and sucked at it loudly.

"Did Fred act unusual on Sunday?" I tried again.

"In truth, yes," Wally admitted. "Apart from greeting our stuffed French shirt in his stocking feet, he was strangely happy. Relaxed. He probably had a hot date waiting for him in the wings. Your water is boiling over." Wally stuck his sucked finger back in the tomato relish.

Dinner was going well. Skinny Gregory helped himself three times to my spaghetti, and Wally had heaped so much on his plate to begin with that he begged off a second helping. Evelyn, like most American women who have accumulated inches and years, didn't touch the alcohol and dabbled with the carbohydrates. I did not hold it against her. I was getting there fast myself. Besides, she didn't need food, she had sex. I buried my mouth and my envy in the spaghetti.

"Does the police suspect anyone yet?" Wally asked once we had passed on to stuffing ourselves with meat loaf. Eight eyes suddenly looked at me. Six wanted an answer. Two, Patch's, wanted meat loaf.

"I have no idea." Mattie was none of their business.

"Well, there are dozens of possible suspects," Wally said, tugging at the napkin covering his protruding belly. "Let's first rule out the unlikely murderers. Julia Monsanto and Evelyn head the list. Evelyn didn't do it because it wouldn't suit my needs to have her carted off to jail, and Julia didn't because she'd probably forget about it before carrying out the foul deed. Unless she intended to kill one of the two H's and got Fred by mistake. Now that I think of it, that's a real possibility. They've been trying to fire her as head of the TV department for years."

"Why haven't they?" I asked.

"Fred wouldn't let them," Evelyn interjected before Wally had a chance. "She got him his first job with Leo Burnett, and she also introduced him to Harland when the real third H died." She paused for breath and lost the floor.

"Who had the decency to die after a respectable heart attack," Wally continued. "Ev is correct about our warble-throated Julia though. Fred considered her his muse."

"Warble-throated Julia?" Evelyn cried out. "Christ, your copy stinks."

"Hmm, you might be right again," he conceded. "I have you to blame for that. The negative effects of love. Far too relaxing."

The splotches on Evelyn's face seemed to melt into one even layer of embarrassed red. She tried to hide behind her salad.

"Love would do wonders for you, Gregory," Wally

74

said. There was no stopping him. "You know it's not too late to try again. Not all women are stinkers. Simona's a good example of the nonstinker type. She has the whipped dog syndrome — totally harmless. Ev, I fear, not only barks, she bites, which I find irresistible." He tried to give her backside a slap but only managed to hit the rim of the chair seat.

I stopped eating. Gregory smiled. It was his only defense. Wally ignored our reactions. He was far too busy rubbing his throbbing hand under the table.

"Stinkers, Stinko, great name for that perfume," he went on. "Ann Lester loves it. She finagled the one and only bottle in the country from Fred. If Janick knew, he'd have 'le crise de foie.' " Wally moved his eyebrows up and down à la Groucho Marx. "I wonder what she had to do to get it?"

Evelyn bared her canines.

"No matter," he continued, raising a calming hand. "What does matter is that now she practically floats through the office on the strength of that smell. She positively stank at last Sunday's meeting. I'm amazed Janick didn't notice. Thank God he doesn't want any copy for that stuff. All I can come up with as a headline is SINK WITH THE STINK. After all, I do believe in truth in advertising." He got up and released a great quantity of crumbs to the animal contingent waiting below.

"Since when are you big on truth?" Evelyn pushed her empty plate aside and reached for a cigarette. "Your words convinced me to buy some stupid cream that promised to give me 'the complexion of an English rose in the dewy morn.' Instead I look like a rose who's barely survived a hailstorm."

"I'm making it up to you, aren't I?" Wally gave her an embarrassingly lascivious grin and poured the three of us wine from magnum number two. Evelyn's glass remained empty.

"I liked the perfume," I said.

"When did you smell it?" Wally asked.

"Yesterday. She drowned herself in it for her meeting

with the detectives."

"Trying to seduce two hard-working policemen? That sounds like her." Wally nodded his head in approval. "For a minute I thought you might have been the hot date Fred was so happy about. Seriously though, I do consider myself lucky that Janick thinks just the word 'Free' and gorgeous photos are going to do the trick."

"You'll have to come up with something for the TV commercials," Evelyn quipped.

"A full orchestra and a few bons mots at the end delivered by a cognac-hued male voice should suffice. Things like 'Free for love, Free for life, Free for happiness.' "

Evelyn applauded and Wally beamed. It didn't even dawn on him that she might be making fun of him.

"This is a classic case of 'cherchez la femme,' " Evelyn said. "I'll bet anything that this is a crime of passion. Fred was killed by a woman, you just wait and see." She dug into the homemade ice cream Gregory had brought to the table. She could resist spaghetti and wine, but not dessert.

"Women always like to take all the credit." Wally took the floor again. "I read in the *Times* that 85% of murders are committed by men, so logic says you are wrong."

"To hell with logic," Evelyn countered.

"Typically female," I said before he could. I continued quickly for fear of being interrupted by another flow of words. "How did it go on Sunday?" I asked. "What was the meeting all about?"

"Fred was unusually gallant and charming with Janick," Wally answered, filling my wineglass again. "He explained that he didn't want to interfere, but he needed to know the scheduling since such an important campaign would affect the entire agency, and he had to plan other ads for other clients, and so on and so forth. It went surprisingly well. In the past I've sat in on meetings between those two that were so unpleasant, I was reduced to silence."

"Then they couldn't have been all that bad," came from Evelyn. Wally lifted an arm as if to hit her, but refrained. I think he was scared of hitting the chair again.

"Fred wasn't very happy on Friday," I said. "Did any of you talk to him that day?"

Gregory shook his head.

"I was locked in my room trying to come up with pure Shakespearean copy," Wally said.

"You could have spoken to him on the phone," I ventured.

"The only person I exchanged greetings with was Bertrand, scout's honor."

"What's it to you?" Evelyn wanted to know.

"Apparently he got very angry a phone call, and I was wondering why." And what had happened to his ring?

"Well, he sure got over it by Sunday. Right, Wally?" Evelyn asked for corroboration. He nodded in assent.

"What's much more important than the deceased's erratic moods," he said, "is whether you've come up with any models yet?"

"Four are coming on Monday, but there just isn't enough time."

"Oh, cheer up," Evelyn said. "We can always do a Dana ad. Big hairy hand on a white gooselike female neck, face conveniently off screen. Or even better we can shoot a mysterious shadow. That's what she originally came up with for the Merry shirt ad being shot on Tuesday."

"Dana is shooting the Merry shirt ad on Tuesday?" I asked in surprise. "On Thursday she asked me to let go of the photographer, Paul Langston, and we hadn't finished picking models yet. She certainly worked fast. Who's shooting it?"

"Beats me," Evelyn said. "I don't need to know who it is. That's your department. All I care about is that she meet her deadlines, which she hasn't been doing lately. Dana's getting nuttier every day. She's beginning to remind me of Julia."

"I think Ev has a point," Wally said. He hadn't spoken for two minutes. He needed to exercise his jaw. "She certainly had a wild Ophelia look on Sunday. When I asked her what she was doing on the seventeenth floor in front of the ladies room on a Sunday, in a very friendly way, mind you, she fled toward the stairs, but of course they were locked. I could hear her jiggling the door handle. She was gone by the time I came out of the meeting. She was probably waiting for Papa Fred's approving nod on some ad or other."

Or she was Fred's hot date. But that should have made her look very happy, not suicidal.

"Why can't these women do the job on their own?" Wally asked Gregory rhetorically. "You don't see Bertrand running in to Fred's office. You do your job without Fred. I had my best thoughts away from the man and . . ."

"You're full of it again, Wally," Evelyn interrupted. "Bertrand didn't run in to Fred because he didn't have to. He had Mr. Harland behind him and you had Bertrand behind you. Dana owes her career to that man. So do I to a certain extent. He thought we had talent and gave us a chance. He was the man behind us and we went back out of gratitude."

Wally shook his head slowly. "You went back because you had no choice."

Instead of answering, Evelyn clamped her mouth down on another cigarette.

"We're all cowards," Gregory said quietly. He reached for his full glass and drank the no longer cold wine in long deliberate sips. "Cowards," he repeated.

"Not me," Wally said. "My life's an open book." He shifted in his chair to face me. "What about you, Simona? What was Fred shaming you with?"

"I don't know what you're talking about."

"Then I guess Fred died just in time." Wally leered. "Lucky you."

"If he says one more word, I swear I'll leave him," Evelyn announced, standing up. She looked like she meant it.

When she reached the door, she said, "Thanks a lot, both of you. The meal was super. And Simona, I'd appreciate it if you'd keep your mouth shut about Wally and me." Instead of a good-bye, she regaled us with one of her trumpet sneezes and a slam of the door. Wally rushed after her without saying a word.

"What was that all about?" I asked as I cleared the dishes and Gregory rinsed them off.

"Too much wine, on top of his innate penchant for spinning tales."

"All of that," I said through my own wine haze. "All of that and much more."

"He means well, you know, even though he says unpleasant things." Kind Gregory immediately came to his defense.

"Do you like him that much?"

"He makes Evelyn happy and she's a good friend."

"Why is her affair with Wally such a secret?"

"Because it's just that—an affair. She knows she can't keep him for long, and I suppose she thinks the loss will be easier to take if no one knows she had something to begin with."

"Is that what happened to you?" I asked bluntly.

"Maybe tomorrow, Simona," Gregory answered without visible signs of annoyance. "I'm tired too."

Chapter Nine

I woke up with white wine fuzz on my tongue, garlic on my breath and ringless hands on my brain. I felt great. When I went to the bathroom to remedy the state of my mouth, if not my brain, I draped a towel over the mirror as if I were in mourning.

As I was about to walk downstairs, I found Mamma Cat in front of Gregory's door protesting loudly and a note from Gregory saying he had gone to get the Sunday *Times* with Patch and to wait for him for breakfast. Mamma Cat wound herself around my legs, her worn-out tits flopping against my ankles, beseeching me to do something. The mystery of her despair was soon solved when I heard a weak echo of her cry from the other side of the door. The minute I opened the door an inch, a fur ball jumped out. I had intended to open the door a few inches, enough to free the locked-up kitten, but not enough to invade Gregory's privacy. I didn't make it. It's useless to make excuses for myself so I won't. I stepped into the room unashamed. It was just an ordinary room, with a few of the same baskets and pottery found in the kitchen. As I stared around, I wondered why he needed to keep the door closed. The sheets were clean, the bed made, the floor swept, no dirty underwear lying about, no sinister secret seemed to be lurking. And then I saw the photographs pasted on the wall next to his bed. You couldn't see them until you walked into the heart of the room. I stepped closer and saw they were all of the same girl, and my heart started beating itself into an aerobic frenzy. There was my model for the perfume campaign, the unknown Paulina that I was looking for. I didn't know who she was, where she was, what she was in relation to Gregory, but I knew that she was perfect. There were at least twenty pictures of her in many stages of growth. In the grown-up ones she couldn't have been more than twenty-two years old. In some close-ups she looked like a darker version of the young Rita Hayworth; in others, especially when she laughed, her eyes had the crazy twinkle of Bette Midler. She was beautiful because her face spoke, it told you whatever you wanted to hear. She was vibrant, alive, moody, sensual and I don't know what else. She was all those advertising words blended together into one face.

I heard Patch's nails come tearing up the stairs and reality took over. To be more honest, it was fear rather than reality. I didn't want Gregory to catch me in his room, and yet I had to know about this woman he so obviously adored in secret. Patch stopped outside the bedroom door and looked at me, his tail wagging. He was waiting for a word or a gesture; even the dog needed permission to enter the sanctuary. I felt so awful I turned my back to the pictures and walked out quietly. Gregory had stayed downstairs and had not seen me; the animal family would keep my secret. I walked down to the kitchen firmly convinced I could forget her.

I riffled through the Sunday paper and drank my coffee, but when Mamma Cat jumped on my lap and gratefully licked my hand, I burst. I blurted out words about locked-up kittens, betrayal of friendship, deception, and forgiveness. I was so upset myself that I didn't notice what Gregory did with my words. Carefully I averted my eyes from his face, and he sure didn't pat my hand and say it was all right. I think I

81

finally stopped speaking when the empty space around me sounded louder than I did. It was as if the warmth of the house and its inhabitants had been sucked away by a gigantic vacuum cleaner.

"She's my daughter, Ellen," Gregory finally said. "Ellen Price." He raised his voice when he gave her full name as if he wanted to prove to me she was indeed his.

"Where is she?"

"She grew up in Nebraska with my sister. She's still there, in Omaha, working in an office." Gregory made no mention of her mother and I wasn't about to ask, but I did wonder if she was the stinker Wally had mentioned the night before.

"Does she ever come here and visit you?"

"No, we only see each other when I take my yearly vacation. I don't want her here. I don't want her here," he repeated and banged his coffee cup on the table. I gave it a try anyway.

"I'm not the one who does the final choosing, but I really do think she would be perfect for the 'Free' campaign. We could fly her in for a few days, have some shots of her taken by Scriba, see how she reacts to the camera, show the shots to Janick and it's done. If it doesn't work out she will have had some fun, glamorous times in New York with her old-fashioned Dad." I gave Gregory a patronizing kiss on his bald spot. I was beginning to feel very good about the whole thing. "But," I added, a big resonating "but" that filled the room. I was playing Faye Dunaway in *Network* full force. "But if she is right, then, my dear illustrator of other people's dreams, her life will become a dream and you can retire."

"Sure, she can sell her looks for money, let herself be used as bait in fancy restaurants so the owner can attract a trendy clientele, dance at the Palladium every night and snort with the guys, or have her face slashed like that Hanson girl. Some dream. Sure, why don't

82

we fly her in tomorrow."

"So maybe it isn't a dream," I admitted. "It still is a great job possibility. Why shouldn't she earn a lot of money if she can. There's nothing wrong with that. And you're going to be here to help her. Why not try, Gregory, please. She is so perfect. And who knows, if she likes acting, it may even lead to that. If not, after ten years of work that will take her all over the world, she can retire and buy up half the state of Nebraska. Would that really be awful for her?" He didn't answer me.

"Let me have a picture of her at least," I pleaded. "Let's show it to Bertrand and see what he says. He may not like her at all. I could be totally off. Come on, Gregory, showing her picture isn't going to do any harm. You can still say no." As soon as I said that I realized his permission wasn't needed. Ellen was an adult, she could make up her own mind. All I needed was a picture.

He said "no." And I blew up.

"Who the hell do you think you are, dictating other people's lives? Do you think your life is so perfect? Take a good look at yourself, Gregory. You're a small man who's gone into hiding behind Magic Markers. Yes, like kids' crayons. You have a talent that should have been showing in some SoHo gallery, but it's so much easier to draw pretty pictures of other people's ideas, isn't it? You surround yourself with cats and dogs instead of having your daughter next to you. She's beautiful so you bury her in some obsolete state with your sister. Why the hell didn't you bring her up?" I was practically spitting on him. "Oh, I know, it's the old classic. She reminded you of her mother, who is either dead or fucking someone else, so you've chased her away, except for three measly weeks a year. Or is it the wicked city that isn't the right atmosphere for bringing up baby? For Christ's sake, Gregory, you should be so proud of her. She's so beautiful and I bet she's great too. Why aren't you showing her off to everybody?" I ran out of breath.

Gregory sat at the kitchen table and stroked his favorite ginger kitten. I didn't look too closely because I suspected he was crying. I was having trouble with my eyes too. I turned around and went upstairs to pack my bag. When I came downstairs Gregory and the animals had disappeared, but a nice close-up shot of Ellen lay on the table.

Back in my studio I undressed, took a very hot shower so that I would feel cool when I got out, and then lay on my loft bed staring at Ellen's photograph. The open windows brought 96 degrees of air into my single room. Staring at beautiful Ellen in my sweat wasn't doing anything to help my mood, so I closed my eyes and soon fell asleep.

I dreamt of Ellen running naked in the sand with Fred chasing her. He caught her and started choking her. I could see a close-up of his hands on her throat. They were white and swollen. The hands of a drowned man. And there was no ring on his little finger, just a purple welt, as if the ring had been wrenched off. I woke with a start to the intercom buzzing continually. I stumbled naked to the door, realizing too late I was in full view of the windows opposite me. My body was greeted by anonymous hoots. They did not sound appreciative, and what's more, Detective Stanley Greenhouse was downstairs requesting permission to come up. I was sure he was loaded with another set of embarrassing questions. It was turning out to be a perfect Sunday.

"Just a minute," I yelled through the intercom, then quickly ran to the bathroom to get dressed.

With underarms as dry as the desert, a mouth as fresh as mint, and an unforgettable face by Revlon, I buzzed him up and waited nervously by the door. I was also dressed.

He made it up the stairs in seconds. "You get quite a workout everyday, Miss Griffo." He wasn't even out of breath, so how did he know?

"Simona. Surely on a Sunday it can be Simona. Can I offer you something? Coke, iced tea, Sambuca, Amaretto?" I added the liqueurs just to see if his was an official call. They always decline alcohol when they're on duty. I'd seen that in the movies.

"No, thanks, I'm fine," he said, which wasn't very helpful.

He took three steps into the room and sat down on my makeshift sofa. Looking at him atop two mattresses, camouflaged by a white *matelassé* spread I had brought from Italy, I forgot he was a policeman investigating a murder, and I began to feel better about the day. Greenhouse was perfect sitting there, framed by the wooden scaffolding of my loft bed hovering above. He gave the apartment that extra touch, that *je ne sais quoi* that all decorators seek and few find. He was dressed casually, an alligator shirt, khakis, Timberlands. Very different from the efficient tan suit, button-down shirts and ties I had seen him in at the office. He looked softer too. Less tucked in, more simpatico. He even had a twinkle in his eye. Actually it felt more like a flashing Times Square neon sign, beckoning me to buy. I sat on my trunk, just a few feet away from him, and enjoyed the view.

"I just came by on an impulse," Greenhouse said. "I mean, I was in the area. I went to see that movie you mentioned, the one playing just a few blocks away, at the Waverly."

It's also playing in half the movie theaters in town, I thought to myself. "You were right, it was very funny," he said and then stopped dead. He was looking at my graffiti wall.

"Valuable paintings?" he asked, referring to the clean white rectangles the pictures left behind, making

85

the wall look as if it had been stripped of so many Band-Aids.

"No, just photographs."

He walked over to the door and examined the lock. The wooden jam had already been fixed by a carpenter. "Get a Fox Police lock put in, with a Medeco cylinder. It comes with a bar that locks into the floor. It's the best for a wooden door." With a few long steps and a stoop, he was back on the mattresses, looking as if he'd always belonged there. "Did you report it?"

"No, it happened Monday, and with Fred's death and everything . . ."

Greenhouse looked at me with soft eyes. "You don't take very good care of yourself, do you?"

I took a deep breath. Why should I? I thought. Out loud I said, "By going to the Waverly, I guess you were checking out my alibi? Not that an alibi is needed," I added.

"What do you mean?"

"No one needs an alibi. It's not as if the killer had to be there. Fred wasn't shot or stabbed. All the killer had to do was put the cyanide in the capsules and leave the pills on his desk."

Greenhouse shook his head. "You're wrong about the alibi. It's needed all right. The killer had to be sure that Fred, not someone else, was going to take those capsules. If they were just going to be left in Fred's office, anyone could have taken them. Someone at that Sunday meeting could have had a headache and asked for a capsule."

"Not for a headache," I corrected. "They were antihistamines."

"And that's the funny thing," Greenhouse said. He leaned back, his head almost hitting the wooden frame of the bed above. "Fred apparently didn't suffer from allergies. We checked with his doctor and everyone who was with him on Sunday maintains he didn't have a cold. So why did he take two Nozphrees, and how

86

did the killer know he was going to take them? He didn't stuff them down his throat."

"Did you come here to ask me that? I'm afraid I can't answer."

"No, I was just thinking out loud. That's not why I came. I just don't get down here a lot anymore." His face was flushed, but I didn't know if that was from the heat or from shyness. "When you mentioned you lived in the Village, I thought, why not, let's go see what it's turned into."

"Well, do you like it?"

"Sixth Avenue is a little dirty." He pointed toward the TV set sitting next to me on the trunk. "Is that what was used for the art work?" The Krylon spray can was standing on top of the TV like an Oscar on a marble mantle.

I nodded. He got a handkerchief out of his back pocket and reached over to pick up the can. "Do you have a bag I can put this in?" He didn't even ask if he could take it. I liked that. He was taking care of me.

"I saw him," I said, handing him an A&P bag from the kitchen corner next to the bathroom. "I wouldn't be able to recognize him. It happened too fast. But he was wearing a leather jacket."

"And you think he's the same guy who stole in the office."

"It's possible."

Greenhouse put the Krylon can into the bag and retrieved his handkerchief. "This city is full of leather jackets. Even in July." He looked toward the open window overlooking a FOR SALE brownstone across the street. "Most people have air-conditioning." He looked back at me. A nice, open face. "Where's that Steve's ice cream place you mentioned? Raf says I really ought to try the stuff."

"Two blocks up on Sixth. Just around the corner."

"Want to join me? It'll cool us both off." Then he realized what he'd said and he became even redder. I laughed happily.

"Don't worry, Greenhouse, I know what you mean. It's broiling in here."

The line in front of Steve's was so long that we had to forget about the benefits of air-conditioning and wait outside. It didn't help the conversation any. Someone leaving the store with a big sundae knocked into me, and I was pushed against Greenhouse. Touching him was wonderful. I just wanted to stay there, leaning against him. I think I did, longer than was necessary, but he didn't push me away.

"Is the ice cream worth the wait?" Greenhouse asked.

"Definitely. Besides, I love this place. See that bulletin board by the window? That's how I found my apartment. A student flunked out of NYU Law School and needed someone to pick up his lease quickly. I got a bargain considering New York prices."

"Funny place to advertise an abortion clinic," Greenhouse said.

"Where?" It was his turn to lean toward me as he pointed to a corner of the bulletin board. I stared at the printed cardboard. "No one will know except you," it promised in English and Spanish with the doctor's name printed underneath. Pretty courageous to advertise so openly in these times, I thought, getting an odd, uncomfortable feeling. The address was close by, a few blocks into the East Village. Maybe a Right To Lifer was going to blow the whole place up.

"Do you want to write the name down?" Greenhouse asked, his hand wrapping around my forearm.

"Oh, no, there's no way I could be pregnant," I blurted out. His skin was touching mine and I didn't know what the hell I was saying. "What I mean is," I swallowed for stability, "at the moment, I don't need that. I was staring because there's something familiar about the ad, but I now realize the place is very close to me and I walk by there all the time." I wanted to kick myself for letting him know a man hadn't been anywhere near me in ages.

Greenhouse looked back at the sign. "I guess a lot of teenagers eat ice cream, and a lot of teenagers get pregnant." He let go of my arm. "Do you have kids?"

"No, I just eat ice cream. How did you become a policeman?" I asked, steering him into safer territory.

Greenhouse gave me a twisted smile.

"You've been asked that before?"

"A couple of hundred times," he answered.

I was annoyed. "I'm sorry, but I was only trying to make conversation."

"I know," he said soothingly. "The New York party. First comes the introduction, then the 'and what do you do?' When I tell them I'm a cop they quickly head for the bar."

The idea of Greenhouse standing abandoned in the middle of a party was highly unlikely, no matter what his job was. There were too many hungry females about. "I think it's a pretty rude question myself," I said, "but I might not mind it if I could answer vice president, Chemical Bank."

"Art buyer is nothing to be ashamed of," Greenhouse said and moved up five inches in the line and five inches closer to my heart.

"With my salary? Anyway, I never say art buyer. Everyone thinks I'm buying paintings. I say I'm a casting director for print ads. They're very impressed."

Greenhouse laughed. I guess he didn't like party snobs either.

"My pet peeve number two is 'And where do you live?'" I said, feeling encouraged. "That gives people an instant replay of your bank balance. Saying I live in the Village has brought mixed reactions, though. One eager girl said, 'How exciting, are you an artist?' A woman with diamond rocks in her ears said, "With a doorman, I hope." Then there was the man, I've erased his face from my memory, who looked me up and down and then snarled, "You're not one of those dykes, are you?"

Several people in line turned around and looked at me. I had been talking a little too loudly.

"My favorite answer," I continued almost in a whisper, "came from a dark pin-striped suit and vest I met at a party. You know, the lawyer type. He was somewhere in his forties and good looking. 'The Village?' he said. 'That's a bit low, isn't it?' I still don't know if he meant low in life or low in the geography of Manhattan. And all the time I was talking to him I was hoping vainly he'd treat me to an expensive dinner."

"Serves you right then," Greenhouse said, gripping my shoulders and shaking them gently. We had finally reached the inside of the store and its powerful air conditioner, but I wasn't feeling the cold at all.

"I'm going to ask again," I said once his hands left my skin. "How did you become a policeman? You look so Ivy League to me and I've always thought of policemen as more the Marlboro man type."

"I have a feeling that wasn't a compliment," Greenhouse said and continued smiling.

"I've never liked those big gruff men, really," I lied.

"I went to NYU. Had I made Columbia, you would have been right about the Ivy League. I was going to go into my father's printing business. I even had plans for an MBA."

"When did you graduate?" I was wondering about his age. I had the unpleasant suspicion he was a few years younger than I was.

"I didn't. My father died and I couldn't go on."

"Did you run out of money?"

"No, there's money still there. More than enough. It just didn't make any sense getting a degree."

"What'll it be?" a pale, overworked teenager asked us with a tone of infinite patience. He looked like he

90

hadn't seen the summer sun since his birth. I had my usual, but Greenhouse took some time choosing. He looked so helpless as he studied the wall with all the flavor listings that I just wanted to hug him. I licked my spoon instead.

Once outside we didn't know where to head with our very full cups. The apartment was out, the heat would have melted us down. There aren't any places to sit in the Village without ordering something, except Washington Square Park. On Sunday it's a perfect zoo, wild animals and staring onlookers all congregated on one square block of concrete interspersed with a few tufts of drugged out grass.

"Let's go to my old college campus and watch the junkies ply their trade." Greenhouse said starting to walk south with a heaping cup of ice cream in one hand, and a incriminated spray can in a plastic bag in the other. "It's my favorite spectator sport. If we're lucky, we'll find an empty bench."

The bench he chose once we got to the park wasn't exactly empty. A young couple was mushed together at one end slobbering kisses on each other. We silently slobbered our ice cream, trying not to look.

Greenhouse leaned over toward me and whispered dangerously close to my very sensitive ear, "NYU students meeting their Phys. Ed. requirement." I turned my face quickly to look at the couple and came within three millimeters of kissing Greenhouse somewhere around his chin. I wished I hadn't missed.

"Wouldn't your father have wanted you to finish college?" I asked, turning quickly away.

"My father always wanted me to do what was right for me. He didn't encourage me to follow in his footsteps. He'd say, 'Go with your gut, but use your head to satisfy that instinct. And never forget the people around you. They're just as important as you are.' He was an all-right man. He helped a lot of immigrants come over after the war, sponsored them, helped get

91

them jobs. He believed in helping people." Green-house spoke and continued to enjoy his ice cream. One did not exclude the other. There were no sighs, no nostalgic hesitations. He was at ease with his memory.

"After he got killed by some doped-up mugger in the elevator of his office building one night, I got to know the police force pretty closely. I liked what I saw and both my gut and my head said yes, this was the way to go, this was my way to help people."

"Did they ever find the killer?"

"No, he's somewhere in this city, if he isn't dead of an overdose."

"Isn't that the real reason you became a policeman? So that you could find your father's killer or take out your anger on the guys you pick up? Aren't you full of hate?"

"No to all of the above. You've been reading too many psychology books."

I looked at his face. His eyes had shut off the neon. They were clear, sincere brown, and they looked back at me with confidence. I believed him.

I searched my purse for a pack of cigarettes, then my skirt. I needed one badly and that's when you never have one. To give myself something to do, I took his empty ice cream cup and walked to an over-flowing garbage can. I stuffed both our cups in there as best I could. I felt funny. The conversation had turned serious, and I didn't know quite how to handle that. Should I start talking about myself, get personal and risk scaring him off, or should I just play light and fluffy, forever happy? And why was his face so likeable. Somehow finding room in the garbage can for my two empty cups was becoming increasingly difficult.

"Why don't I do that for you," said wonderful Lancelot to nervous Guinevere, as she fumbled with her bra. Greenhouse put the cups in the garbage can with one assertive push of his forefinger. My make-believe bra fell to the ground.

"I'll walk you back," he said in a tone that offered no choices. I nodded my head in agreement despite his tone and wished I lived on Two hundred and Tenth Street.

"Are you coming to the office tomorrow?" I asked after a block of silence. We were walking very slowly, our arms brushing each other.

"No, I'm also working on another case with Raf, but I'm glad you brought that up."

Please let him ask me out tomorrow night.

"We never did get a chance to talk to Dana Lehrman on Friday. She didn't show."

"We?" I said sarcastically. No date. We were back to official business. "You're the one who's always in charge. I think you have Detective Garcia tag along just for comic relief."

"Who are you trying to knock, me or him?" Greenhouse asked with an unamused face.

"I'm sorry," I said. "I get very crabby at the end of Sundays. And this one's been worse than most. What were you going to say about Dana?" As I spoke, I put the palm of my hand on his arm and held it there for a few seconds. I just needed the reassurance of his skin again. It was warm and smooth and it helped.

"We need to ask Dana Lehrman some questions. Can you make sure we'll get hold of her on Tuesday?"

"She's shooting a print ad that day on the lake in Central Park. She won't be too happy to see two policeman coming."

"She should have shown up on Friday," Greenhouse said.

"At least Detective Garcia will be happy."

"You're right. He can't wait to see some models. He wants to show off to all the guys in the precinct. I'm assuming there are going to be some models, or will it be just a romantic photograph of the lake?"

93

"No, there'll be models. Four models. One male, three female. But I doubt they are the kind that Detective Garcia is going to like." I don't know why we kept talking about Raf. I was sure Greenhouse was just as interested.

"What do you mean?" Greenhouse asked.

"Dana is going for the sophisticated look on this ad, so the girls are very tall and thin."

"You mean string beans with no tits? That's too bad. Maybe we should wait for her next shoot." When he saw my look of dismay, he laughed. "I was only kidding. If Raf isn't satisfied, he can always look at you."

Greenhouse must have thrown out caution along with the empty cups. What he was pointing out was the fact that I am well-endowed, which is my mother's euphemism for top heavy. What he didn't know was that normally I would have given anything to look like one of those sophisticated string beans, but by the way Greenhouse was looking at me, I had an inkling that he and Raf shared the same tastes and at that moment my body suited me just fine.

"Will you meet us there?" he asked me, his face shifting to serious.

"Sure, I like nothing better than getting out of the office." I wanted to add "with you," but didn't. "By the way, I remembered something this weekend that might be important to you."

We had reached my building by now, and we stood in front of the stone steps that led to an old town house that had gone the way of Gloria Swanson in *Sunset Boulevard.*

"HH&H gives a signet ring to all employees who have been there ten years. Fred had one. He got it shortly before I joined the agency, and he always wore it. He didn't have it on him when I saw him dead."

"Thanks, we know about the ring," Greenhouse said. There went my great contribution toward solving the mystery. "The ring left an indentation on the

94

little finger of his left hand which means it couldn't have been off of his finger that long."

"Did you ask the people who saw him on Sunday whether he was wearing the ring?"

"No one remembers noticing it one way or the other, except the head of the TV Department, Julia Monsanto. She swears he was wearing it."

"Good luck with Julia," I said, throwing my arms up in the air. "She has little pieces of her brain misplaced about the city."

"So everyone tells me."

"I'll bet you anything that ring has something to do with the killing. I'm sure of it," I said excitedly. I wanted to help him, get involved in his work. I also wanted the murder relegated to the "Finished and Over With" file.

"I wouldn't say that if I were you," Greenhouse warned.

"Why, don't you think it has something to do with Fred's death? Aren't you going to look for it?"

"We have found the ring, and I don't know what to think." His voice was flat, no expression. The sound of it made me look at him closely. He did not have a happy face.

"What is it?" I asked.

"Fred Critelli's signet ring was found hidden in a Kleenex box, in the second drawer on the lefthand side of a desk. Your desk."

I ran up all four flights of stairs as fast as I could. He didn't follow me.

Chapter Ten

It was already nine o'clock in the morning, but I couldn't get up. I couldn't face climbing down the shaky wooden ladder next to my bed, touching the bare floor with my feet and being forced to face the nauseating light of a bright July morning. I preferred to lie there, staring above me, curling my toes and sucking my thumb. I didn't know how that ring had gotten into my desk, and I was frightened. Fear wasn't the only feeling I was drowning in. I felt thoroughly humiliated. Greenhouse's friendly visit had been a sham. I had made the usual mistake of building an entire Hollywood screenplay, complete with a walk into the sunset holding hands, based on the misconception a man had come to see me because he wanted to enjoy my company; instead what he had really wanted was to see if I could be a murderer. If I hadn't volunteered the information about the ring, probably I would have been under lock and key at that very moment, instead of tossing and turning in my bed. How did the ring get into my Kleenex box? I knew I hadn't put it there and I hadn't killed Fred, but my assertions of innocence wouldn't be enough for Greenhouse, at least not Greenhouse the policeman.

After a while the picture I painted on the ceiling

fifteen inches above my nose looked too bleak, and my thoughts wandered in search of some comfort. "He has such a nice face it couldn't be capable of deceit," I told myself. And there was no denying the beckoning neon in his eyes. Maybe he really did like me. He had looked so sad when he told me about the ring. Sad and disappointed. Maybe he felt I had let him down, not the other way around. "Damn it," I said to myself as I slid out of bed with the renewed energy of hope, "I'm going to find out who took that ring." I was happily into screenplay II.

In the office, a nervous Bertrand was waiting for me.

"Where've you been? There are some models downstairs waiting to be seen."

"Can't you see them on your own?" I asked testily. "You're the one who has to like them." I had completely forgotten about the 'Free' campaign.

"No, I want to discuss them with you. I need a woman's opinion." Bertrand pushed me into his office and phoned Mattie to send the girls up, one at a time. Luckily, only four were scheduled to come that morning. Now that I had Ellen's picture, I wasn't going to look for other models, but I did want more time before showing Bertrand my discovery and another chance to convince Gregory that I wasn't out to ruin his daughter.

"Look, Bertrand, I've got some big problems with this murder. I need some time out. What about calling down Ann Lester? She can help you narrow them down. After all, she's the account supervisor of this thing."

"Marble-hearted Lester? What does she know about femininity and charm?"

"In my opinion, a lot," I countered.

97

Bertrand was as stubborn as a mule. "No, darling, I need a real woman to help me. Besides, I like your company better. You're younger, prettier, sexier." He reached over and squeezed my hand. My mouth almost fell open. That had been a definite come-on and a complete surprise. I wondered if Fred's ghost wasn't playing tricks on both of us. Besides, I would have sworn Bertrand would have only been interested in the Muffys and Puffys of his restricted world. I mean, I was 100 percent WOP, not WASP. I retrieved my hand and tried to look nonchalant.

Model number one walked in dressed in jeans that had been cut off to show half her ass, knee-high boots that, given the weather outside, could only be justified if they hid bad ankles, and a loose shirt that hadn't seen a washing machine in a long time. I peered at the yards of shirt suspiciously and deduced that the only rotundity she possessed was in her ass. It was a great-looking ass, but that alone doesn't necessarily sell perfume. Bertrand was busy being very charming, while I wondered what the hell had possessed me to call her in. Even her face was buried by a mass of unruly red-brown hair. I looked over Bertrand's shoulder as he leafed through her portfolio, and I saw the picture that had intrigued both of us. It was a shot of her from the waist up, looking at an off-camera point to her left, her head leaning against a beige sofa. Her hair had been pulled straight back to reveal a small delicate face with porcelain skin. That particular photographer had done a superb job. I looked at her in real life, and all I saw was an aggressive pout and skin that was gasping for fresh air.

"She must give her parents a bad time, that one," was Bertrand's only comment after he had given her retreating back the attention it commanded. How quaint of him, I thought.

Model number two entered the room in stages. First a bangled arm appeared on the doorjamb, then a long leg, followed by the rest of the six feet. Apart from her rehearsed entrance, she was pleasant to look at. I could see that Bertrand was interested by how slowly he looked at her portfolio. He even sat her down and offered her a cup of coffee, which she declined. He placed his chair very close to her and asked to see her hands. As he held them, he told her a joke. After the terrible punch line she gave a little closed-mouth smile of politeness.

"I want you to laugh for me," Bertrand said, trying the direct approach. "Can you do that?"

She tried several times. "I'm sorry, my teeth aren't that great. I guess I have a complex about them." Her teeth looked toothpaste-ad-perfect to me, but you can't fight someone's opinion of themselves.

"That's all right, don't worry about it." Bertrand said, finally letting go of her hands. "You've got a great-looking portfolio." He took a comp (a composite picture of her) for our files and returned the book to her. "Thanks for coming by."

She stood and looked at him eye level. I think Bertrand was a little disconcerted by her height; he was used to looking down. Her departure was much more rapid than her entrance. She must have sensed that her chances had died with her inability to laugh.

"Why did you have to hold her hands for so long?" I asked only out of curiosity.

Bertrand came over and stroked my hair. "I like to touch. I'm a sensualist at heart." I moved my head from his hand.

"I held her hands to see how her face would react to my touching her. How someone reacts to touching says a lot. She didn't like it. And she wasn't able to laugh. For this campaign I need someone who is at ease with herself, happy, curious. Who likes to touch and be touched. A sensualist, like me. And I suspect, like you."

That remark made something stir in my tummy. It was the memory of my hand touching Greenhouse's arm the night before. I stared at the carpet and buried that thought in a soft wave of gray pile near my right foot, and then I forced myself to concentrate on the business at hand.

Would Ellen Price fit the bill? I thought efficiently and then said, "I would have hardly defined you as a sensualist. You always look so proper, uptight."

"See how little you know of me, Simona?" Bertrand said very softly.

Wally walked in, grinning, with model number three. The interruption was very welcome.

"We met at the elevator and Miss Lucas looked lost. I thought I'd escort her here." His hand was firmly attached to her elbow, and she didn't mind it at all.

Miss Lucas was as pretty as a magnolia and had a figure and a drawl to match. She simpered, sighed with her breasts and fluttered her long lashes like fans fighting the Mississippi heat. I decided she must have been in New York all of two hours, and I was ready to send her right back home. The men did not agree with me. The three of them hovered over her shots. By the way she let the two men bump into her she sure looked like a sensualist to me, and I almost hoped Bertrand would love her. Then I could forget about Ellen, and Gregory and I could be friends again.

Evelyn poked her head in with the excuse she was looking for Ann Lester. Women's instinct is fantastic, I thought to myself. How had she known that Wally was in Bertrand's room rubbing himself against an eighteen-year-old Southern Belle? It was that good old jealous tension that keeps all our senses in a constant state of war alert. I remembered the feeling well.

Wally didn't bother to move away from the model. In fact, he didn't even bother to look at Evelyn, and I felt sorry for her. Nothing of what she must have been going through showed on her face as she closed the door behind her.

Miss Lucas was finally released and wobbled out of the room on her three-inch white heels. If she was going to pound the sidewalks to show her wares to the New York advertising world, she was either going to have to take lessons from Jenny Fenton or buy a pair of sneakers like the rest of the Manhattan women.

"Well, she certainly likes to be touched. She knows how to laugh. In fact, she never stopped laughing. And all of her is gorgeous. So what do you think?" I asked Bertrand.

Wally said, "We forgot to look at her toes. Let's call her back." He ran out the door as if pursuing her. He didn't come back.

"She is all of what you say, Simona, but she has one very big flaw."

"And what is that?" I asked, expecting him to say she had a mole on her left shoulder that bothered him.

"She's stupid and it shows in her pictures. I don't want women to envy our model's looks; I want them to want to be her. Whoever is going to model for the perfume is going to end up doing all the Janick product line, so she has to be fantastic."

"And you're shooting at the end of next week?"

"That's right. Don't give me that look, Simona. That's what advertising is all about. You must have had impossible deadlines dubbing movies. You're not new to this."

"Don't remind me. I nearly died each time. We

101

were either trying to open for Christmas Eve or Easter or trying to get to the Cannes, Venice, Berlin, or whatever film festivals. Yes, I'm used to deadlines, and I hate them. Friday you didn't even know what you were shooting except for maybe a beach scene. Have you and Mr. Janick come up with something definite while cavorting at Nell's? I'm assuming Scriba is doing the photography."

We were waiting for model number four to show up. She seemed to have disappeared between floors.

"Jean wouldn't use anyone else," Bertrand said. "You'll be happy to know that Scriba and his group are taking care of all the location scouting."

"If I'd had to help with locations too," I said sweetly, "I would have sent the whole bunch of you to the Fulton Fish Market. I'm sure they can use a little perfume."

"Seriously, we've come up with a good idea," Bertrand said. "The Grand Canyon. We're going to stand her on a ledge looking out at the dawn. We'll cover her from every angle possible and in long shot, medium range, close-up. I also want to shoot the sun coming up in various stages, from the merest hint of light to a full blown burst of sunlight. We want to be able to develop a whole campaign using the Grand Canyon. Once we've firmly put the perfume on the market, we'll move into other concepts."

"Is she going to be naked?"

"No. I would have liked that, but too many people would object. It's a pity, really, because the nude figure does represent freedom nicely. But we can't ignore the sensibilities of people like my mother. She would choke on the family pearls if she knew her son was in someway connected with the 'divulgence of obscenity.' No, our model will be wearing something long and flowing. A slip of a thing that blends in with her skin and the color of the rock. We don't

102

want her dress to stand out."

"What's the headline?" I asked.

"Wally has to come up with something by this afternoon, when Jean gets here. I only told him about the Grand Canyon idea this morning, so he's not too happy with me either. I tried to call him at home yesterday from East Hampton, but he was never home."

Maybe not even Bertrand knew about Wally's affair with Evelyn.

Ten minutes had gone by since Mattie had called saying she was sending up body number four, but there was still no sign of the model. I left the room and walked along the corridor, thinking Wally was probably hidden with her in the obscurity of some office. Instead I found her sitting in a chair in my office, alone. Mattie had given her my name instead of Bertrand's.

"I'm sorry about the mix-up," I said, after introducing myself. "Have you been waiting long?"

"Not long enough," she said ruefully. "I've been at it since eight o'clock this morning, and it's great to get off my feet."

Her portfolio had obviously been retouched. In the fluorescent light of the real world, the creases of her neck gave her age away just as surely as the number of rings in a tree trunk. She would never last in a campaign that we hoped would continue many years, but I brought her to Bertrand's office anyway. After she left he asked me to keep looking.

I went right to Gregory's office instead. He was hunched over a salad.

"What, no gourmet lunch from home?" I said, as I sat down uninvited.

"It was too hot to cook yesterday." Which I translated to mean he was too upset to cook.

"Look, Gregory, I'm sorry about what I said. I got

carried away with the idea of finally getting some attention in this office. Really, I'm sorry. I'd give anything to take it back."

"No, what you said was right. At least, seen from your point of view. You don't know the whole story and even if you did, you would probably still think I was a selfish bastard. Let's just leave it alone."

"I haven't shown Bertrand the picture. I couldn't bring myself to without your blessing. I was really hoping one of the girls he saw this morning would satisfy him."

"But they didn't. And you still want Ellen, so you came here to relieve yourself of any guilt feelings. You want your cake and you want to eat it, too. Is that right, Simona?"

He was making me feel awful. I didn't say anything.

"No, I won't give my blessing. I don't believe that being a model for Janick, Inc. is going to bring Ellen any more happiness than she has now. Money yes, happiness doubtful. But I don't know for sure and, as you said, who am I to stand in her way? Besides, you don't need my consent. She's twenty-one years old. What you really want to know is if I will still be your friend." He looked at me and thought a little while. I heard the crunch of the iceberg lettuce between his teeth. Nothing stopped him from eating. "I think I am man enough not to resent what you've done," he said, after he had swallowed. "Give me a little time, though." He bent over his food so I could no longer see his face. I said "thank you" to his bald spot and walked out quietly.

In the corridor I still found myself hesitating about the photograph. If Ellen were to be selected it would certainly change her life radically. Would she weather the change well or would her solid, rural values disappear under layers of New York soot? I had no way of knowing whether she was strong or weak, emotional or sensible. Jenny, busy at the Xerox machine, helpfully wiped away my doubts.

"That sounds so neat," she said excitedly after I filled her in. "Just like a TV miniseries. Now Simonaaa, stop worrying. It'll be fine. And just think how nice it will be for both of them. Father and daughter finally together. Don't pay any attention to Gregory. He's just being a fussy old bachelor." I smiled at her gratefully.

I went back to my office to check on my status with the NYPD. Neither Raf nor Greenhouse had called. Had I become suspect numero uno? With my luck, Raf was probably busy writing out the warrant for my arrest with his stub of a pencil. Screenplay II, the life and loves of one art buyer and one quasi-Ivy League policeman, was definitely on hold until someone solved the mystery of the ring and Fred's death. I applied my supposedly international wits to the problem, but couldn't even contemplate who the murderer was, and as to the ring, Fred could have easily given it to someone. But if that had been the case, why had it turned up in my desk? Was someone trying to implicate me in Fred's death to confuse the police, or was it done out of spite? I had no way of knowing, except that I didn't think I had made any real enemies. Even whiny-mouthed Dana had no reason to get me into trouble. I was sure she begrudgingly appreciated my Madonnalike patience with her. Suddenly I remembered I hadn't told her the detectives were going to visit her on the shoot the next day and I reached for the phone. There was no answer in her office, and when reception picked up, I was told she had left for the day and could not be reached. All I could do at that point was imagine the look of dismayed disbelief on Dana's white face when I interrupted her shoot with two cops in tow.

105

I rushed to Evelyn's office and barged in without knocking. "Can you tell me where Dana is? I need to let her know something."

"Shit" was her only answer. One hand disappeared under her desk too quickly for me to see what it was hiding. With her free hand she started shifting through some papers piled high on her desk, making noise and confusion. Finally she seemed to find the sheet she wanted, and she stood up with relief. "Thank God she doesn't have any deadlines today." She showed me both her hands now. The mysterious object had been safely stashed away. "Can't help you. She disappears a lot these days." Evelyn's lips tightened in disapproval, which takes some doing since they're so full.

"What else is she working on?" I sat down without an invitation. "She has the unpleasant habit of not clueing me in, and then at the last minute she expects me to know everything and help her. All I know about is this Merry Shirts ad tomorrow, but if she was here working on Sunday, she must have some other ads coming out."

Evelyn laughed and lit a cigarette. She even offered me one. She had obviously forgiven me my rude intrusion. "So that's why you came barging in here all hot and bothered."

"Well, since Saturday . . ." I started in my defense.

"I thought you were going to forget Saturday night." It was a bark with a bite close behind it.

"You mean pretend we never had dinner together? Why? I'm not going to talk about, well, you know . . ." I didn't dare even mention Wally's name.

"I do know. First you say dinner, next it's 'Wally and Evelyn.' Much easier to forget the whole thing, not just parts of it." She sucked at her cigarette.

"As you wish," I said, getting up. What had she wanted to hide from me?

106

"Where are you going? I haven't answered your question yet," she said with the rush of friendliness that comes with the relief of having gotten away with something. "I'm just as curious as you are as to why Dana was in the office on Sunday." She gestured me back into the chair. "She's preparing a new presentation for a sock manufacturing company, but she's got time on that. My guess is that she'd give anything for the Janick account. I'll bet you she hung out by the bathroom hoping to overhear something or just to spy on the comings and goings." Smoke came out of her nose in angry spurts. "She's a spoiled brat from Long Island, who went to Europe when she was thirteen, wore Gucci at fourteen, and Tiffany diamond-stud earrings at fifteen. But I'll bet you anything she didn't get screwed until she was thirty." Evelyn parted her full lips and picked tobacco from her tongue. "I enjoy that thought. It makes me feel there's some justice in this world after all." The red spots of her blotchy complexion glowed with satisfaction, and she looked like she enjoyed a lot of things: sex, drink, smoke, whatever came along. Even pimply, obnoxious Wally.

"Could she have had a date with Fred?" I asked her.

"You mean an appointment?"

"No, a date. She might have been the hot date Wally was talking about."

"He couldn't have been that hard up." Evelyn laughed, short and sharp like a cough. "Who the hell am I to pass judgment, right? But at least Wally doesn't have Fred's looks."

"Why do you dislike her so much?"

"She has a big mouth." Evelyn shut her own full mouth tightly, and I knew I wasn't going to get anything more out of her on that subject.

"Did you see Dana here on Sunday?"

"If you're thinking what I'm thinking, forget it," she said, dismissing my thought with a smoky wave of her hand. "She couldn't kill a mosquito. One drop of blood and her pudgy face would hit the floor fast."

"There was no blood," I reminded her at the same time thinking that it would take a lot to make Evelyn faint.

"Don't be so fucking literal." She started batting those long lashes, her contacts bothering her again. "By the way," she added, "you can forget about this conversation too."

"Next thing I know, you'll be asking me to pretend you don't exist at all."

"The nice thing about this hole in the wall is that it's got real walls and a door that closes. You can come in here any time; just make sure you knock from now on."

So that I won't catch you by surprise, I thought. At that moment, Wally walked in carrying a huge, white teddy bear that could have passed for his twin, at least in girth. It had a big pink bow tied at its neck and the famous metal clip on one of its ears. Neither of them had knocked.

"Is Gund a new account?" I asked. I couldn't think why else he'd be carrying a bear around.

"No, my sister just had a baby over at Queens General, and I forgot to buy a present." It was the first time he had ever mentioned a sister, and I was surprised. I had always seen Wally as a lonely child, not brought up by family warmth. One of my stupid assumptions.

Wally sniffed the air. "Oh, Ev," he said with soft reproach in his voice. He walked around the desk, still holding his giant bear and kissed her forehead. It was the first time I had seen him be tender with Evelyn.

"You'll never guess who I saw in the maternity

ward cooing over a black baby," Wally said with loud glee, wiping away the nice moment. I thought of Mattie, but Wally's slurping smile told me it wasn't going to be that obvious.

"Our little Jenny Fenton. I guess those high heels of hers aren't the only thing she bounces on." He laughed and kissed his bear.

"You don't mean you think Jenny's the mother of that baby, do you?" Evelyn asked patiently and slowly, as if speaking to a retarded child.

Wally winked at her, a repulsive wink with the eyelid slowly sliding down over the eyeball as if caressing it. "At her age," he said, "she's lucky she can get it in any color."

He wasn't talking about a baby.

Evelyn's skin turned an even red. My face felt like hardened plaster of Paris.

"Which reminds me," Wally said, hugging his bear tightly, "I really didn't appreciate that interruption in Bertrand's office. I mean, we were only working. There was no need to snoop. Don't let that bark I love turn into a whine."

It was time for me to get out of there.

"Please don't leave, Simona," Evelyn said. I closed the door and sat down again.

"Remember the bite, Wally, I'll always have that," Evelyn said calmly. "No matter what."

"With you I thought I was free at last of these petty jealousies," Wally countered, sounding like a pompous trumpet. "That's why I wanted a middle-aged, mature woman who . . ."

"Middle-aged?" Evelyn roared. "What makes you think you're so young? Thirty-six is middle-aged too." She punctuated it with a point seven sneeze on the Richter scale. No timid gestures for her.

Wally just stared at her as if in shock. "What did I just say?"

"That I was a middle-aged, jealous dog."

"No, damn it, my exact words."

"I make it a point to forget your exact words."

I wanted out so I gave Wally the coup de grace. I only wished I had real bullets, not just words. "You said, 'I thought I was free at last of these petty jealousies. That's why I wanted . . .'"

"At last! That's it! Oh, Ev, I love you, I will always love you. I bless you forever." Wally blew her a kiss and rushed out of the room. I was the one to recite his immortal lines, but Evelyn got the thanks. On that Monday, it made sense.

I went out to get some lunch and I bumped into Jenny, literally, on the street. She was right about having trouble being noticed. We were heading in the same direction.

"What's this business about you and a black baby?" I blurted out from the heart of my foul mood as I attempted to keep up with her cheerful rhythm.

By the look on her face it was clear "the business" was none of mine. I backed off. "You're right, Jenny. I'm sorry. You're right. It's just that today's the worst Monday of my life." I had obviously forgotten about Fred and the previous Monday. Jenny stopped walking. She stood still on the sidewalk, with the lunchtime crowd rushing past her, trying to look tall in her heels, waiting for me to explain. And I loved her for it. For her patience, her interest.

"Greenhouse thinks I stole Fred's HH&H ring. He found it in my Kleenex box. For all I know, he probably thinks I killed Fred."

Jenny gave me a wonderfully reassuring look of total surprise. Her whole face lifted up in astonishment. Even her nose stopped drooping. I could have hugged her. She sure didn't think I was a thief or a killer. And her complete surprise also told me she had not planted that ring in my desk.

"But listen," I continued, also wanting to be friendly and helpful and resuming our walk toward food, "you'd better go put some tape over Wally's mouth if you don't want all of HH&H to think you've become a mother overnight."

That stopped her again. This time her face was noncommittally blank, but her nose gave her away. It turned bright red, ready to snap.

"You go on, Simona. I forgot something." She walked away quickly, without bouncing. Something was weighing her down. I hoped that for a change she had come up with plain, healthy anger and those sharp red heels were going to kick Wally's mouth in.

Chapter Eleven

That Monday lunch, I treated myself to two pizza slices with extra cheese and pepperoni. Pizza always did wonders for my mood. After the first half hour of elation, it would plunge me into such horrible feelings of guilt that I would forget any other problems my life might be facing. Just like the first times I had sex. That's why I kept going back for more.

Luis met me at the door and with a proprietary gesture only a Latin male is capable of, wiped one corner of my mouth with his handkerchief.

"Good pizza, eh," he stated. All the ingredients must have been hanging out of my mouth. "When are those two cops coming back?"

"I don't know," I answered honestly. "Why?"

"I have those lists they asked for. They said it was important." I could see Luis mentally twirling his mustache with self-indulgent abandon. Having no idea what lists he was talking about didn't deter me from wanting to see them.

"Thank you for cleaning my mouth, Luis." I took a deep breath and watched him glance down at my heaving blouse. "I know you always want me to look my best and that makes me feel good." He preened like a cock. Women aren't the only suckers for flattery. "I don't know when the detectives are coming back to HH&H. I do have a meeting with them tomorrow morning, so if you like I could take them the list." I gave him my best "I'm-only-doing-you-a-favor" look which consisted of keeping my face a total deadpan.

"I don't know. This is a police matter. It's important."

I didn't have much patience. My pizza-gorging regrets were beginning to settle in and predominate. "As you wish. If it's that important you will have to go down to police headquarters and deliver it personally. I'm sure they'd appreciate it, and that way they'll be able to question you some more."

Keeping my fingers mentally crossed, I walked toward the elevator. Without looking at him, I stepped in, and just as the elevator door was sliding shut on me and my bluff, Luis's hand appeared with a gray HH&H envelope. The metal panels recoiled, as if allergic to human contact, and Luis informed me gravely that he could not leave his post. The envelope disappeared into my skirt pocket before he could change his mind.

Once upstairs, Mattie called to let me know Bertrand had been looking for me, and that there had been no calls from policeland. She also warned me the "Frenchman" was on his way. Luis's lists would have to wait. It was Ellen Price's turn now. I wanted Bertrand to see her before Mr. Janick did.

He stared at the photograph a long time. He placed it close to his face and looked. Then he pushed it far away from his desk and looked. After ten more gray hairs grew on my head, he placed the photograph on his lap and tapped his heels slowly on the floor as if lulling that face to sleep. Finally he got up and said, "She's nice." He threw the photograph on his desk. It fell face down. He turned her around so that Ellen looked up at the whole room. He started pacing, and each time he passed the desk he would give her a quick glance. I think he was getting

113

acquainted. I watched silently as the pizza slices churned into pure acid in my stomach.

"Get Wally." As I turned toward the door, he added a forgotten "please." I was beginning to feel that Ellen had hooked him.

I found him in Gregory's office, in good health and without his teddy bear. Evidently Jenny had inflicted no visible damage.

"Wait 'til you see my headline," Wally said before Bertrand had a chance to speak. "I'm having the shop print it up in various typefaces, although I think it should be in Optima like the print on the packaging. Gregory found this awesome picture of the Grand Canyon he's getting blown up, and we both thought you should . . ." He stopped speaking when Bertrand stood and held up the photograph. He looked. I saw Gregory standing just behind the door jamb.

"Yes, 'tis the sweet face of heaven," Wally said, "but does she have tits and ass?" I didn't have to look to know Gregory was wincing.

"Wally, we're not selling sex, we're selling perfume," Bertrand said, still holding Ellen's photograph against his chest for Wally to enjoy.

"Same thing, Bertie, except your proper Protestant upbringing won't let you see it. Well, where is she? Let's have a look at her in the flesh. We'll pinch her a bit and see if she fits the bill."

"There are a few complications." I spoke up before Wally could get a chance to pursue his lecherous line of thought. Gregory had not budged from the door. "She lives in Omaha. She's never modeled before, so we'd have to fly her in, get Scriba to do a test, then present it to Janick and see if he likes her. And I don't know if she's willing to do it yet."

"Those don't sound like unsurmountable complications." Thank God for Bertrand's calm approach to my confusion. "Where did you find her?"

114

I turned to the door and said, "Gregory, you might as well come in here and join us."

Bertrand looked at Gregory without a trace of surprise. The sensualist kept his emotions well hidden. "Ellen is Gregory's daughter. I saw her photograph at his house."

"Well, well, well." Wally was warming up for one of his trumpet concertos. "So that's what our dearly departed meant when he said the ugly duckling had given birth to a swan." Wally caught my look of horror. "Don't look surprised. I told you your beloved Fred liked to find out ugly little tidbits about people to use as he saw fit. Well, this particular morsel certainly isn't ugly, but then who knows the whole story, huh, Greg?" He took the picture from Bertrand and furrowed his brows in heavy scrutiny. Wally looked at the picture again. "That Magic Marker of yours got some good results this time. Not a bad drawing, but she doesn't look a bit like you. Why I'd say that . . ."

"Congratulations, Gregory," Bertrand interrupted and walked to Gregory to shake his hand. "I'm sure you're very proud of her." Bertrand had been quick enough to see Gregory's clenched fist as it was getting ready to hit Wally's face. His own outstretched hand stopped Gregory, who quickly recovered and pumped Bertrand's hand gratefully.

"Would you object if we brought her to New York?" Bertrand asked.

"No, Simona and I have already discussed it. It's entirely up to Ellen."

"Do you mind, Gregory?" Bertrand asked, indicating the door with a slight uplift of his chin. "We'd like to discuss Ellen's possibilities, but with you here it becomes a little embarrassing." Bertrand spread out his hands as if asking forgiveness.

"Of course," Gregory replied. He looked down at his feet and reluctantly followed them out.

"Wally, what do you think? Is she right for 'Free'?" Bertrand sat down and swung his chair to face us. We were now down to business.

"How the blazes do I know. All I can say is she's beautiful. But then so was that peachy thing this morning."

Bertrand frowned.

"Okay, okay," Wally admitted. "This one has class. There's no doubt about it. Where she got it only her photographer knows for sure. From what I've heard of the mother . . ."

"It's none of our business." It was my turn to shut him up.

Wally stared at me, surprised by my anger.

"I think you're right," he said slowly, "and I think I owe my friend, Gregory, an apology." Wally had some redeeming features after all. "To me almost all women are beautiful, but I'm a copywriter. Don't ask me about faces, ask me words."

"Simona, what do you think?"

"I think she's great. I have one advantage over you. I saw her in a lot of pictures. I saw her look happy, wistful, bored, making faces at the camera. I've seen her at all ages, from naked, gurgling baby on fur rug on up to this close-up of a young woman waiting for life to happen. She looks wonderful in all of them. She's not only beautiful. She's *simpatica*."

"Which means?" Bertrand asked.

"Which means you want to get to know her, she's nice, she's fun," Wally said, taking the words right out of my mouth. "Did I get it right, my angry *Italiana?*"

"Perfectly," I had to concede.

The phone rang. Bertrand picked it up and listened. "Well, Jean is on his way up. I want to show this photograph right away. No, Simona, I want you to stay. This is your baby. Just call Ann to come down. I'm sure Jean will want her opinion too. Maybe we should lighten her hair. That might give her a softer look." Bertrand had picked up Ellen's photograph again. "I don't know, I can't judge from just one photograph. But she's definitely worth the expense of flying her in for a few days."

I was one step closer to solving one of my problems, and I happily reached for his phone to dial Ann's extension.

Bertrand had gone to meet Mr. Janick at the elevator, and when they walked back into the room, side by side, they looked like twins. Their individual features did not resemble each other, except their height, perhaps. Mr. Janick was a scant inch taller than Bertrand. It was the air they exuded that tied them together. Confidence and affluence, with a brush stroke of snobbery included. Mr. Janick was not as thin as Bertrand; he had the European corpulence of the well fed. The rage to diet was only now reaching the youth of Europe, and Mr. Janick, in his double-breasted, glen plaid suit with a thin blue stripe and silk shirt the color of linen, belonged to an older Europe. He was in his early fifties, and untidy streaks of gray marked his dark hair, worn slicked back tight on his head like a swimmer's cap. I was mesmerized by his aura of strength. He looked like the king of the jungle sheathed in an aristocratic distinction that belonged to a Louis XIV parlor. Bertrand introduced me, and he leaned forward and brought my hand to his lips. As his head moved down, I recognized the scent that had once breathed from my ex-husband's face and pillow. This time the memory didn't bring the usual slash of pain. I smiled a welcome to both the man and my newfound strength and gratefully breathed in *"Eau de Cologne du Coq"* by Guerlain. Janick, Inc. hadn't moved into a men's line yet, but I didn't think the company could have come up with anything more appropriate for its owner. The cologne came in a beautiful glass bottle etched with bees. The imperial bees of Napoleon. What better symbol of strength and ambition?

Guerlain was quickly overpowered by the scent Ann Lester brought in with her. Remembering what Wally had said, I presumed it was Stinko. It was definitely the same perfume she had left in the corridors of the seventeenth floor on Friday. She and Mr. Janick kissed on both cheeks, and she suggested we go to Fred's office where there would be more room for all of us. As she led the way, Mr. Janick reached for his handkerchief and held it to his nose for a while. I was sure it was steeped in his Guerlain, and he was taking a long sniff to protect himself from Ann's scent. Something wasn't making sense.

"Isn't Ann wearing your perfume?" I asked Mr. Janick.

"Oh, no, no, Madame. If my nose does not betray me, I believe that what Ann is wearing is 'Obsession.' "

"I had no idea," Wally chimed in as we walked down the corridor. "I thought she was wearing our one and only. I have been following her about every day, inhaling deeply to seek inspiration. Now I'll have to rewrite all my copy."

Mr. Janick did not even project a shadow of a smile. "I specifically stated to Mr. Critelli that I did not want anyone to wear my scent, but I did leave him one bottle to enable you to seek the inspiration you need." He walked ahead to join Bertrand.

"The man has no sense of humor," Wally moaned.

"I thought he didn't want any copy for his ads." I said.

"Last week he didn't. This week he does. So what's new in advertising?" Wally started whistling *La donna è mobile.* The notes of the aria filled the corridor. He

118

didn't care who heard him.

"If there's only one bottle around, what made you think Ann was wearing Stinko?" I asked in a whisper, between phrases.

"Because she told me she was."

"Well, you'd better get hold of that bottle and refresh your nose."

"Don't tell anyone around here, Simona, but I can't tell one perfume from another. My inspiration comes from banging you know whom. But lately it's been more banging and less inspiration." He didn't look at all upset by that fact.

We had reached Fred's office, and though I was glad I wouldn't have to listen to Wally anymore, I did find it difficult to walk into a room I still considered Fred's sanctuary. Jenny held the door open and looked down at her bright red heels. I couldn't tell what she was feeling.

The vertical blinds of the picture window had been drawn, letting only oblique afternoon light illuminate the vast gray room. Behind wide strips of expensive, textured fabric, the jagged Manhattan skyline lay in waiting.

"Thank you, Jenny," Bertrand said from behind Fred's desk, the crown of creative director sitting comfortably on his head. The transfer of power had taken place very smoothly. I didn't know who had suggested using Fred's room as a meeting place, but at this point it didn't matter. Bertrand, by the simple act of sitting in Fred's chair, had shown us he was the man in charge now. Maybe the time was ripe. Fred had been dead a week, and his body was on its way to be buried in the Sicilian hometown of his parents. The wall that only a few days before had still displayed Fred's lifetime achievements had been bared and once the police found the murderer, all traces of Fred would slowly disappear from the agency and people's memories.

"Wally, show us what you've come up with. Jean, I want you to know I didn't have the time to see anything. He found the scrap based on our idea, and he's thought up the headline. We even have a face to show you."

"And I haven't been told anything at all, so it's going to be an exciting surprise," added Ann, sitting on the leather sofa and settling her light pink silk skirt neatly around herself. Ever since the program *Moonlighting* had come on TV, Ann had adopted the Cybil Shepard look: carefully coiffed blond hair with pale clothes to soften and minimize her wrinkles. It worked. Everything Ann tried worked.

Wally reached behind Fred's desk and propped up a four foot by two foot comp against the window ledge. It was a photograph of the Grand Canyon at dawn; the foreground was all the shades of brown imaginable, from a deep russet that almost turned purple in the shadows to the pale beige of clean sand. The headline was placed in the pale yellows and pinks of the dawning sky in the background, the words looking as if they were helping to push the night away. They read: FREE. AT LAST. The product shot, a close-up of a light green, miniature champagne bottle with 'Free' etched on the front with the same burst of multicolored drops as the package, was stripped in the lower lefthand corner. The word CELEBRATE sat beneath it. The only thing left to our imagination was the model. No one spoke. Mr. Janick sat in the armchair, looking at the comp, while one finger gently tapped his pursed lips. We all waited. The silence lasted an eternity. Wally didn't make it.

"Gregory got this picture from an old *National Geographic*," he said too loudly. "I bet Scriba can come up with something just as good."

"I'm sure he thinks he can come up with something

120

much better," Bertrand said with a smile. He looked at Janick, betraying no nervousness. "Scriba should have been here, but he had to fly out to California to do a shoot for *Harper's* in Carmel. Supposedly Clint Eastwood agreed to pose with the models. He'll be back tomorrow."

There was more silence, more finger tapping on fleshy pursed lips. Then Mr. Janick shifted his portentous weight.

"*C'est bien fait,*" he said. "*Oui, oui,* it is very OK. I like it. Bravo, Wally. 'Obsession' has inspired you well." Everyone smiled.

"What's this about 'Obsession'?" Ann asked, her suspicions aroused.

"*C'est ne rien,* just a little joke between Wally and me. He has been obsessed by this whole campaign, have you not?"

"Indeed, it has been an obsession. Oh, the smell of it," Wally said not too subtly, obviously enjoying the joke at Ann's expense.

Ann shook her beautifully dyed golden hair disdainfully, releasing another waft of strong perfume. Mr. Janick pulled out his handkerchief from his pocket, and I remembered what I had in my pocket. I reached in and held on to Luis's envelope.

"What do you think of this face?" Bertrand asked abruptly. He held the photograph to his chest, the way he had with Wally.

Ann, sitting next to Mr. Janick, inhaled sharply, but didn't say anything. Mr. Janick reached out an arm for the photograph.

"You hold her up as if she were a work of art," he said as he took the photograph. "Let me examine her closely." With a legerdemain, gold-rimmed glasses appeared on Janick's patrician nose. "Wally, we have the darkness of the pharaoh's tomb in here. Do you think you can enlighten us?"

121

Wally scurried to the windows and shifted the blinds. Sharp slices of Manhattan and the sky erupted into the room.

"Ah," came from Janick as the sunlight reached Ellen's face. "She is a small work of art. We must see more of her. Is there more?"

Ann reached over and took the photograph in her hand. "She's a knockout. I've never seen her before. Who is she?"

"She's not a model," Bertrand said. "We're flying her in to test her. I think it's worth it. I just wanted to make sure you did too."

"Absolutely." Janick nodded and his glasses, ignoble evidence of age, disappeared into his breast pocket. "But we do not have much time."

"Simona, to whom we owe this discovery," said Bertrand, forever the gentleman giving credit where it was due, "will get her here in a flash and help us set up the tests. You can reach Johnny, Scriba's agent, in the morning." Bertrand was now addressing me directly. "He's going to be back in New York late this evening. Don't call him before eleven in the morning, or he'll bite your head off. Keep me posted."

Bertrand leaned back in Fred's chair and finally relaxed. "Thank you, all of you." We filed out of the room. Only Janick stayed behind. Before the door closed, he crossed his legs and settled back into the comfort of the flannel armchair with a proprietary air.

Jenny was sitting at her desk in front of Fred's office, a faithful reminder of the previous reign. At the sound of the closing door, she jumped up like a Jack-in-the-Box, with a wide smile stretched across her face. "How did it go? Did Mr. Janick love her?"

This time I was the quick one with the apology. "Forgive me, I can't talk right now. I'll catch up with

122

you later."

"It went beautifully," I shouted as an afterthought while practically running to the bathroom.

Although the bathrooms at HH&H do not afford total privacy (all you need to do is look down at the shoes to know who's in the booth), they do have the advantage over my office of having doors that lock. I quietly sat down on the tip of the toilet seat and opened Luis's sealed envelope. He had not written anything on it, therefore all I would have to do to cover up my misdeed was to replace the envelope. I mentally thanked Luis for his forethought. The first piece of paper I came across was a list of the people who had used the first aid room during Mattie's vacation, when Luis had had the keys. Quite a few people had gotten headaches during that two-week period. Dana, Jenny, and Evelyn had gone in. So had Gregory, Julia, and Bertrand. The people who worked with Moneybags seemed to need an endless supply of aspirin. Some receptionists and mailroom people had also raided the medicine chest. There were thirty names in all. I didn't think that particular list was going to help Greenhouse narrow down possible suspects. Besides, there was no guarantee that Luis's memory was reliable.

The second list showed who had entered and left the agency, and at what time. This is what I read:

Employee	ID #	IN	OUT
Bertrand Monroe	1765/74	11:30	14:31
Wally Burgh	1254/74	11:45	14:17
Ann Lester	3298/28	11:47	14:08
Fred Critelli	3333/74	12:00	17:27
Julia Monsanto	7639/75	12:10	14:15
Gregory Price	1143/74	16:03	16:48

123

Why had Gregory come in on a Sunday all the way from New Jersey and his beloved garden? And why hadn't he mentioned it? Wally had said Dana had shown up on Sunday, but the sensor said she hadn't. Who was right?

"Simona, are you all right? You've been in there an awful long time."

I jumped at the sound of Jenny's voice. "I'm fine. Just trying to get my thoughts together."

There was a third note, a small piece of scratch paper on which was written, "For now no leather jackets, but I don't give up." Signed "Luis." How wonderful of Greenhouse. He was looking for my thief.

Having flushed the toilet to cover the rustle of paper, I put everything back into my pocket and stepped out. Jenny greeted me with an unwary smile and got in the booth next to mine.

"I know what you mean about johns. I do some of my best thinking sitting on the pottie," said two bright red heels. I drowned out any further comment from those cut-off legs by turning on the water and washing my hands.

"How about dinner tomorrow night?" Jenny asked as she popped out of the booth.

"Love to. What kind?"

"Oh, anything. I love everything," she said with her usual Frank Capra outlook.

"Wally is alive and breathing. How come?" I asked. She did not understand. "You left me in the middle of the street at lunchtime when I told you about the hospital, and I thought you were going to drill his head with a heel or something."

She burst out laughing. "You have the weirdest sense of humor. What made you think I would do that?"

"You looked angry. Your nose turned red."

124

All of her blushed. "I was a little upset," she admitted. "I thought he was making fun of me and I got enough of that in high school to last me a lifetime." She looked in the mirror and started to nag her perfectly combed hair. "The guys always used to call me skimpy. They said I was so small because my dad held out on my mother at the big moment."

"No wonder you're still reaching for the moon," I said, looking down at her new shoes.

"Aren't they gorgeous?" Jenny tapped her heels sharply on the tile floor several times, as if the sound helped confirm her presence. "I've gained half an inch with these." She straightened up to her limit and playfully measured herself against my five feet six inches.

"Too bad," I said. "Wally got away with it one more time."

"He doesn't mean anything by what he says," Jenny said. "Everyone knows he's got hoof and mouth disease and he's always putting his hoof into his mouth." She looked at me wide-eyed. "Hey, that's pretty good for me." She started laughing, then stopped herself. "You're wondering about that baby, aren't you?"

"Sort of," I admitted.

Jenny shook her head vigorously. "That baby's not mine. Those are boarder babies. The city puts them in hospitals because their mothers are unfit. They might be in prison or on drugs or alcoholics. Who knows what else." She added some lipstick to her already red mouth. "It's nothing special," she told my reflection. "Lots of women go. We're sent by foster care agencies." Trying to make it sound like just another job, a baby to be rocked, another letter to be typed. I wondered if I would ever rock my own. The thought hurt.

"You should be proud of yourself," I said and walked out.

125

Luckily Gregory was still in his office, straightening out his room and capping all his Magic Markers.

"Why were you here the Sunday Fred was murdered?" I went straight to the point.

Gregory looked at me with sad eyes. "Think I did it?"

"No, I don't think you did it, but you could have seen something?"

He shook his head. "I went directly to my office to finish a layout for Dana. I didn't have all the colors I needed at home. What are you staring at?"

"That spray paint." A can of Krylon stood in the middle of his desk. "I didn't know you used spray paint."

"I don't. That's coating to protect my illustrations."

"Does anyone here use spray paint?"

Gregory picked up the can and placed it behind a double row of Magic Markers. "Not the art directors. Maybe down at the studio."

I was fixating on that stupid thief. The murder was much more important. Besides, those cans could be bought at any hardware store.

"I didn't know Dana had anything urgent on the agenda to warrant weekend work," I said. Evelyn had ruled that out.

"I didn't say she did." Geoffrey looked at me evenly. "Didn't you give her the layout that Sunday?"

"I didn't know she was in the office, and I don't have a key to get to her floor. Then with all the brouhaha over Fred's death, I forgot to give her the layout until the end of the week." Gregory picked up his satchel, ready to leave. "That'll save you the trouble of checking with Dana."

I shook his arms in frustration. "Hey, we're friends, remember?" He didn't look convinced.

126

"They want me to get Ellen here right away," I said, changing course. "Janick thinks she's wonderful. I'm just about to call her. Want to stick around? She'll want to talk to you."

"No, leave me out of this. I have to go or I'll miss my bus." He walked toward the elevator with his red plastic satchel over his shoulder. Just as the elevator door opened, he called out "good night" to the floor in general. Forgiveness wasn't going to come easy to Mr. Gregory Price.

Chapter Twelve

Back in my office, I reached Ellen after having been put on hold for what seemed ten minutes, but might have been only two. She had a gentle, well-educated voice with no trace of any regional accent. Ellen wasn't going to need any diction or voice lessons to sound good on a TV commercial or a guest appearance. Julia in the TV department was going to be very grateful. Any extra assets beyond beauty were very welcome.

She was flabbergasted by the news. Who wouldn't be? It was the "Lana Turner discovered in a drugstore story" all over again. This time a photograph hidden in an obscure house in New Jersey had done the trick.

There was a long moment of silence while she thought over my invitation to fly to New York the next day.

"What does Gregory say?" she asked. Not Daddy. Gregory.

"He says it's up to you, that you're twenty-one and old enough to make up your own mind," I answered.

"Is he there? Can I talk to him?"

"No, he's on his way home. He didn't know I was calling you," I lied. She sounded so forlorn.

"Let me think about it overnight, please. I couldn't leave tomorrow anyway. It wouldn't be fair to my employer. When is the latest I can come?"

"We would definitely need you here by Wednesday," I said. She had just been offered the possibility of becoming a model, with her picture plastered in all the best magazines and the earning capacity of $100,000 the first year, and she wanted to be fair to her employer who was probably paying her $12,000 a year. That said something about the Omaha education that Gregory had been extolling. Having lived in overaggressive New York a few years, I wasn't sure whether it was a negative or a positive something.

"Why don't I call you at nine-thirty tomorrow morning, your time? I'll expect your decision then." She agreed and hung up, and I was left with a guaranteed sleepless night.

I called Julia Monsanto in TV and got her after one ring.

"Hi, it's Simona. We may have our model. I thought you should know."

"What lovely news," she said in a breathless, shaky voice, "but I'm not sure I know what you're talking about."

I reminded her of Bertrand's perfume campaign.

"Yes, yes, of course. That is a relief. There were so many pictures to sort through. It was getting to be very tiring." She regaled me with a long sigh.

"Don't stop your search," I warned her. "I won't know if she's coming until the morning, and then she still has to do some tests with Scriba. I just thought you should know what was going on up here on the seventeenth."

"You are sweet. May I come up to see?"

"Of course, Julia, be my guest."

After half an hour, she still hadn't come. By then it was past closing time and, for all I knew, forgetful Julia could have blithely gone home. Wally's inexhaustible voice shattered the silence of the floor like a radio suddenly turned on to maximum volume. I peeked out and saw the perfume group minus Janick standing by the elevator obviously ready to wrap up the day.

"Ellen's going to let me know in the morning," I shouted out to Bertrand.

He nodded. "Don't worry. She'll accept. Why don't you go home now like the rest of us?"

"Julia's on her way up."

"Good thinking. I'm afraid I forgot all about her."

"If only we could," Ann said in her coolest tone, just as the elevator shut the three away from me. I started to clean up my desk for the day.

"Where are you, dear?" her winded voice asked me from afar. I poked my head out of the opening and Julia gave a small laugh of relief. She walked her heavy body slowly down the corridor, holding up her hand as if fending off onrushing cars. On her other arm she carried an old-fashioned leather purse, the kind that closed with a snap. It never left her side. Margaret Thatcher and Queen Elizabeth came to mind, except that Julia looked like she had had fun in her life.

"I was sure you said the sixteenth floor."

I had specifically mentioned the seventeenth floor. Besides, Julia had been to my office several times before.

"These offices are so confusing," she continued in her come-and-go voice. Julia's voice, like her memory, is not something one can depend on. Most of the time it is barely audible, as if the act of being in that large frame is taking up all her energy. At other times it weaves in and out, now loud, now soft, as though her antenna isn't picking up the right waves.

"There are no distinguishing signs to tell you where you are. And I'm afraid I did forget your name, dear, so that didn't help." She placed herself into my chair with a very audible sigh of relief and looked at me.

"You have a nice face," she said apropos of nothing. "I wonder what you could sell?" Her sixty-year-old face stared at me in childlike concentration. Her excessive fat had pushed away any wrinkles and the smooth roundness made her look the child even more. Baby-fine dyed red hair curled around her head in benign, lacy wisps. I half expected a magic wand to appear between her fingers.

"You would never do for detergents. Not the housewife type, really. No, no . . . smile at me . . . yes, that's nice . . . like that. Why yes, of course. Animals. You could sell 'Bark of Happiness Chow.'" She stopped, not convinced. "Perhaps something more feminine. 'The Purring Munchies' should do, I think. Yes, quite nicely. I can just see a big tom licking your face gratefully." Satisfied with having placed me in the right TV commercial, she started rummaging through my desk drawer. I let her be. She might produce a rabbit, I thought, or make a nasty ring disappear.

"They all say I'm scatterbrained, but I'm not really," Julia said with an unusual burst of energy. She didn't look up from the drawer. "I'm merely tired. Can't they understand that? Forty years of commercials, nothing in my life but commercials." She looked up and saw me listening. For my attention I received a shy smile. "Well, yes, I did have some gentlemen friends," she admitted. "But even then, they were all in the business, so it was a caress or two stolen between stockings, cereals, sanitary napkins. I'm bound to get them mixed up a little. The commercials I mean." Her search had now extended to the top of the desk.

"Why don't you quit?"

Her eyes opened in amazement. They were of a blue so light and transparent, it looked faded. "I love my work. Much more than any of the men. Of course now" . . . her voice lowered into a mutter— "it's more than likely . . ." She sat up as if someone

131

had slapped her back hard. "Dear, I'm looking for a cigarette; do you have one?" I handed her my pack. She took three. Two she stuffed in her handbag, one she put in her mouth and started rummaging again looking for a match. I did not volunteer one. I was curious to see how long she'd keep it up.

"It's been hard," she said with a trembling sigh. "So unfair really. He was trying to change." She continued her search. "He didn't get a chance, now did he?" Julia leaned back in the chair for a moment, short of breath. "Poor girls. Hard on all of us."

"I don't know about that," I quipped. "I think some people are glad he died." I was thinking of Bertrand now firmly installed in Fred's sunny office.

"Hmm, yes. If nobody else, the murderer should be glad. At least I hope he is. It would have been such a waste to have killed him and then regret it. There is no going back, is there, so what is the point of remorse?"

What could I answer to that? "Did you see Dana here in the office on Sunday?" I asked instead.

"Oh, I'm sure she was there if Fred was there. I don't remember seeing her. Though I might have." She had given up on the drawer and was scrutinizing the floor. As her head bent down, I could see her scalp through the thin wisps of her hair. I took pity on her and slipped my matches on the desk.

"I have a terrible memory, I'm afraid," she said as her head came back up. She did not question how the matches had suddenly appeared on the desk. She was just happy to have found them. She lit her cigarette and with a snap of her handbag made the matches disappear. She smiled like a child who had just licked her favorite ice cream cone. Her mouth let go of short, billowy puffs of smoke.

"I don't inhale," she said catching my eye. "I wouldn't have any voice at all. Like my memory. All going. I'll go too. They'll put me down as if I were an old fretting poodle. That's what they'll do. Fred isn't going to be very happy about that." Her eyes glazed over. "If only the letter could help."

"What letter?"

"It doesn't matter now, dear. One has no power behind a tombstone," she whispered.

I wasn't sure I agreed with her.

"He was so young. Such talent," she said with renewed vigor. The cigarette rested forgotten between her short fingers. "He could make any woman feel beautiful, you know? I'm sure he worked his magic on you." I gave a small acknowledging nod. "But he was unfair sometimes. Misused people." Julia wheezed into a laugh. "I've known him for years and years, but there was nothing between us, you understand. When I met him he was almost indecently young." She sighed, a trembling sound that made me think of Wally's "warble-throated" description. "It was so much better that way. It let us stay friends through the years." Her cigarette had gone out and she patted the papers strewn on top of the desk looking for the book of matches. I pointed to her purse. "He started out as a reporter, you know," she went on to say, once she had taken several puffs to make sure the cigarette was burning. "He would have been good too. He had a natural curiosity, always wanted to know everything. But he changed his mind and wanted advertising. And I did what I could. I was well established by then. People listened to what I had to say. I helped with a job, helped him with his moods. Held his hand . . ." her voice trailed off into memory. I remembered too. Not Fred, he was too close for memory. I remembered the man who was so like him, the husband I had helped, the man who had left me. I wanted so badly to put everything to rest, Fred's death, my husband's desertion. Somehow they had mingled together to form a solid dull ache I had to get rid of once and for all.

"Now where's that photo?" Julia abruptly asked, shouting me back into the present. "I don't have all day." She tugged at the thin strands of hair on her forehead and looked at me crossly, as if I'd been holding her up. I gave her Ellen's picture. She took a deep breath. "How very lovely." Julia put the picture down and looked at me. "You could be too," she murmured. "If only you'd smile."

I'm getting there, I thought. First let me get rid of those shadows.

"Shampoo would be nice," Julia said in a loud, firm voice. "The girls are always so happy and pretty in shampoo ads." She heaved herself up and walked out of my office with a firm grip on her handbag. "Thank you for showing me her picture. It's nice to know I haven't been forgotten all together."

"You're welcome." I noticed that her knee-highs needed pulling up. "By the way, my name is Simona."

She waved her free hand in the air without turning around. "Shampoo is next," her quaking voice assured me.

My phone rang and I rushed to get it. Maybe Ellen had already made up her mind. It was Raf.

"Hi, did you cook anything good lately?" he asked, without introducing himself. "Listen," he went on, without giving me a chance to answer. "Stan wants you down here for some fingerprinting."

Oh, *mio dio*, it had come to that.

"What about right now?" Raf asked.

My body temperature dropped to zero. I didn't answer.

"You prefer coming in the morning before we meet Miss Lehrman in the Park? Hey, I sure can't wait to meet those models. Well, what about it? When are you coming?"

"I might as well get it over with," I said.

Fingerprinted. The United States Immigration Service had done that. But I was an immigrant then, not a suspect. "I'll come right away. What's the address?" What was I going to say? They weren't going to believe anything I told them.

"Two Thirty East Twenty-first Street, between Second and Third. South side. I'll be here waiting for you. And do me a favor, start thinking of a recipe for me. My girlfriend's coming over tonight and she wants Italian."

"How about elbow twists with fox glove pesto?" I suggested to the dial tone. Raf had already hung up.

Chapter Thirteen

The ink pad was open, ready for me.

"Hi, welcome to the Thirteenth." Raf grinned. "Sorry to get you dirty, but what can I do?" He shrugged philosophically and reached for my hand. "Hey, relax, this doesn't work unless the hand's limp. That's better. So, what'd'ya come up with?"

"I didn't kill Fred," I said through clamped teeth, acrid sweat beginning to form in my armpits. I felt just like that day in Naples, half-naked, stripped of clothes and pride, lined up with countless other women, waiting to be X-rayed, waiting to be blessed with entry into the United States of America.

"Have you ever had tuberculosis?"

"Have any of your family been insane at one time or other?"

"Have you ever been a member of the Communist party?"

"Have you or do you intend to practice prostitution?"

"What if I lie?" I had asked.

"That would be reason enough to deport you to your country of origin."

Banished for a lie. And now I was a suspect. Would I lose everything?

Raf had finished with my fingers and was handing me a towel. "Over and done with. Now how about that recipe? Make it pasta, she loves pasta."

136

"I didn't kill him." I blinked, aware I was losing my battle with tears. "I didn't steal his ring." I only wanted a raise. A well-deserved raise.

Raf stared at me dumbfounded. He opened his mouth to speak, but shut it again when a warm hand touched my shoulder.

"Thanks for coming up here on such short notice." Greenhouse appeared in front of me. The hand stayed on my shoulder. "We got some clear prints on that spray can of yours. Now we have to figure out which is whose." He leaned against Raf's battered desk and let go of me.

"You mean, that's why you wanted my prints?"

"Sure," Raf said with an encouraging smile. "Why else?"

"Besides the fun of seeing a pretty lady dress up this place," Greenhouse added, and all I could think of doing was to hold my burning cheeks and laugh the shame away. He reached over and removed my hands from my face, shaking his head and smiling at the same time.

"Ex-pretty lady. Now you've got a beautiful set of prints on your cheeks." This time Raf produced two paper towels and my face turned even redder. Greenhouse consulted his watch and stood up from the desk. "I've got to pick up Willy for dinner," he said. "Raf, get a description of the thief and show Simona where the bathroom is." He began a thorough search of his pockets. "Ah, here it is." He fluttered a piece of paper in front of my face, which reminded me, that in my anxiety, I had forgotten Luis's lists in the office. They would have to wait until the morning.

"Twelfth Street, just east of Fifth. Mike's a good locksmith. Mention my name and he might just give you a discount. If not, he'll at least install your lock well." A soothing pat on the same shoulder and Greenhouse disappeared behind a tall row of filing cabinets. I noticed my surroundings for the first time. The detective's room was medium-size with baby blue paint covering the cinder block walls. Blue for boys or blue for the sky they couldn't see beyond the dirty barred windows? Five metal desks, old-fashioned wooden chairs, phones, manual typewriters, laughing detectives in a corner; what had looked like the hallway to hell only fifteen minutes before had turned, thanks to Greenhouse's words, into a familiar Cagney and Lacey set.

I gladly gave Raf what description I could of the thief. All I could remember was that he had been of medium height and weight, light skinned, and wore regulation street hightops. Bright white ones. Probably just stolen. Like the leather jacket. Raf dutifully wrote it all down.

"You know, you should have reported this to the sixth," he said after we were finished. "But don't worry. Stan'll take care of things. He likes to take care of things. You should see him with his son, Willy. Great dad. I hope to be like him when I have kids. Now what about tomorrow morning?"

I was busy cleaning my cheeks with a blackening paper towel. Raf reached over and helped me aim. "Want the bathroom? It's just outside."

I shook my head no. Those detectives in the corner were already laughing hard enough. They didn't need to see my ink-dotted face.

"Hey, you're getting a real healthy look with all that rubbing. Beats that stuff Tina is always putting on. Tina's my girlfriend. How's about us meeting you at your office at nine forty-five? That okay with you?"

I had to think quickly. I couldn't have them meet Luis. They might find out I had tricked him into giving me those lists. "I'm not coming to the office tomorrow morning. I have to go to the dentist." Lousy lie, but I'm not good on the fast think. At least not in a police station, having just narrowly escaped being a murder suspect. "Why don't you meet me directly by the bridge at the lake in Central Park at ten o'clock?"

"Okay," Raf said. "Your face is fine now. See you ten o'clock sharp. Stan likes people to be on time."

"Yessir."

"By the way," he added, just as I was getting up to go. "You didn't have to worry about that ring we found. It was wiped clean of fingerprints and Stan doesn't think you'd have done that."

"Why not?" I couldn't help asking.

"You wouldn't wipe the ring clean and then stick it in your drawer, would you? Stan thinks you're too bright for that."

God Bless America, I thought as I looked at the large American flag partially covering the windows at one end of the room.

"And that's what I say, too," Raf added and gave me his familiar grin.

I blew him a kiss across the desk, took a clean paper towel and happily wrote out the recipe for *Spaghettini Aglio, Olio e Pepperoncino*. My father's favorite.

Chapter Fourteen

It was a perfect day for an outdoor shoot. The sky was clear of clouds and the usual New York July heat had been replaced by 85 humidity-free degrees. As I walked to the lake from the southern end of the park, I saw some people setting up lights and a van parked on the road nearby. It was only 9:30. I had wanted to get there early to warn Dana, but she was nowhere in sight. Inside the van, Chantal, Dana's favorite make-up artist, was busy putting violently pink lipstick on a strawberry blonde whose hair fell about her face like a lion's mane. Eric, who did hair and was almost always teamed with Chantal, was in the process of covering his hands with some white goo which he then massaged into the short black hair of model number two. I hadn't prepared the shoot, therefore I didn't know the models' names. I waved hello to Chantal and Eric and introduced myself to the others. One smiled back, one was nowhere in sight, and Lion Mane waved. Her lips were too busy to smile.

"Where's Dana?" I asked. I was watching short black hair turn into shiny sleek black hair as Eric combed the white goo through her hair. The wet look was his favorite. Eric was from Punksville, and the only thing about him that looked like it had seen water in the recent past was his brown hair. He wore it slicked back as if he had just surfaced from a dive in the pool. Even the English dialect he spit out sounded dirty, but Dana thought he was the best. I liked him because he hadn't reached stardom yet. His hourly rate made Dana's usually tight budgets more comfortable. He got for an hour what I earned in ten. It seemed fair to me.

"She's late," Chantal said. That much I knew for myself. I looked around the van. It was spacious, with mirrors all around and good lighting. To one side there was a small sofa that one could actually curl into and fall asleep. On the other side was the kitchenette area with hot plate and refrigerator. Dana's clothes stylist, Arnold, was next to the kitchenette, hovering worriedly over a skirt with an iron in his hand.

"I do wish she'd get here," he said. "She hasn't selected the skirts that go with the Merry shirts yet, and I don't want to have to iron them all. I mean, my life is difficult enough." He pushed a strand of blond hair back with the arm that held the iron. The other hand was busy holding up a very wide taffeta skirt. Dana called him affectionately the "fey gay."

The shirts we were advertising that day were evening ones. Merry Shirts, Inc. had started its business selling mostly sport shirts for men and women. They had only recently moved to a more sophisticated line. I looked at the shirts hanging on a small clothes rack. There was a fuchsia number that looked like satin but wasn't. I was sure it was destined for Lion Mane. The seams were crooked and the blouse was terribly made, but I knew that Dana would make it look like something that should cost a thousand dollars. Then there was a tight, black, sleeveless beaded top that was perfect for Shiny Sleek Black Hair. The third blouse was all white ruffles from *Gone With the Wind* days, made with a lace that felt like pumice stone. Not exactly what you would want to wear dancing breast to breast with your one and only, but then it might give him the urge to want to tear it off you, which might be the whole point of the blouse.

The door to the van opened and model number three walked in. It was Miss Lucas, better known as Magnolia Blossom, the one Wally had found wandering the halls at HH&H the day before. I should have known Dana would have picked her just by seeing the lace blouse. She was not the titless stringbean Dana may have wanted, but then it was July and most of them were at the couture shows in Paris. Raf was going to like her a lot.

"Why, it's downright cold in here," Magnolia Blossom said. She reached for a terry cloth robe to cover a white leotard outfit that was tighter than her own skin. "I don't want to get goosebumps on my poor skin."

There wasn't any room for goosebumps; that leotard was going to flatten them right out. I left. I told myself the van wasn't made to hold seven people, but I knew I would have walked out of an empty Madison Square Garden had Magnolia Blossom walked in.

Near the water's edge, I saw the back of the photographer leaning into a camera that was set up on a tripod and aimed at the bridge and the lake. Underneath the bridge was a rowboat with a male model dressed in a tuxedo sitting in it. He had his back to the camera. The layout of the ad was three girls, dressed for a romantic evening, leaning over the bridge and waving at a solitary man as he was about to appear from under the shadow of the bridge. The idea behind it was that if you wear a Merry shirt, there's always the possibility of romance. I looked all around the lake for my possibility, but I didn't see my two policemen. Dana hadn't shown up either.

The photographer shouted to the male model to move the boat slightly to the left, and I recognized the deep voice immediately. It was Paul Langston, the photographer a tearful Dana had asked me to call to cancel the commitment she had made with him. When he turned around I knew why Dana had been in tears. His face matched his voice. Tom Selleck was nothing compared to Paul.

"Were you a model?" I asked, too surprised by his looks to know what I was saying.

"No," he laughed.

"I bet you get asked that a lot."

"Yeah. Where's Dana? We're almost set up."

He didn't seem very friendly. I went ahead and introduced myself. "I'm Simona Griffo, the art buyer at HH&H."

He took my offered hand and smiled in recognition. "You're the one who phoned to call off the whole thing—what happened?"

"I'm sorry, but somebody got things a bit mixed up."

"No harm done." He looked at his watch nervously. "I want to shoot before noon. The sun casts the worst shadows on your face then."

"Don't worry, she'll be here. She's never missed a shoot yet." Just as I said that I saw Dana hurry toward us. She was wearing a knit outfit by Sonia Ry kiel of pale yellow cotton which badly matched her very green face. To make matters worse, her wide, bottom-heavy frame had turned the signature stripes and bows into ripples and waves. No wonder she looked seasick.

"I'm sorry, Paul," she said. They hugged like long-lost friends. "Simona, why the hell didn't you tell me those two were coming," she screamed at me, her large, red mouth acting as a natural megaphone. I looked where she was pointing. Greenhouse just stood there, his arms clasped behind his back, perfectly relaxed. Raf waved.

"I tried to, Dana, but you weren't in your office

yesterday."

Her face changed color from green to cottage-cheese white. She got defensive, but the voice stayed loud. "I was at the doctor's." Sure, like I was at the dentist's.

"Have you talked to them yet?" I asked.

Her anger turned into a self-pitying drone. "Why do you think I'm so late? It was so unfair." She twisted a long black curl around her finger nervously. "He kept asking me about Fred, and I got all upset. How am I supposed to produce a happy ad now?" She looked at me as though I could provide some relief.

"I'm sorry, Dana," I said helplessly.

"It was just awful," she said and walked away. I followed. I knew she was crying. I see tears and I become guilty putty.

"Dana, I'm sorry. I really am. Is there anything I can do?" I reached for her shaking shoulder.

"I'll be fine." She shirked from my touch. "It's just that I'm so tired. All these deadlines." She shook her long, full hair several times as if to jerk all the tears away. "I better get in that van and see what they're up to. The client is coming any minute."

"What happened with Paul Langston?" I asked. That stopped her dead. She had obviously forgotten about the phone call. She just stared at me for a few seconds, her face a blank. She was trying to remember what excuse she had used with me. Then her eyes widened as if someone had just used a flash on her. That's when she remembered.

"He and the client made up," she said and turned to go. I didn't believe her.

Raf came up to me. "Hi, where are the girls?"

"You'll have to wait awhile. They're still dressing."

Raf turned around to the approaching Greenhouse. "Don't we have anything to ask them real urgent? Like what they're doing tonight?"

144

Greenhouse laughed and shook his head. When he reached me his face turned serious.

"Hi," he said.

"Hi," I said, looking up into that nice, clean face. Paul Langston couldn't hold a candle to him. That morning Greenhouse looked like Tom Selleck, Paul Newman, Robert Redford and Alain Delon combined. All I needed was a smile and my life would be complete.

"Thanks for yesterday," I said.

"Nice clean cheek," he said.

"Even nicer, discounted Fox Police with Medeco cylinder on my door."

"Good." His hand brushed mine. That was even better than a smile.

"Hey, you two," Raf said, "this is a police investigation, remember? We're here on official business." I think he was enjoying himself just as much as we were. We paid no attention to him and continued to examine the pupils of each other's eyes. Then the van door opened and the girls and their attendants starting streaming out. At that point I lost both of them. As I had predicted, Raf was very much taken by Magnolia Blossom in her White Ruffle. He followed her like a lost puppy seeking a home, and as she teetered in her heels, she wiggled her tail in the air to make sure he caught the scent. Greenhouse seemed fascinated by Shiny Sleek Black Hair.

"She looks like she could do mean things to you," he said in a very low voice. Dana, in her tireless soprano, was shouting instructions and so was the photographer. Arnold was squealing to the girls not to muss up their skirts, but I had heard Greenhouse all right.

"If you like that sort of thing," I answered in an equally low voice. He blushed and moved away.

The client came, a big fat man from the Midwest somewhere. I watched Dana introduce Paul Lang-

145

ston. It was clear the two had never met before. Dana had lied and at that moment I didn't care. I was too happy sitting on the grass, having sexual fantasies in Greenhouse's proximity.

Greenhouse got up, wiped the grass from his slacks and said, "It's time to go," he said.

"Don't you have to ask Dana anything else?" I asked hopefully.

"Nope."

"What did you have to ask her?"

"Aren't you the nosy one," he said and brushed his forefinger against my nose. Good fairy Julia had been right. The time had come for the real thing. I beamed back at him. I didn't feel like holding anything back. It was too beautiful a day for that.

"There's one thing I want to know from you," Greenhouse said.

I'm free tonight.

"Do you know of any man in his right mind who would wear a tuxedo to row a boat in Central Park at eleven o'clock in the morning?"

"Eleven o'clock? Oh, *mio dio,* I have a very important long distance phone call to make at eleven-thirty. I've got to get back to the office." I picked up my purse from the grass.

"Boyfriend?"

"No, female model."

"Good." He smiled at me. Heaven.

I was floating on my way to the subway when I remembered. I ran back and met him walking down Fifth Avenue with Raf.

"I forgot to give you this," I said as I pushed a freshly sealed HH&H envelope into his hand.

"Hey, wait a minute, what's this?" he asked.

"Luis gave it to me."

"That's the stuff I asked Luis for yesterday." Raf's face lit up. "Great," he said.

"What do you mean, you asked Luis for yester-

146

day?" My feet were glued to the sidewalk, dread spreading up my calves.

"I called yesterday afternoon," Raf explained, "same time I called you."

"What did Luis say?" I asked in a trembling voice. If Greenhouse knew I had those lists since yesterday afternoon, it was going to be *ciao, ciao, bambina* for me.

"He said they weren't ready yet."

"Thanks for bringing them," Greenhouse said.

"Sure, any time." I fled guiltily toward the subway.

Luis stood by the elevator, smoothing down his double-breasted blazer. It was his favorite place. With brass buttons shining, he looked like a general reviewing his troops.

"*Ehi*, Luis, *grazie*," I said. "You're a real *amigo*."

Luis gracefully waved some people into the elevator and winked at me. "We Latins got to stick together. They got it now?"

"Resealed and delivered."

"And I'm still looking for a leather jacket," he reminded me, laughing, as he escorted my elbow to the waiting elevator.

"I talked to Gregory," Ellen Price said over the telephone. I held my breath.

"Yes," she said, "I would like to come to New York." This day was continuing to be glorious.

"I've already looked into the flights to save you the trouble." She was too good to be believed. "I could arrive tomorrow at LaGuardia at four-fifty-one P.M. I really can't get away any earlier. I hope that's not too late."

"No, Ellen, that would be perfect. I'm so happy you're coming, but I do want you to remember that the whole thing might not work out. I mean, I don't want you to build your hopes up too much."

Ellen laughed. "You sound just like Gregory. Don't worry. I'm not really counting on becoming a famous model. I'm just happy to get to New York. I've never seen it, you know. Well, I guess I must have seen it since I was born there." She laughed again. Bertrand was going to like her laughter. It came so easily. "But I was taken away when I was so little, I don't remember. And I can't wait to see my father and where he lives." I was glad to hear her finally acknowledge her relationship to Gregory.

"You just reminded me I have to make a hotel reservation for you. I have to set a few things in motion, so I'd better hang up."

"No hotel room for me. I'm going to stay with Gregory in New Jersey. That's not an inconvenience for you, is it?"

"Not at all. He doesn't live that far. We'll just hire a limo for you. Does he know you want to stay with him?"

"He's the one who insisted."

"That's great." I was glad Gregory had welcomed her. "I'll meet you at the airport with your father. Have a good trip." I hung up and ran to Gregory's office. He sat there, his usual tight hunched self totally absorbed in drawing a band of marching socks. I stood behind him and kissed his bald spot. He didn't stop drawing.

"What's that?" I asked.

"Some new client we're pitching."

"Cute idea."

"Nothing new." He didn't sound very excited by the ad or by the fact that his daughter was coming to New York and staying with him.

"I just came in to tell you I love you," I said.

"That's nice." Gregory was used to hearing my indiscriminate declarations of love whenever I was happy.

"Hungry?" he asked and reached for a small packet

148

wrapped in foil. Sweet, nurturing Gregory. He had forgiven me.

"No, I'm in love."

"You already said that."

"No, I mean I'm really in love. I'm so nervous about it, I couldn't eat a thing. Just think, I'm going to get beautifully thin."

Gregory lowered his head and looked doubtfully at me from above his glasses. He put the silver packet in my hand. "That'll keep twenty-four hours in the fridge. Eat it when the dieting romance is over. It's chocolate cake layered with Bavarian cream."

"Don't make fun of me, this could be the real thing." I was already beginning to feel a slight longing in my stomach as I looked at the packet.

"That cake's too good to pass up for a cop," he said.

I gaped at him.

"Don't look surprised, Simona. I'm not that dumb. Besides, Jenny's been spreading rumors."

I made a mental note to strangle her that night. After dinner. I don't like to eat alone. "You're going to the airport with me tomorrow."

"No, I've got too much work to do," he said, without much conviction.

"The socks will just have to march away in protest. Bertrand's campaign takes precedence."

"What do I have to do with it?"

"You, my dearest sourpuss, can make Ellen smile. I know that much from talking to her on the phone, not that I can figure out why. All I want is for that girl to be happy."

"So she'll look better in front of the camera?"

"Why not? And thanks for the peace offering." I ran out before a Magic Marker hit the door.

I gave Bertrand the good news and then rushed to my office to make the arrangements with Johnny, Scriba's agent. He had already reserved Thursday

149

and Friday for the tests and had put Scriba's favorite hair and make-up people on hold. Scriba's studio was located in a loft on Sixteenth Street just off Union Square. That whole area is crowded with photographers' studios, and I often see models of both sexes, portfolio in hand, hurrying to an appointment when I walk to work in the morning. Having the studio so close to the office made Bertrand's life easier. He could pop in and out of the office in the middle of a shooting day to check his mail or OK something from the type shop. I looked forward to popping in and out on Thursday and Friday. This was a shooting test I wasn't going to miss. I wasn't going to let anyone forget that Ellen Price was my discovery.

I looked at my desk empty of job folders, lit a cigarette, thought of Greenhouse's nice warm brown eyes and was really beginning to enjoy life, when Evelyn appeared.

"What the hell happened in the park?" She sat down and lit one of my cigarettes. She hadn't knocked, but then I didn't have a door or anything to hide either.

"Nothing,. why?" Except that I think I might have just fallen in love with a healthy, kind, warm, trusting New York City policeman of all the unlikely people.

Evelyn slouched back comfortably in the armchair. "Her clothes stylist, what's his name . . ."

"Arnold."

"Arnold." She made a face. "How could I forget. Anyway, he called in hysterics. You had just left the shoot. Dana was throwing up in the van, she had screamed at him, called him a stupid fag. For no reason at all according to him. He was going to walk off the shoot, wanted me to find another clothes stylist. Immediately. Couldn't wait." She looked at me and did her blinking routine. "So nothing happened, huh?"

"I don't know what was going on, except that the police may have upset her. They questioned her just before the shoot, and she wasn't very happy about it. I wouldn't take Arnold too seriously. He flies into a rage if a model runs one of his precious stockings. You'd think he was paying for them instead of the client. Did you calm him down?"

"Sure, I promised him more money. You'll just have to find it somewhere in your budget."

"Thanks for taking over."

"No problem. Listen, I'm staying over in the city tonight . . ."

I gave her my I-know-what-you-are-up-to smile.

". . . and I want no comments from you."

I still smiled.

"What are you doing for food?"

"Jenny and I are going to a Chinese place near me on Christopher Street. You're welcome to join us."

"Will do," Evelyn said and stood up. "I didn't think Jenny would venture into Chinese, she's more the waffles with syrup type." With that she left, taking my last cigarette with her.

Chapter Fifteen

The three of us were comfortably settled in a corner of Uncle Hsu's. Pepper red walls and ceiling, lacquered to a brilliant shine to reflect the dim light of paper lanterns, boxed us in safely.

"I hope the food's as hot as those walls," Evelyn remarked.

"You have your pick," I said and signaled that we were ready to order.

After the waiter patriotically refused to understand Jenny's need for a Black Russian, we both settled for white wine spritzers. Evelyn settled for water.

"Do you come here a lot?" Jenny asked, looking around the small room and twitching her shoulders.

"When I can afford it, yes. It's got a nice, cozy feel to it."

"Well, yes, I guess," Jenny said doubtfully. "At least, no one's going to bother you here." And she looked pointedly at the male couples that surrounded us.

"What's the matter, Jenny?" Evelyn asked. "You got problems with gays?"

"Sshh," Jenny whispered, which of course drew the immediate attention of our neighbors. She tried not to look at them. "No, not at all." Jenny sat straight up in her chair to make herself taller. "It's just, well,

Fred couldn't stand them, you know." She rested her case.

"That's the first I've heard of it," Evelyn said, "but it doesn't surprise me. That man was crammed full of prejudices."

"He was not!" Jenny exclaimed. "He just had definite ideas of what he liked and disliked."

Evelyn gave Jenny one of her rare, unblinking stares. "Yeah, he hated the world and worshipped himself."

"Thanks for spreading rumors that I'm in love with Greenhouse, Jenny," I said in mock anger to divert attention.

"Oh, I'm sorry, I didn't mean to upset you. I just thought it was so great the way you've been glowing in the dark."

"Anyway," Evelyn added, "it sure beats spreading rumors you were in love with Fred."

My face must have done something.

"For Christ's sake, Simona, you act as if you've got a lemon stuck up your ass. Take a laxative or something." Evelyn sometimes liked to wrap her words in sandpaper. "What's wrong with Jenny saying you've got a crush on that detective? It's about the only time she's got something right."

Jenny looked down and played with her chopsticks.

"By the way," I said, "he's taken me off the hook, doesn't think I took the ring."

"What ring?" Evelyn asked.

"Some sweet soul, probably the murderer," I spoke slowly, looking at Evelyn carefully, "dropped Fred's HH&H ring in my Kleenex box." All I got was her usual blinking eyes.

"That's wonderful. About the ring, I mean," Jenny said and bobbed her curls in approval. "I think he's so cute, and I think . . ."

"I'll admit he has a great ass," Evelyn contributed.

153

Jenny ignored the interruption. "I really think it's about time you started thinking seriously about a man." She rearranged the objects on the table in a neat symmetrical fashion. She was going to have a harder time with my life.

"You can't wait too long to have a baby." She turned her concerned face toward me. "You do want one, don't you?"

"Isn't this getting a little personal?" Evelyn asked, shifting her weight in the rickety chair.

I didn't answer either of them. I was thinking of Jenny in that maternity ward, cradling a baby. Small Jenny with a handful. "Jenny spends time caring for boarder babies," I said. "Isn't that wonderful of her?"

"They just lie there in their cradle all day and night long." Jenny putting herself down. "Someone's got to pick them up." She began wiping imaginary crumbs from the white tablecloth.

"Sure, but what happens to your gut when you put them back down and walk out of there?" Evelyn asked. "That's what I want to know. I think I'll drink to that downer." Evelyn raised her glass. "And to you, Jenny. I didn't know you had it in you." She took a long swig of water.

"Well, as for my wanting a baby," I said, getting back to Jenny's question, "I haven't found the possible father. Or to be more honest, he hasn't found me."

"Well, you're not going to find one by just sitting around and waiting. You've got to adopt the American way. Go get 'em." Jenny shook a clenched fist in the air, an urchin ready to mount the barricades, ready to fight someone else's battle. "But why did you leave Italy? The men there are so gorgeous. I mean, look at Marcello Mas . . ." Two helpless hands went up in the air. "I can't even pronounce his name."

"Yes, they are handsome," I admitted, "but they tend to slip in and out of women's beds like olive oil,

154

and please don't tell me they don't mean it, Jenny."

Evelyn looked at me in sympathy.

"What about you, Jenny?" Evelyn asked, shifting the spotlight. "Let's see the wrinkles in your gut."

"There's nothing to tell, really," she said sadly. "I've always had to take care of my mother. That didn't leave much room for anyone else. She died only two years ago and now it's too late for me to have babies, so why get married?" She saw nothing wrong with that logic.

"I'm too selfish to worry about anyone else, young or old," Evelyn volunteered before anyone could ask and stuffed half an egg roll into her mouth, as if to prevent further revelations.

We all dug into our food in silence for a few minutes.

"Hey, what's happening with the investigation?" Jenny asked me, suddenly finding her bounce again.

"They asked Dana some questions this morning, and she got all upset."

"Really?" A small barbecued rib stuck out of her mouth. "Do you know why?"

"I tried to find out, but I didn't get anywhere." We had polished off the hors d'oeuvres, and I already felt full. "I don't think I can eat another thing."

"Stop depriving yourself," Evelyn barked. "You're not getting him tonight, so you might as well eat. It's a pretty good substitute." She piled Moo Goo Gai Pan and Pork on her plate as if to encourage me to do the same, but she wasn't playing fair. She had both.

"I'm going to find out who killed Fred," I said out of the blue, surprising even myself.

"Oh, no, Simona, don't." Jenny's face puckered up with worry. "It's such an ugly thing. Let the police take care of it."

"No, Fred's ring was found in my desk. I have first

155

rights."

"Is that the only reason?" Evelyn had a way of seeing through things.

"No. I think I want to put him to rest."

"Someone's done that already," quipped Evelyn.

"I mean put him to rest in my mind. Put everything to rest."

"That's a tall order."

"Yes, it is." I took a deep breath and looked at Evelyn's full plate. "But I think I'm ready to bury the bad men in my life."

"Good luck."

"I wish you luck too," Jenny said doubtfully. "I just hope you don't get into any trouble. What are the H's going to say?"

I waved a dismissive hand and asked, "What do the two of you know about Giovanna?"

Evelyn looked at me in surprise. "What about Giovanna? You should know more about her than we do. You both come from the same place."

"I'm talking about her relationship with Fred. She's taken his death very badly, hasn't she?"

"Well, she's bound to be more upset than most," Jenny said. "Giovanna lived with Fred."

"The ideal setup." Evelyn added in her typical rasping way. "Not only did she work a full day at HH&H, but then she'd go and take care of His Highness. Do his laundry, cook his meals, run his bath, have his espresso ready at six o'clock in the morning."

"Doesn't she make enough money at HH&H to survive without working at night too?"

"Money had nothing to do with it," Jenny said. "Giovanna was devoted to Fred. She owed him a lot. She wouldn't have been able to come to this country if he hadn't sponsored her. He had a right to expect something back for it. I feel so sorry for her. She's

156

going to be lost without him." And I pondered if she was also speaking for herself.

"Yeah, it's like losing your pet cobra."

"Oh, Evelyn, you don't really mean that."

Evelyn blinked nasty signals back at Jenny.

"Bertrand asked me out to lunch on Thursday," I said. It was my turn again to change the subject. "He dropped a note on my desk this afternoon."

"How romantic," Jenny said.

"That's the least he can do after all the work you're doing for him."

"I don't think it's that kind of a lunch," I ventured.

"Then what kind of a lunch is it?"

"I don't know, but he's treating me differently. He seems to have noticed I'm a woman all of a sudden, and I'm completely thrown by it. Did he just break up with someone?"

"I don't know anything about Bertrand's private life," Jenny said shaking her head regretfully. "I don't think anyone does in the office."

"That would be a first," Evelyn remarked.

"Actually, Fred must have known something," Jenny admitted reluctantly.

"Mr. Busybody himself," Evelyn added.

Jenny leaned toward me, as though wanting to exclude Evelyn's caustic remarks. "About a month ago, they were locked up in Fred's office and I heard Bertrand shout, 'My private life is none of your business.' Jenny slowly nodded her head several times, as if physically confirming her memory.

I remembered Wally's words in Bertrand's office. Had Fred been trying to find another "ugly little tidbit to use as he saw fit?"

"Maybe it's none of our business either," Evelyn reminded us. "Tell me more about this lunch," she asked me, getting into more comfortable, innocuous territory.

157

"For several years I've drawn a complete blank as far as the other sex is concerned," I said, "and now, in the space of a week, I've met one man whose twinkle makes me rush to the bathroom to dry off, and another, successful and rich and all the things one should want out of life, who invites me to have lunch with his mother at the Colony Club. I'm very confused."

"I thought Bertrand's mother lived in New Canaan," Jenny said. So much for not knowing anything about his private life.

"She comes into the city every Thursday to have her hair done at Elizabeth Arden, and she expects to lunch with her son come hell or high water."

"So why were you invited?" Evelyn wanted to know.

"Because Bertrand thought that Mummy and I would get on splendidly. I'm quoting him."

"I can just hear him," she jeered.

"Well, Evelyn, I'm rather flattered," I said.

"What about your Greenhouse with the great ass?" Evelyn went on. Wally's ways were rubbing off. "Ready to forget him for old Boston money with no ass at all?"

"One's got nothing to do with the other." I wanted to drop the whole subject.

"That's the point," Evelyn said. "They come from two different worlds, and I'm hoping you're not snob enough to be swayed by chandeliers and candlesticks." She tapped her fingers on the tablecloth to the rhythm of her tired eyes. "I'd stick to that nice, little, middle-class ass. You can't go wrong with him. Wops and Jews don't belong on New Canaan estates."

"That's terrible," Jenny gasped. "Don't listen to her, Simona." Jenny pointed her long nose at Evelyn and looked very much like a worried mother hen. "You know something, Evelyn? I really think you should

158

take a drink or two. It might make things a little easier for you." Her face softened into genuine concern. "Fred can't do anything to you now. He's dead."

Evelyn's eyes and fingertips froze together. "Do me a favor, take those sharp red heels of yours and stuff them down your throat." With that request Evelyn threw a twenty-dollar bill on the table and walked out.

"I'm sorry, but she really does need a drink," Jenny said with a resolute shake of her curls. "She's gotten so rude and mean."

"What's Fred got to do with it?"

"He just knew she had a drinking problem, and I guess he held it over her." She didn't seem very happy to admit it.

"How did he find out? Did she get drunk in front of him?"

"Oh, no. I don't think she ever did that. Dana just caught her drinking in her office several mornings in a row and reported it to Fred." Sweet Dana of the big, red mouth. Somehow I didn't like what Jenny's mouth had done, either.

"It's getting late," Jenny said, checking her watch. "Do you mind if we get our fortune cookies and leave? In five minutes, you'll be asleep, but I've got a train to catch."

As Jenny had predicted, I was asleep in no time, but I kept having nightmares. Greenhouse rowed under the bridge and came out of the shadow as Fred, then quickly transformed himself into Bertrand; my ex-husband's face, with his steely blue eyes grinning, surfaced from the depths of the water to stare at me; a naked baby came floating by and as it neared it turned into a thin strip of white paper, a cookie fortune telling me I was "Better alone than in bad company." Another fortune floated by exhorting me to "Go get 'em."

My mother was right. Never go to sleep on a full stomach.

Chapter Sixteen

"Mattie's been arrested," Evelyn announced the next morning. She was standing in Gregory's doorway.

"That's ridiculous. Who told you that?" I asked belligerently.

"I saw it downstairs twenty minutes ago. Those two friends of yours came and took her away."

"Maybe they just want to question her," Gregory said quietly.

"In handcuffs? Gregory, make me the blackest coffee possible on that contraption of yours. I'm completely bowled over." Evelyn dragged the weight of her body into the room and let it fall in Gregory's spare chair.

"I can't believe Mattie killed Fred," Evelyn said. She frantically reached in her pockets for a cigarette she couldn't find. I silently handed her one of mine. I was too stunned to speak. I couldn't believe Greenhouse would make such a stupid, cruel mistake.

"She didn't." Gregory looked at Evelyn and his face became a white blank. His voice didn't betray the slightest doubt.

"Well, Gregory, if she didn't, who did?" Evelyn asked, leaning forward and inadvertently blowing smoke in his face.

He started to put the caps on his Magic Markers, and said nothing. We both stared at him; he did not look up at us. Did he know?

"Any one of us could have killed him," he finally said. "We all had reasons."

"Mattie included," I added.

"She didn't kill Fred." Color suddenly flooded his face. "He deserved to die. He goaded people. He loved to sit there and peel layers of skin with his words. He always found out your weakness and spit . . ."

"Shut up, Gregory, please shut up," Evelyn cried and burst into surprising tears.

"I'm sure they'll release Mattie soon," I said lamely, trying to soothe. "They just made a big mistake, that's all. Just a big mistake."

Evelyn rubbed her nose with her hand, not bothering to reach for the Kleenex box that was in plain view on Gregory's desk. "Yeah, that's what it was. A big mistake." She laughed loudly. "My stupid contacts are floating."

I watched silently as she removed them without ever letting go of her cigarette. Gregory seemed lost in an ugly world of his own.

She looked up, her eyes finally at rest. Some random tears still stuck on the roughness of her face. She didn't wipe them away. I think she had already forgotten them. "Luis told me they arrested her because she was seen going in the delivery entrance the Sunday Fred was killed."

"Who saw her?" I asked. Gregory continued to stare at the wall. He looked too drained to speak. I didn't even know if he was listening.

"The Indian newspaper vendor on the corner. He knows who she is and where she works because she gets the paper and candy from him every day. Apparently your duo asked the vendor a lot of questions about the comings and goings on that Sunday. He knows us fairly well. Practically all of HH&H buys from him. This morning he told Luis he wouldn't

162

have said anything about Mattie to the police if he had known about the murder. Said it wasn't good for business. Can you believe that? Who's he trying to kid?" She finally threw what was left of her cigarette in an empty coffee cup and licked her finger where it had just been burned. "Of course, for reasons unknown, Mattie hadn't said anything to the police about being here on that Sunday, which makes the whole thing suck."

"What took them so long to arrest her?" Gregory finally spoke, color stroking his face again.

"That's what I asked Luis, and he said the vendor had gone to Florida on vacation. That's why he didn't know about the murder. He just opened up this morning." She sat back in her chair and put her legs up on the rim of the chair Gregory was sitting in. Her shoes touched his slacks. He moved slightly to make more room for her. "I know it gets hot in India, but Florida in July is crazy."

"How did Mattie get the keys to the delivery door?" I asked.

"She's always had them." Evelyn said. "She, Luis, and the agents that manage the building are the only ones who have the key, besides Mr. Heffer. Luis and Mattie are the first to get to the office. Luis watches the front door, Mattie the delivery door." She removed her feet from the chair and sat up. "Gregory, where's that fucking coffee? I'm dying here." Evelyn had gone back to being rude Evelyn. It was reassuring.

"Sorry, but there's no time for coffee." I looked at my watch. "Gregory and I have to go to the airport to pick up his lovely daughter. Right, Daddy?"

"Don't call me that. I don't even let Ellen call me that."

"I noticed. How come?"

Evelyn snapped her eyes at me.

"Sorry, none of my business," I said quickly. "Meet

me downstairs in five minutes. I just want to let Bertrand know we're going."

Instead of going to Bertrand's office, I headed straight to the refrigerator and took out the slice of chocolate cake and Bavarian cream Gregory had given me yesterday. He had said it would last twenty-four hours and the time was up. I figured I might as well eat it. What had gone on in Gregory's office had completely frazzled my nerves. Mattie had been arrested; Gregory and Evelyn had acted very oddly, and Simona had done her usual number of tripping all over herself in apologies, instead of asking what the hell was going on. To top it all off, there didn't seem much point in getting thin anymore. Greenhouse was slowly and clearly going down the drain. I didn't think I could ever look him straight in the face if he started arresting people I liked. I gobbled down my first big bite, and as the cream slowly melted in my mouth, I decided that I could never deal with a boyfriend who was in the business of drugs, corpses, and arresting people. If I was forced to see Greenhouse again, I would just ask him to put on sunglasses. I wasn't going to let that twinkle get to me again.

The slice of cake Gregory had given me was enormous, and I took it with me to Bertrand's office knowing it would fall into a welcoming mouth. To my surprise Dana was sitting, her back to the door, showing Bertrand some rough layouts Gregory had sketched for her. Apparently Dana had not needed an official memo from the nineteenth floor to know who the new creative director was. She had come to pay her obsequious respects. I wondered if she thought she could get to Bertrand's bed too.

"Hi, my love," I said loudly. Dana jumped in her chair. Bertrand, bless him, didn't flinch at the term of endearment.

"Oh, it's you," she said shaking her heavy hair. I

164

half expected her to drip gel on her designer-covered lap. "You scared me," she added with a short laugh. She did not go back to her layouts. She continued to stare at me, red mouth quivering. It took me a moment to realize she was looking at my cake.

"Would you like some?" I couldn't help but offer. She looked starved.

"It's chocolate, isn't it?" I didn't answer her. What else is an almost black cake made of?

"Oh, I musn't, I'm getting so fat," she said, rubbing her hand over her stomach and looking at both of us. I wondered if she expected us to disagree with her.

"Well, I brought it in to offer it to Bertrand. Now the two of you can fight over it."

"I'm not at all hungry," Bertrand, the gentleman, said. He winked at me behind her back.

"Here, Dana, it's all yours." I proffered the slice gingerly, as I might offer a bone to a pit bull. She surprised me by accepting it graciously. I refrained from patting her on the head.

"I'm off to the airport with Gregory. Do you want to come and take a preview glimpse of her?"

"No, Dana has to show me some of her ideas for a new ad for Lington which she has to present in the morning." Dana smiled with her full mouth. "Anyway, I'd rather see Ellen tomorrow morning in Scriba's studio, rested up and ready for the camera. I'm going to stop over in the office first. I don't think I'll get there before nine-thirty, ten o'clock. Just make sure they don't put any make-up on her face. I want photographs of her completely natural. Then I can see what I've got and what to do with it."

"I've already told Johnny, but I'll be there to make sure."

"I'm counting on that," he said with a serious face. "And you won't forget about the other thing, will you, Simona? No blue jeans allowed." This time he laughed nervously. He was referring to the luncheon date, and he was trying, in his embarrassed way, to tell me to dress properly. I couldn't tell him I don't even own a pair of blue jeans because my buns are too big.

"Italy's finest," was my answer. I had planned to wear an expensive-looking, conservative, beige linen suit left over from my Italian days. I had tried it on that morning and happily discovered it still fit me if I held in my stomach and didn't eat dinner that night. I think that was the real reason I was being so generous with my chocolate cake slice. Starvation wasn't the only thing I had planned. I also intended to spend my whole evening trying to iron out the wrinkles that always cling to linen with great ardor, and ironing on a July evening in a small room with no air-conditioning was guaranteed to sweat a few pounds off me. I was going to do it gladly, because I knew Bertrand would be pleased with my choice of dress. It was the kind of "I'm such a goody-goody" suit that even a nun would approve of.

"On your way out, Simona, would you mind telling Mattie to have one of the boys bring me some empty cartons?" Bertrand asked in his official business voice. "I have to start thinking of moving out of here."

I opened my mouth to say something, but Dana's whine beat me to it. "Mattie told me not to call them boys. She says it's degrading. She said if they are old enough to serve their country, they are old enough to be called men. I just thought I'd warn you, because she gets very upset about it." She looked pitifully happy that she had been able to give Bertrand some advice.

"Mattie's been arrested, and I have to get out of here or I'm going to be late." I stayed long enough to see Dana's mouth hang open, her tongue foaming with cream. I said "Ask Evelyn" to Bertrand's ques-

166

tioning face and ran to the elevator. An unhappy Gregory was waiting for me, and I linked my arm in his and dragged him toward the cleaner air of New York streets.

Chapter Seventeen

She was standing perfectly poised and confident, even though we were half an hour late. When she saw her father her lovely face disintegrated into a thousand smiles, each component of her face straining with happiness. She took a few steps forward shyly, then threw her arms around him without letting go of the raincoat and small suitcase she was carrying. Her embrace narrowly missed a rushing passerby. Gregory responded by holding her waist and leaning toward her slightly. He wasn't going to commit himself to a big, welcoming hug. She was a good two inches taller than he was, which made her around five nine. I breathed a sigh of relief. In all the excitement of the discovery, I had never thought to question her height, which was a very important factor. Five nine was the ideal height for a model, neither too tall that she would tower over a man who might appear with her in an ad nor too short so that clothes would not flow elegantly from her body. I studied her back while she held her embrace. I had a feeling Bertrand would ask her to go on a crash diet to lose three pounds. Her behind was too seductively round in the flesh, and the camera always added a few pounds of weight. The layout I had seen showed her body in profile and her gorgeous derrière would be a real eyecatcher, too distracting by far. Of course, if she didn't lose the weight in time, the retoucher could always work his magic.

They parted, and I stepped forward to introduce myself. She turned a perfectly sculpted face in my direction and studied me, happiness and excitement betraying themselves now only in her light brown eyes. I gasped out loud. Paulina and Isabella Rossellini could just wipe their faces clean with cold cream and call it a day. Once Ellen came out in print for Janick, Inc., the faces that represented Esteé Lauder and Lancôme were going to be forgotten. She had no make-up on. Natural, just the way Bertrand wanted her, and she was stunning. I can't describe her, because no woman can really see an incredibly beautiful woman without the distorting feelings of embarrassment and envy. I was envious of her looks and embarrassed by the sensuality they conveyed. All I can say is that I can't even imagine waking up in the morning and seeing a face like hers in my mirror. The world would be too different.

We didn't have to wait for any luggage. She had everything with her, and I ushered them both to the waiting car. As we drove into Manhattan on the Fifty-ninth Street bridge, she didn't speak. Her eyes were busy jumping from one window to the next, taking in the silhouette of the city. The colors were gray and pink as the day was preparing for a demure sunset. The haze left by the day's heat made Manhattan look as if it had just been lightly dusted with baby powder. It was spectacular and a wonderful way for Ellen to see the city for the first time in her adult life. Once the car plunged into the darkness of East Sixtieth Street, the magic was gone and I got down to business.

"Get to bed early tonight, Ellen. Tomorrow is going to be a gruelling day. The car will pick you up at Gregory's house at seven-thirty. We want you in the studio by eight-thirty. I'll be there to greet you and don't worry about breakfast. Scriba, he's the photographer, loves good food and has wonderful croissants, bagels, donuts. Whatever your heart might desire."

I asked the driver to drop me off in front of the office

on his way to the Holland Tunnel because there was one question I was determined to ask before the day was over. I got out of the car, closed the door, and poked my head through the window on Ellen's side to say good night. "Sleep well, Ellen. I think you'll do just fine. Your father is going to be very proud of you."

The car drove off and I was left with the memory of a frowning Ellen. Something was very wrong between father and daughter, and I resolved to find out what it was as soon as I got to know her better. I didn't have much doubt that she would be staying around for a while.

Chapter Eighteen

Julia's office looked like a greenhouse. She had a small room on the eastern side of the ninth floor which she had filled with hundreds of small pots of African violets. They huddled together on the windowsill; they climbed along and above the window with the help of green plastic; they crowded her desk.

"It's just perfect for them here," she told me with a welcoming smile and her quavering voice. In one hand she held a small, enameled watering can painted with bright-colored flowers that almost got lost in the many folds of her dress. Only the long spout stuck out. I was again reminded of a fairy with her magic wand. Good or bad I didn't know.

"They don't want too much sun, you know." She removed her glasses from the tip of her nose and hid them in a pocket.

"Julia, did you see Fred on the Friday before he died?" I asked, for once getting right down to business.

"I don't know. It's hard to remember." She stopped her watering and shook the can. "Oh, dear, I have to fill this again. There's never enough water to go around."

"Why don't you buy a bigger can?"

"This one's much too old to discard," Julia said and gave it a reassuring pat. She slowly sat her large body in a wide, worn-down armchair that had clearly

171

come from home. "Helps my back," she said as if I had asked. She placed the watering can on her lap as if it were a beloved pet, gave a long sigh of comfort, and seemingly forgot about her plants.

"Jenny said that on the Friday before he died Fred received a phone call that made him very angry, but no one seems to know anything about it," I said.

"He was so happy on Sunday. I'm the first person he told, you know." Her voice had faded to a whisper.

"Told you what?"

She took a deep breath to get the words out. "That he was happy. I want you to know he was happy on Sunday. You seem to care so much about his moods."

"I just thought the phone call might have something to do with his death, since it made him so angry. At least Jenny said he was angry." I was beginning to think Jenny had made the whole thing up.

"When did you say that was?" Julia asked softly.

I looked at the shooting schedule that was taped to the wall behind her desk to help her pinpoint the day in her vague mind. "It was the day after you shot the commercial for the new Belvino wine account."

"Oh, dear, yes. Belvino. I'm afraid I did upset them a little." She tugged at the thin red wisps of hair falling on her forehead.

"What happened, Julia?"

"I waited and waited. I couldn't understand why no one came. It was so unlike everyone. But then, of course, it was my fault. I was in the wrong studio, you see." She looked at me with her faded eyes. "I got muddled and I never thought to call the office."

"Were they able to shoot the commercial?"

"Yes, yes, thank heavens for that. Fred rushed in to save the day. He was good at that. I remember the time we had to present a whole new ad concept to a new fashion client . . ."

172

"Was he angry?" I interrupted.

"It's really a wonderful story," she said, suddenly having gone deaf. "All the art directors had searched their minds for weeks, but the only ideas they had come up with were stale and terrible. Fred had just been with HH&H a few days so he hadn't been asked to contribute." She stopped to take a long breath and I settled back in my chair for the Once Upon a Time. "The morning of the meeting we were sitting in the conference room in a panic. We had nothing to show, you see. No copy, no layout, not even a hint of a good idea. Mr. Harland was about to deliver one of his artful speeches full of some excuse or other, when Fred burst into the room dressed in black from head to toe." She narrowed her myopic eyes as if to see him better in the distance of her memory and smiled. "He looked dashing. He had all the lights turned off except the podium light, which he turned to shine in his face. That's why he wore black, you understand? He only wanted his face to show.

"Fred waited for silence and then started narrating a story." Julia wheezed for breath. "It was a wonderfully sad love story where the heroine kept changing her beautiful dresses, hoping each new dress would bring her closer to her lover." She clapped her hands in childlike glee. "We all applauded at the end. It was pure genius. Fred had offered the client the idea of running a series of commercials as if they were sixty-second soaps—a love story always looking for that happy ending. When they aired, a voice-over at the end whispered"—she lowered her voice to a murmur—" 'Just one more dress,' as if that were the solution to all our problems." Having come to the end of her story, she rewarded herself with a deep, satisfied breath.

"That was wonderful, Julia, but I really do need to know why Fred was angry on that Friday."

She looked crestfallen by my insistence. "Well, he was a little angry with me."

"Angry enough to fire you?"

Julia gasped. "Fred would never fire me. Never. He was a friend. I got him his first job. He wouldn't, he just wouldn't."

"Here, let me fill that for you," I said, reaching for the watering can on Julia's lap. She was nervously stroking it as if to calm an angry cat.

"Whatever for?" she asked.

"You haven't finished watering your plants," I reminded her, taking the can away from her gently.

Was Julia telling the truth or did she have a good reason for murder?

When I got home I took out my ironing board and settled down for a night of hard, hot work. The phone rang while I was struggling with the left armpit of my jacket. Armpits are difficult to iron, linen armpits impossible.

"Hi, Simona." Greenhouse slurred my name as if he weren't quite sure how to pronounce it. I was not prepared to hear the sound of his voice, much less for the effect it had on me.

"I can't talk to you unless you put your sunglasses on."

"At night? In my apartment? On the phone?"

"Yes," I insisted. "I promised myself I wouldn't talk to you unless you put your sunglasses on."

"Am I allowed to ask why?"

"Your eyes bother me." I couldn't keep it up. "Oh, I'm sorry, Greenhouse, I know I'm being silly, but I don't know what to say to you after what you've done."

"You mean Mattie?"

"Is it that bad for her?"

174

"I'm sorry, but I'm not free to talk about the case."

"Then why did you call, Greenhouse?"

"Look, my name is Stanley. Most people call me Stan."

"I call you Greenhouse."

"I know you do, but it sure doesn't sound very friendly."

"Oh, it is friendly. In Italy, a lot of people call each other by their last names. We get used to it in school. The teachers just use your last name without a Miss or a Mr. in front of it, never the first name. If I wanted to be unfriendly, I would be formal and call you Detective Greenhouse."

"You know, you're funny. You sound so American I forget you're not. No, I take that back. Your hands are a dead giveaway."

"What do you mean?" I asked, beginning to feel pleasantly light-headed. I reached over to unplug the iron and steadied myself on my two mattresses.

"When you talk your hands are all over the place." Everywhere but on you, I thought.

"What's wrong with calling me Stan?" Greenhouse wanted to know.

"Our relationship hasn't come to that point." I made a face after I said that. I was presuming again.

"Well, I'm glad there is a relationship. It seems to be a little touch and go with you."

"With me?" I screamed in his ear. "What about you? One day your eyes are beckoning like the neon signs in front of those topless bars, and on other days it's the KGB-off-to-Siberia look. One time you brush against me twice in five minutes, making me think it can't be an accident, and then the next time I see you, you stay away as if I were a ticking bomb. It's always been that way with us."

"What are you talking about?" he asked, his voice slightly hoarse and constricted. I could tell he was ly-

175

ing on his stomach. Fourteen years dubbing films teaches you these little things. "You make it sound as if we've seen a lot of each other."

"I know we haven't." Damn it. "Don't be so literal. I always exaggerate a little," I explained. Exaggeration and fantasy keep me alive.

"That's Italian too, huh? Like the hands."

"Mm-mm." Why couldn't he be lying on my two mattresses? I knew Mattie wouldn't have held it against me. I could even hear her say, "Simona, honey, you get what lovin' you can outta life."

"I'll remember that in the future," Greenhouse said. I was going to dream about that word—future.

"Now I better go. The movie's about to start."

"What movie?" I asked, wanting to hold on.

To Each His Own. It's on Channel Eleven. You should see it. I've already seen it three times." He was going to hang up the phone so that he could see a movie that he had already seen three times? Oh, if I only had Ellen's face. He'd be groveling then. "It was made in 1946 and it stars Olivia deHavilland and John Lund. Great movie. I'll call you soon."

"Greenhouse," I called out to stop him from hanging up.

"What is it?"

"Mattie didn't do it. How could you arrest her? And why the handcuffs? Is she too big and black for two soft-white policemen?"

Silence on the other end. This time I had overdone it just a little, even for an Italian.

"Mrs. Washington gave us no choice." Icicles, instead of words, slowly dripping into my ear. "She refused to come with us and became verbally abusive."

"She was scared. Can you blame her?"

"In the case of resistance to arrest, it is normal police procedure to use handcuffs. It had nothing to do

176

with her size or color."

"But it's all wrong. It's got to be all wrong."

"Listen, Simona, let's get one thing straight right away. I don't mix my social life with my work." I started to gurgle something, but he wouldn't let me get the words out. "No, let me finish. My work is very important to me, and nothing interferes with it. Do you understand that?" He didn't wait for me to say yes or no. "I never want to hear about Mattie or anything about the HH&H murder from you. I'm sorry, but the movie's started and I don't want to miss it. Good-bye."

Damn him. That had been so unfair of him. How could he think I would see him and forget he was the man who had arrested Mattie. The fact that three minutes earlier I had been ready to share the same bed with Mattie's imagined approval slipped my mind entirely. At that moment I decided that inside that hard exterior of his beat a heart of stone. I turned on the iron and banged it around a little. Who needed him anyway. The next day I was going to be wined and dined at the snobby Colony Club, and I was going to be just fine. And wasn't he going to be surprised when I came up with the murderer? Who was going to have the last word then? I plugged in the iron again, determined that I and my linen suit were really going to look like Italy's finest, and to hell with New York's finest. I also turned on the TV set and switched from Channel Four to Channel Eleven. I might as well watch while I was ironing, I thought. I was in time to see the main title, *To Each His Own*. At that moment it seemed a very apt title. I didn't realize until later how apt the whole movie was.

Chapter Nineteen

When I got to the studio on Thursday morning, Ellen had already arrived and was being scrutinized by Scriba, Johnny, and the hair and make-up people. They had sat her down on a low, hard-backed chair, and Scriba was holding her face in his hands, turning it from one side to the other. She look terrified.

"Hi, Ellen," I said cheerfully. "Have you had coffee yet?" Before she could answer, I grabbed her by the hand and pulled her away from Scriba's grasp. He didn't say anything. We made our way across cables and rolls of seamless paper strewn about the wooden floor to a table at the far end of the room. It was covered with breakfast goodies. We avoided the calories, filled two mugs with coffee, and then I walked her around the place, hoping she'd relax. I wanted to see her smile come back before Bertrand got there.

Scriba's studio is essentially one enormous room with bleached wooden floors, bare white walls, and a ceiling twelve feet above us. It is the classic warehouse loft that is so prevalent in downtown Manhattan, and which I would love to own. Coming from my two-by-four studio apartment, all that empty space is mind-boggling.

"Ellen, I'm sorry about Scriba. I should have warned you. He thinks models are just background props that have to blend into his photographs, but he is a wonderful photographer. Just ignore his loathsome personality."

"Shhh, he can hear you," Ellen whispered like a frightened schoolgirl.

"It's all right. He likes to be thought of as loathsome. It makes him feel important. Actually he's a very nice man, after you've known him for about twenty years." I looked at Ellen and realized my sarcasm wasn't helping the situation any. "Come on, let me show you the dressing room."

On the left of the entrance, Scriba had created a dressing and make-up room by enclosing the area with white Japanese screens. In the middle of this space, resting on low tables, he had placed a row of mirrors bought from a beauty parlor going out of business.

"It's just like in the movies," Ellen said, pointing to the light bulbs that framed all the mirrors.

"Well, movies aren't based on total fantasy. Some reality does creep in." I thought of the movie I had seen the night before; the story of a woman whose fiancé dies in the war, leaving her pregnant. A soppy, boring film, I had thought while watching, refusing to like what Greenhouse liked.

"Is this where the women get dressed?" she asked.

"It's unisex."

Ellen looked surprised, but not horrified.

"Models get so used to showing their bodies to all and sundry that hiding them from each other wouldn't make sense," I said. "Besides, Scriba wants as much space as possible for his photography."

"It's such a huge place."

"Yes, but sometimes he has to build a set in the studio, and then he needs all the space he's got."

"What kind of set?" Ellen asked.

"Oh, I don't know. It could be a living room, a section of a restaurant, a nursery. Things like that." Olivia deHavilland had the baby anyway, despite the dead father. No thought of abortion in 1946. Not on

179

the screen at least.

"Does he always wear a hat indoors?" Ellen asked in a whisper, referring to Scriba's constant companion, his beloved black fedora. She had sat down in front of one of the mirrors.

"He couldn't work without it. Black hat and white, silk scarf are his identifying props, just like Fellini. Scriba likes to play the great Italian director."

Ellen took a sip of her coffee and then smiled awkwardly at her own reflection.

"You're not too convinced about all this, are you?" I asked, sitting down next to her.

She lowered her eyes. "I was so nervous about flying out here I asked my doctor to give me a tranquilizer. He suggested a jog around the park instead."

Doctor. Yes, doctor. That's what it was about that movie. It had made me think of the doctor from the abortion clinic ad in Steve's ice cream place. The name had been so familiar.

"It seems so unreal," Ellen continued. "Besides, I know Gregory isn't happy about it." She leaned forward and peered closely into the mirror, as if to confirm her looks. "He's never even told me I'm pretty."

"What is with you and your father? Why won't he let you call him Daddy. Why won't he let you live here with him?"

Ellen looked at me through the mirror. She didn't say anything.

"I'm sorry, I have a habit of asking the wrong questions. Please forgive me." I sure hadn't waited to get to know her any better before digging in.

"That's all right. I know you're a good friend of Gregory's. He talked about you a lot last night. How I owe you this trip and everything."

"You owe this trip to that face of yours, and don't let your father make you think any differently."

"He's so upset. I've never seen him this way. I know I don't see him very often, but . . ." She looked at me helplessly. "I guess I shouldn't have come. He doesn't want me here." She lowered her head and I thought I was going to see tears again.

"Hey, stop that, Ellen." I reached over and touched her arm. "He is upset, I know. But it has nothing to do with you, believe me. Someone he cares for very much has been arrested. That's the reason, not you."

"Are you sure?" A flickering light of hope passed across Ellen's eyes.

"Of course, I'm sure," I lied. I wasn't sure about anything at that moment. "Come on, I better hand you back to Scriba or who knows how he'll sabotage your pictures."

"Ah, there you are, my Nebraska *bella*." Scriba opened his long, thin arms in a gesture of greeting and watched Ellen tentatively walk toward him. "I hope you have not listened to any of Simona's nastiness about me. She is jealous because I too come from across the ocean, from Italy." With that fake pizza-pie accent, Staten Island was more like it. "She is not unique at HH&H. I steal her thunder. That is the right expression, no? Don't be so stiff, *mia cara*," he went on to say without waiting for an answer. "It changes your face." He sat Ellen down in a chair placed in front of a long roll of white seamless paper that he was going to use as a backdrop.

"I'm sorry," Ellen said.

"No, no, no. Never apologize to anyone. You are too beautiful for apologies. Don't worry, Scriba will relax you, make you happy."

Jenny had also gone to a doctor.

Three cameras on tripods placed at different angles stared at Ellen. She looked like she was facing a firing squad.

Of course. It was the same doctor. The name on the calendar and the name on the ad had been identical.

"What music do you like?" he asked Ellen, gently

stroking her long, straight hair, feeling the texture of it. Make-up and Hair watched on the sidelines. Hair was dying to do something to Ellen's limp locks; his mouth was twitching. Make-up looked very happy; his job was going to be easy.

"Oh, I like lots of music. Bruce Springsteen, the Talking Heads, The Police, Phil Collins."

"Johnny, put on Phil Collins," Scriba ordered. "At least he does not scream so much. Why do the young like screaming? Screaming is no good for the nerves."

Yes, age was a factor. Jenny said she was too old to have children. The clock was ticking for me, too. Was I going to make it? But then why go to an abortion clinic?

"In the Air Tonight" came through the loudspeaker. "Now I'm going to go behind the camera, and you will tell me your life, no? I want to hear everything. Tell me the happy moments, the sad. Whatever you wish. I will listen, but I will also photograph. I" — he tapped his forefinger against his chest for emphasis — "I will photograph your life as it passes through your face." His assistants turned on the lights and directed them on Ellen's face.

She looked at me doubtfully, took a deep breath, and started. "I was born in New York City on March 7, 1964. I was sent to . . ."

Bertrand made his entrance just as Scriba started clicking. "Sorry I'm late," he said to the room at large. "Where is Ellen?"

Hair and Make-up parted to offer him a full view. Ellen got up and stood still, not knowing what to do. He walked right up to her and kissed her on the cheek.

"Hi, Ellen, I'm Bertrand Monroe. Welcome to New York. How was your flight?" His face was warm and friendly. I had no idea what he was thinking behind it.

"Very nice, thank you," she answered. I would not

182

have been surprised had she curtsied, she was that inhibited. She had lost all the confidence I had seen when she had first looked at me at the airport. I didn't know whether Gregory had anything to do with it or whether it was the excitement and newness of the situation, but I was afraid she was going to totally freeze. Scriba looked worried too. Bertrand was still making polite conversation with her when he looked at his watch. I instinctively looked at mine. It was eleven o'clock. We would have to leave the studio no later than twelve-ten to be punctual for the Colony Club. I had a feeling Mummy would not like to be kept waiting.

"You must be hot under those lights, Ellen," Bertrand said. "They're already making me perspire." He looked as cool as vichyssoise. "Come take a walk with me. I need to buy cigarettes. It's a great day outside." He held her by the elbow and steered her toward the door. Ellen was already mesmerized, watching every word come out of Bertrand's mouth. As he opened the door, we heard him say, "I'd love to show you Union Square. It's become quite a charming park. They copied the original subway kiosks . . ." His voice and their bodies disappeared behind the closing of the door. The pied piper playing his magical tune, I thought, and liked him even more.

The assistants turned off the lights, Johnny went to a desk in the entranceway to make some phone calls, and Scriba walked over to the table and started stuffing himself with croissants. We all knew we were in for a long wait.

Bertrand came back alone at noon. "I took Ellen to the office and left her in the doting care of Julia."

Not Julia, I thought. Julia's odd. Julia might . . .

"What's the matter, Simona?" Bertrand asked. "Are

183

you worried Julia might misplace her somewhere?"

"I guess so." What else could I say? I was so confused.

"Julia's not as muddle-headed as she likes to pretend," Bertrand said with a laugh, "and they took to each other immediately. That girl looked as if she needed some old-fashioned mothering, which reminds me, are you ready, Simona?"

I nodded. I had used the time of Bertrand's absence to iron the skirt of my suit again. After sitting down to talk to Ellen, it had looked like a worn-out accordion. Make-up and Hair had whiled their time away by "doing me up." After having toned down the make-up considerably, I looked as good I could.

"My compliments. You look very nice." Bertrand said, his expert eye assessing me quickly.

"What do you think of Ellen?" I asked. Bertrand did not get a chance to answer.

"Bertrand, the girl is beautiful, yes, but she will be difficult. Very difficult. She does not react to me," Scriba said with great solemnity. It was the gravest of all sins.

Bertrand laughed. "Omaha does not import your brand of flamboyance, Scriba." Scriba had no first name. He was just known as Scriba.

"It's our fault," Bertrand continued. "Even a professional model would have been scared with what is at stake. We're not going to take any pictures this afternoon."

Scriba groaned and Johnny, forever the greedy agent, jumped up from his desk. "Listen, I canceled *Harper's* for this shoot, Bertrand. Do you understand? Canceled. They were furious with us. Now you're telling me we're not shooting. I just don't believe this." He ran both his hands through his hair and then quickly patted it down. Johnny was always very careful with his appearance, even when he was angry.

"*Harper's* doesn't pay a third of what we pay you,

184

Johnny, so stop the hysterics. Anyway, I'm still going to use the studio, and I want everyone here. I want the girl to get used to us. We're like exotic animals in a zoo to her. First of all, I want you"—Bertrand pointed his finger in Johnny's direction—"to get some beautiful outfits up here. She's a size eight. Call Madonna and have them send up some clothes. Evening gowns mostly. I want her to get excited, to have fun. Maybe we'll take some Polaroids. That way she can see how she looks in different clothes." He walked up to Hair and Make-up. "Don't criticize her hair. I know it needs some work, but we'll worry about that later. Do her face in a few different ways. Show her how her face can change. Let her think she's become a Barbie doll. After this afternoon, I want her to love us and to think that modeling is the best job in the world. So it's up to all of us." He gave us an encouraging smile. "Simona and I have to leave. We'll meet back here at two-thirty sharp. Come on, I've got a car waiting downstairs." He took my elbow as he had with Ellen and steered me out the door.

Johnny came running after us, his short legs working twice as hard as Bertrand's. "Bertrand, I have the greatest pictures to show you of the Grand Canyon. We found the most perfect ledge."

"After lunch, everything after lunch."

The elevator wasn't on the floor and we ran down the four flights. I didn't know whether we rushed because we were late or to avoid the advancing Johnny.

Once I caught my breath in the car, I told Bertrand I thought he was a genius. He shrugged. "She's still a little girl, really, and little girls like to play. So that's what we'll do."

"What do you think of her?"

"If we can get her to overcome her fear, she'll be perfect. She has a perfect figure."

I nodded in agreement, burying the envy that had decreed her buns too shapely.

"Her hair is not very good, but we can change that," Bertrand said, relishing his Pygmalion role. "The important thing is that her face is beautifully expressive, even though I've only seen fear expressed so far. No, I shouldn't say that. She glowed when I bought her a hot dog from a street vendor. Thanks to you, Simona, I think we've got our girl."

I felt as beautiful as Ellen looked.

"When is Mr. Janick going to see her?" I asked.

"Not until tomorrow. I don't want her to be subjected to any more faces or any more foreign accents, for that matter, real or fake."

I gaped at him in surprise. I had never voiced my doubts about Scriba's nationality.

"You underestimate me," Bertrand said in answer to my expression. "By the way, I thought I should warn you that my mother can be rather formidable." He reached for my hand. "And she doesn't see very well, which is too bad, really. Your face is even more expressive than Ellen's." He leaned toward me and looked. "Not as beautiful, perhaps, but just as wonderful."

If only Greenhouse had said that.

Chapter Twenty

Our car stopped in front of a blue awning at Sixty-second and Park, next to two black limousines also depositing people in front of the Club. I looked up at the huge blue and yellow flag fluttering above the awning and as I walked into the grand entrance, I felt I had entered an embassy. It was certainly foreign land to me. The doorman recognized Bertrand and warned him that Mrs. Monroe had not yet arrived. On the way to the guest waiting room, we passed a wall with hundreds of names on it. By each name was a hole. Some of the holes were pegged, and Bertrand explained that the doormen took great pride in recognizing the 2,360 women members and putting a peg by their name when they entered the Club. It allowed the members to know who was in the Club at any given time. I was dying to stop and see who belonged, but I realized it wouldn't do. The only names I managed to catch were four Rockefellers in a row.

We waited for Mummy in a medium-size rectangular room done in baby blue with rose armchairs. Everything looked terribly sweet and genteel. A woman, bundled up in sweaters despite the summer day and wearing a very quaint straw hat, smiled at Bertrand in greeting as she left the room leaning against another woman. Bertrand said "hello" and called her by a name I didn't catch. "That's Mrs.

187

Atkinson," Bertrand said to me in a low voice as we sat down on a blue linen two-seater. "My mother tells me she comes here every day, even though she lives in the city."

"Why, is this club mostly for out-of-town women?"

"Yes. I'm told they have wonderful rooms upstairs where the ladies can rest between their shopping trips. I'll have to bring you here in the winter. They have a nice dining room upstairs, which is closed in the summer."

It was almost twelve-thirty, and I excused myself to go to the ladies' room for a last-minute checkup. I had expected a welcoming room with velvet sofas and damask armchairs. I was a little disappointed. Everything was white and pink and very functional. The only sign of frivolity was in the choice of wallpaper, which was overwhelmed by large pink carnations. As I combed my hair, I noticed the hair pins gathered neatly in a small lucite tray by each mirror. They were all gray.

Mrs. Atkinson was sitting nearby adjusting her hat in front of the mirror. There was no sign of her companion.

"Do you know how old I am?" she asked me abruptly.

"No."

"Ninety-four."

"You certainly don't look it," I said, smiling at her.

She nodded her head in approval and resumed fiddling with the drooping plastic cherries of her straw hat.

When I got back to the waiting room, Mummy had not yet arrived and Bertrand looked uncomfortable.

"I saw Mrs. Atkinson in the ladies' room. She told me her age. Ninety-four. We could use her for a Janick Cosmetics ad," I said, trying to lighten up the atmosphere. "Use Janick Moisture Care and look

188

seventy when you're ninety. That should go over big."

He stood up abruptly and I knew she had come. I turned around and quickly stood too. She walked slowly, with the help of a cane, her long, thin body, Bertrand's body, stiff with pride. She had beautifully coiffed gray hair and a handsome face, her complexion still pink. She was an older female version of Bertrand, except that her face was more striking because it had strength. Until I saw his mother's face, I had not realized that strength had been the missing ingredient in Bertrand's face. She was strong and as enduring as a historic monument.

Mrs. Monroe gave me a perfectly gracious smile as Bertrand introduced me.

"It's so nice when Bertrand allows me to meet his young friends," she said, still standing. Then she narrowed her myopic eyes to look at me better and make sure that "young" was the appropriate adjective. I raised my incipient double chin and gave her a bare shadow of a smile. Too much smile and my skin would have folded back into limp pleats.

"Let's go directly to the dining room," she said. Only her mouth moved as she spoke. The rest of her face was frozen in a benign expression. "I don't want to do too much sitting down and getting up. It's more and more difficult for me." She turned around and slowly started to lead us toward the dining room. Bertrand held her by her left elbow. I walked on her right, next to her cane.

"Good afternoon, Mrs. Monroe," said a smiling, fat-cheeked woman, whose middle age was very recognizable. She accorded Bertrand and me a nod each. "Your usual table is ready."

"Of course, Mary. I wouldn't want any other," Mrs. Monroe said by way of thanks.

Mummy's usual table was by a sealed window, the panes of glass replaced by mirrors. The large room, dominated by two grand old chandeliers, had many

189

mirrors. A long buffet table was set up against a mirrored wall, making the food offered look more abundant, richer. All the attendants, except Mary, seemed to be the same age as the diners. Somewhere over sixty.

As if guessing my thoughts, Mrs. Monroe said, "The club has excellent service. Really excellent. They're all Irish, you know. Good strong stock. A glass of skim milk for me, Mary. You should have the same." She hesitated a second over my name. "Simona, I did pronounce it properly, didn't I?"

"Yes, you did."

"I do know foreigners hate to have their names mispronounced. Although you speak English well. Bertrand's been telling me all about you. You were educated here, weren't you?" She turned around to see Mary still hovering over us. "What is it, Mary?"

"Did your guests want something to drink?"

Mrs. Monroe looked at me with piercing eyes, perhaps piercing only because she had to force them to see me in focus. "Will you have milk also? It's so good for your bones."

I shuddered. Skim milk is like watered-down chalk to me.

"I'm sure Simona would prefer a glass of white wine," Bertrand dared on my behalf.

"Oh, yes, I forgot you are Italian. And you, Bertrand?"

"The same."

"Two skim milks and one white wine." Mary hurried away. I looked at Bertrand, certain he had meant wine when he had said "the same." His face looked innocently blank.

"Drinking milk is an American habit, of course," Mrs. Monroe continued, "but I daresay it's healthier."

I got the irresistible urge to smoke a thousand cigarettes at once and blow them in Mummy's face.

"It is a charming room, isn't it?" Mrs. Monroe said

190

as she saw me look around. Everything was in very good taste, from the gilt wall sconces showing a proud American eagle, to the pink tablecloths and the delicate chairs obviously not made to seat the obese, but they had taken decorum to a lifeless degree. Even the flowers were not real. I thought a club that could boast four Rockefellers in its membership could afford fresh flowers. But perhaps their lively look might give offense.

"Bertrand, dear, I would like the chilled Senegalese soup," Mummy said. "Will you get it for me? When you come back, you and Simona may go up and see what you like. Don't forget those wonderful little toasts, please."

Bertrand stroked my hand and got up to do his mother's bidding. I faced her alone.

"Do you see my son often?"

"Oh, every day," I said, happy I didn't have to lie. Bertrand hadn't briefed me in any way, and I didn't know what role I was supposed to play.

"Of course, I had forgotten you work with him. Do forgive me for prying, but I'm sure you know how anxious mothers can get." She touched my face with her right hand. The gesture was so unexpected, I jumped. "Your mother must be anxious for your future, too."

Her fingers caressed my cheek and I wondered if I was being checked for the wrinkles her eyes weren't able to see.

"Is it an important relationship?" she asked.

"I think it's a little too early to tell," I replied, which also wasn't a lie.

"Oh, no, it's very late, my dear. Very late. I don't have that much time, and I suspect neither do you." She did indeed have the sensitive touch. "He must marry before I die!" She pounded her cane on the floor angrily. Mary came rushing to her side.

"Is there anything wrong, ma'm?"

"No, no, Mary. Thank you, Mary." Mary, rewarded with a dismissive smile, retreated quietly.

"Please forgive me, Simona." Mrs. Monroe looked sternly at her unruly cane, as if it were to blame for her improper burst of emotion. "I'd rather you didn't mention our conversation to Bertrand," she continued. "I don't want to anger him. He can be very obstinate when he's angry."

"Of course not, Mrs. Monroe," I lied.

"Every once in a while, when I threaten him with dire consequences, he dangles a new girl in front of my eyes in hopes of appeasing me. But those girls never come to anything." She sat perfectly still, her face devoid of any feeling. "I thought I could be more frank with you. Latins seem to know more about the passions of life."

"Not if the Church can help it."

"Yes, yes, Catholic." A slight movement of head. "Well, it's not the ideal, but it's more acceptable than some. Of course, the children would have to be brought up Episcopalian."

The woman was stark raving mad.

"Here you are, Mummy," Bertrand announced cheerfully as he arrived with her food.

"Do call me Mother, Bertrand. How many times have I told you? 'Mummy' is perfectly asinine."

"I'm sorry. I thought you liked being called Mummy. It sounds so devoted." Bertrand winked at me as he walked behind her back to help me out of my chair. It was the first sign of life he had given since she had come on the scene. "Simona and I will go and get our food and be right back."

"God, Bertrand, why didn't you warn me," I said when we were safely beyond Mummy's earshot. "She already has us married and having children."

Bertrand blushed bright crimson. "I didn't think she'd go that far."

"I don't know what to say to her." I stopped in

192

front of the long food table and offered an empty cup to the soup man. "I don't think I'm up to this." I moved on to the bread basket, dying to chew the caloric comfort of a dozen buns, but I knew this was not the place for excesses. Instead, I took two of "those wonderful little toasts" that looked like they might break your dentures.

"Don't worry about her. Just keep being your charming self," Bertrand said. Slowly walking back to the table balancing my overly full cup, I began to have serious doubts as to where that charm was going to take me.

Senegalese soup turned out to be a good curry soup with pieces of apple in it. I ate silently, listening to Bertrand and Mummy talk about what needed to be done for the herb garden in Connecticut and stealing glances at my watch in the hopes that two-thirty would come quickly.

"Simona, do tell me about your family. Bertrand was a little vague in that regard," Mummy said as we started on a second course of dry omelettes and various weary vegetables.

"My father is an Italian diplomat."

"How interesting," Mrs. Monroe said, obviously pleased by my pedigree. "Is he an ambassador?"

"No, a consul general."

Her mouth formed a small, silent "oh" of disappointment.

"He was stationed in Boston for many years," I said to cheer her up.

"Was he really? And when was that?"

"Sixty-three to sixty-eight."

"Griffo." I noticed a slight furrowing of the brow. "Of course, Consul General Griffo. I didn't connect your name. Oh, Bertrand, this is perfectly delightful. I know her family." Mary appeared to clear our plates. "Mary, be a dear and get dessert for us," Mrs. Monroe chirped. "I can't possibly manage the long

193

walk, and I don't want my son and this wonderful young lady to leave my side. Did you see what you would like?" she asked me. She placed her hand on mine in a gentle but clear gesture of possession.

"I'd love the crème caramel and some decaffeinated coffee," I said.

"Crème caramel and decaffeinated coffee for all of us, Mary." Her son was not given the opportunity to choose. "How are your charming parents?" she asked, turning back to me.

"They're both well. My father's retired now, and they're living in the hills above Rome."

"Do say hello to them for me when you write."

The crème caramel and the coffee duly arrived and I was surprised to discover that the dessert was served with a large spoon. I liked that. It reminded me of breakfasts long ago—smoking bowls of semolina and spoons, too large for a child's hand, stirring the heat away. I ate cheerfully. Now that Mummy approved of me, I felt almost comfortable. I was even beginning to like her a bit.

"Sorry, Mummy," Bertrand said, putting his napkin down. "We must be off. We both have to be back at work at two-thirty."

"Bertrand, don't fidget. Simona has to finish her coffee."

I gulped it down. "Your son is working on a very important perfume campaign," I blurted out to sweeten our departure. "He must have told you about it. If it hadn't been for Bertrand, the agency would have lost the Janick account."

Mummy's coffee cup, on its way to her mouth, stopped in midair. She stared at her son stone-faced. For a long moment Mrs. Monroe did not move. Not a blink, not a tremor. By the color of her face, even the flow of blood had stopped. The three of us sat in a freeze-frame until Bertrand lowered his eyes. With that minimal movement, Mrs. Monroe sighed and

194

her whole body crumbled in defeat, as if her son had silently sounded Joshua's trumpet.

"Oh Bertrand, your father would have been mortified," she said in a small voice.

Bertrand turned to me with an impassive face. "My mother doesn't think advertising is a proper occupation, especially now that the agency's been so gauche as to have one of its partners murdered." He stood up and faced her. "Mummy, we're going," he said, leaning down for a dutiful kiss. I surprised myself by doing the same thing. As my cheek approached hers, she stopped me with a firm cold grip of my hand. "Have you met that Frenchman?" she whispered to me. "He is evil. The personification of evil."

I extricated my hand gently. "I really must go now, Mrs. Monroe. It has been a great pleasure meeting you. And I will write to my parents to let them know I've met you."

She smiled at me then. "Oh, yes, your father was such a charming man. You must have Bertrand bring you to New Canaan for the weekend. The house needs a happy young woman in it."

At the entrance of the dining room, I turned back and saw her standing tall and straight like a flagless pole in the middle of the dining room. I waved a good-bye she couldn't see and almost regretted having to leave her. Almost.

Outside into the sunshine, I found myself breathing a sigh of relief and feeling as if I had just taken off my bra and was free to scratch all over.

"Does she do that to all the women you introduce her to?" I asked Bertrand once we were headed back downtown in a cab.

"She hasn't met that many." Bertrand turned his head toward the window and ended the conversation. He didn't look too happy.

When we hit Twenty-third Street, he suddenly

squeezed my knee and said, "She's right. You should come to the country for a weekend. I'll find fun things for us to do. Away from Mummy."

I looked at him doubtfully.

"Please come," two brown eyes pleaded. "It's important to me."

What the hell, I thought. Greenhouse hadn't invited me anywhere, and the Connecticut estate was bound to be an improvement over my cat closet in the Village, even with Mummy there. "If that's what you'd like," I said.

"That's what I'd like very much." Bertrand leaned over and kissed me just as the cab stopped in front of Scriba's studio.

Chapter Twenty-one

Ellen was dancing a Strauss waltz with Scriba. All I saw were layers and layers of black lace surrounding her slim torso sheathed in green satin. As she was spun across the floor, she looked like an exotic flower with its tall pistil towering over the petals. Her face was flushed with excitement, and she kept laughing. One of Scriba's assistants was unobtrusively clicking away at various cameras placed about the room. The music stopped, and Ellen saw me and Bertrand standing in the doorway.

"Scriba is the most wonderful dancer," she said as she swayed toward us, the rhythm of the waltz still possessing her body. Bertrand reached out to steady her.

"You look very beautiful in that dress," he told her softly.

"Do I? Isn't it glorious-looking?" She straightened out to her full length and swung around. The black lace whipped us. She had regained her confidence completely. "Everyone has been so nice. Julia entertained me by showing me all the commercials she had filmed for the agency, and then I came back here, and Johnny showed me these wonderful dresses. They even put make-up on me, but I wiped it all off. Scriba asked me what I liked doing most. I said dancing and we've been dancing for the past half hour. I love this very much, but when are we going to start working?" Her face was perfectly serious. "I'm ready now."

"All right, then we'll start. Scriba, I want some head shots, no make-up, hair loose, unpretentious. From there we'll escalate to day make-up, evening, various hairdos. Let's concentrate on her face today. Both black and white and color. And I want slides and contacts by tomorrow afternoon. Don't worry, Johnny," Bertrand said, anticipating Johnny's groans, "we'll pay for overtime, the rush, and whatever else is necessary."

The phone rang and a relieved Johnny scurried to answer it.

"It's Evelyn, for you," Johnny shouted from the far end of the room, pointing a short arm at me.

"Great news," she barked into my ear. "Mattie just called to say they're letting her go. Thought you guys should know."

"Did she say anything else? Did she explain the sudden change?"

"I didn't get to talk to her. She called down in reception." Evelyn laughed. "She wanted to warn her staff she was coming back to work tomorrow and to stop 'messin' around.' As for the change, she was innocent and that cop friend of yours finally grasped that simple thought." She hung up still laughing. She was right. It was a happy occasion. Mattie was free and Greenhouse was perhaps just a little bit more approachable. I ran over to whisper the news to Bertrand, who acknowledged it with a nod, then went back to conferring with Scriba. Work. It was time to think of work.

The studio looked like it was preparing for battle. Ellen was whisked off to the dressing room, cameras and lights were moved about by silent assistants, and an air of industrious tension settled upon the room like heavy dust. For Janick, Inc., and everyone connected with it, there was an ad to be produced.

Nothing else mattered to any of them.

Ellen showed herself to be a real trooper. She did not squint once in front of the intensity of the lights. She followed instructions patiently. All she heard for two hours was: "Chin a little higher, no, higher, too high, turn left, turn right, look up, look down, tilt your head left, right, center." It was enough to make a Pavlovian dog tear his master to shreds, but she didn't seem to mind. Bertrand watched silently, munching on his lower lip, letting Scriba give out all the instructions. At each click he would nervously pull at his straightened curls. If he continued to pull much longer, he was going to end up looking like a sheared poodle surrounded by his own clippings. I released my tension by sneaking into the dressing area and smoking my cherished cigarettes. Once I even called the office to check if anyone had called. Greenhouse stayed silent and I hated myself for having hoped.

If it hadn't been for Ann Lester, I don't know how long they would have gone on immortalizing Ellen.

"Hello, everyone, guess who I brought along?" she announced gaily. Behind Ann's tall, crisp figure, wrapped in a Galanos, stood the even taller and ever elegant Jean Janick. Scriba did not stop stooping over his camera, despite the visitors. Ellen's tired eyes quickly tried to steal a look in the direction of the new voice, but they were instantly reclaimed by Scriba. I politely acknowledged their arrival by standing up, but Bertrand did much more. He quickly ran both his hands through his hair, and then he smiled a smile that competed with all the lights Scriba was using to illuminate Ellen's face. It was a smile so intensely happy that it caught me off guard. I quickly looked toward Ann, but she had stepped aside to use the phone. The smile had not been meant for her, or for me, or for any woman. Jean Janick stood still and let himself be adored. His lips barely moved in response to Bertrand's welcome. His eyes did it all.

Their gaze of love lasted only a few seconds. They quickly shifted back to their usual look of casual cool, but I wasn't going to forget those seconds easily. What I had seen was beautiful, strong, and so unexpected that I was gasping for breath. It explained Mummy's behavior and that, in turn, explained Bertrand's false interest in me. It also hurt. Why me? I thought. Why was I always being lied to? Did I really have "sucker" written all over my "expressive" face?

"Jean, what a surprise," Bertrand said, affecting nonchalance. "Your timing is perfect. I think Ellen is exhausted and would be quite happy to meet you. Let's call it a day, Scriba, all right?"

Scriba shrugged his wide shoulders fatalistically, as if Jean Janick's entrance had ruined his best shot, and reached for his fedora.

"You must all forgive this interruption on my part, but I could not stay away. I had to see the beautiful Ellen," Janick said. He greeted her with a bow and raised her hand to his lips. Ellen looked too tired to be impressed or flattered. "You will do my perfume honor."

"We haven't seen how she photographs yet, Jean," cautioned Bertrand.

"She photographs *bellissimo*," Scriba said. He gathered his fingers and kissed the tips with gusto, as if he were talking about the delights of a good pasta dish.

"*Benissimo*," I corrected loudly, snapping at him. "She photographs *benissimo*."

Scriba was too happy with his day's work to let me upset him. He grabbed my chin and gently squeezed it. His face was an inch away from mine. "It is useless for you to correct me," he whispered. "I speak a different language from yours, *mia cara*. I speak the language of the artist."

From across the room it must have looked as if we were having a romantic tête-à-tête because Ann flew to our side on her Galanos wings, the champagne-colored jacket flapping jealously. "Darling, stop breathing your garlic breath over poor Simona and come and give me one of your wet, sexy kisses," she said. I suspected they were used to sharing more than the aromas of Little Italy together, and at the moment my chin was very grateful. Ann embraced Scriba and whisked him away with the grace of a sea-soned hostess repossessing her recalcitrant guest.

"Speaking of unpleasant odors, *chère* Ann, I have brought you and Ellen and Simona a present. I could no longer put up with the odor of that 'Obsession' that you insist on wearing. It was an insult to my profession and my person, *et alors voilá,* 'Free,' for the new American woman." Janick held the bottle high for all of us to see. "A gift from France to the United States that rivals the Statue of Liberty. Please open and put a little on your flesh." Ann obeyed and im-mediately raised her arm to her nose.

"No, no, no. Perfume is like good red wine. It should not be tasted right away. Give it time to ab-sorb into your body, to share with your own per-fume. I assure you the two will mingle and produce an exquisite aroma."

"I only wish Wally were around to listen to you. You have just spoken perfect ad copy," Bertrand teased happily. "Perhaps a little too rich for our more plebeian American tastes, but good nonetheless."

Janick was too intent with his presentation to even acknowledge Bertrand's words. I got the feeling that Janick, Inc. was his number one priority.

"Now you may observe with your nose. Slowly, *je vous en prie.* Enjoy the quiet sensuality."

"I know exactly how it smells on me, Jean," Ann said. "Divine, it is absolutely divine. Here, Scriba,

201

take a sniff. Bertrand, smell." Ann waved her arm around for the whole room to smell. "It is absolutely my perfume. And you know I'm not saying that because I'm your account supervisor. 'Free' just happens to be my perfume. The only reason I was wearing 'Obsession' was because someone swiped my bottle of 'Free.' "

"You had a bottle of 'Free'?" asked Janick, astounded. "How? There was only one. Fred had assured me that he would lock it up in his safe. I did not want anyone to smell it. It was strictly forbidden. Only Wally and Bertrand were allowed."

"My dear Jean," Ann said, "you know perfectly well that the dear, departed Fred was not exactly a friend of yours. After all, you almost left us, remember?" She tossed her golden Bruno Dessange coiffure in disapproval. "Don't blame Fred. It was my fault. He let me smell it and I just fell in love. I had to have it. I admit I also loved the idea of being the only one in this country to have that perfume. You'll be happy to know, Jean, that the smell of it did drive a few friends of mine wild. It does what 'Obsession' promises." She flicked her tongue over her parted lips and looked as wicked as she could.

"That's not the image I want at all," Janick said, horrified. "I want a much fresher approach."

"I wasn't talking about image," Ann said in her most soothing tone. "I was talking about what it really does. We'll sell it any way you want us to."

Janick did not look appeased.

"I was only trying to tell you what a fabulous perfume it is. I didn't mean to be immodest." Ann smiled sweetly.

"Ann, I thank you. Yes, it is a great perfume, but I am worried about the missing bottle. Why would someone steal it? Unless they wanted to give it to the Lauders or the people at Lancôme or Chanel. This is very serious."

202

"Isn't it too late for anyone to steal your idea?" Ann retorted. "After all, Jean darling, you just brought us a bottle as a present. You can't be too worried about keeping it a secret."

"I wasn't going to give you a bottle," Janick said indignantly. "I was going to let you smell it on your flesh, that is all. No, no, this stays with me." He gripped the bottle of "Free" tightly.

"No one knew I had it," Ann protested. "It was in a plain bottle that didn't even look like perfume. It could have been mouthwash or nail polish remover for all anyone knew. I'm sure the cleaning lady broke it and doesn't want to own up. I kept it in my desk drawer. No one knew," Ann repeated. Her face had turned an unflattering pasty white, the skin separating from her make-up. Her rouge, usually artistically blended to appear natural, now stuck to her cheeks like the make-up of a gaudy clown. "No one would ever do something like that at HH&H. Fred knew about the missing bottle, and he laughed it off. It happened the Friday before he died. He's the one who told me not to worry." Ann, in her discomfort, was even beginning to perspire. Bertrand laid a hand on her shoulder to quiet her.

"It happened the Friday before he died," Ann had said. The Friday he was so angry. The Friday he received the phone call.

"Ann's right, Jean," Bertrand said in his warm Pied Piper tone. "It was probably the cleaning lady or one of the secretaries who wanted to impress her boyfriend with Ann's perfume. I cannot believe we have a spy in our agency."

"And why not?" Janick asked. "You have a murderer."

The party quickly broke up after that statement. Bertrand murmured reassurances to Ann. I called the car company to pick up Ellen and take her to New Jersey. Janick stood brooding by the doorway.

203

Scriba muttered sweet nothings to Ellen, and she politely listened, while his assistants turned off the lights. The enormous room was left as it was, ready for the next morning's work. Just as Johnny locked the door, the phone inside started ringing.

"Enough, Johnny," Scriba boomed. "Let it go. For Scriba, they will call back tomorrow."

We left the ringing phone and trundled down the stairs together, the elevator having disappeared somewhere into the reaches of the building. After hours of artificial light, I was surprised by the gentle light of the July evening. We muttered "good nights" and "see you in the morning." Ellen got in her limo, Ann hailed a cab, and Bertrand and Janick walked uptown sharing their worry and their secret love. I was left alone to think. It had been a very full day, and I was ready to call it quits.

Chapter Twenty-two

A ringing phone greeted me when I got back to my apartment. I picked up and heard a sonorous sigh.

"Oh, thank God I got you. I tried at the studio, but no one answered. Listen, you've got to come to the office right away. The cops are on their way, but Giovanna's hysterical and gibbering away in Italian, and no one can understand a word she's saying. Don't waste time with questions now, just get over here."

I grabbed a cab on Sixth Avenue and got to the office just as Greenhouse and Raf were walking in. Evelyn, standing guard at the entrance, grabbed my arm and pulled me inside.

"What seems to be the problem, Miss Dietz?" Greenhouse asked in the cool tones of command, taking the words right out of my mouth.

"I was just on my way out when I heard the commotion," she said as she led us across the empty lobby toward the stairs. "When I got down to the basement, I found Luis pacing in front of the storage room door, and Giovanna weeping and screaming unintelligible Italian over Fred's broken typewriter. Luis shouted for me to call you, and I thought I'd better get Simona over here to help with Giovanna."

We climbed downstairs and faced a long, narrow corridor with closed metal doors on either side. From the far end loud thuds and the rattling of a doorknob reverberated toward us. Luis and Giovanna stood at the end of the corridor, in front of a door that someone was desperately trying to kick down from the other side.

"We got him," Luis said, stepping forward to meet us. "The thief. The two of us got him."

Giovanna shrank against the wall as the four of us reached her. Her face was streaked with tears and white with fear. The rest of her was shrouded in mourning. She had removed the white ruffled apron from her usual black uniform and added black stockings. Even her heavy coral and gold earrings, Sicilian family heirlooms, had been discarded. Everything black except her ashen face and red-rimmed eyes. Her lower lip trembled as she pointed to the door.

"Ladro! Assassino," she accused in a whisper and started crying quietly. As if he had understood her, the man behind the door stopped kicking.

"She got a real scare, *mi amiga* did," Luis said as he put a protective arm around Giovanna. She moved into his body gratefully. He smiled proudly, his mustache stretching with his lips, as if growing with self-importance. "I don't know about the leather jacket yet. I mean he's not wearing one now, and he doesn't answer my questions, but he's a thief all right."

"I want to know exactly what happened," Greenhouse said. Raf whipped out his stub of a pencil and a notebook.

"Well," Luis started, straightening his spine, "I heard Giovanna scream, lucky for her I was at the top of the stairs, I ran down here and she was struggling with the *hijo de puta* in there," Luis underlined his insult with a swift kick at the door. The person behind it remained silent. "Mr. Critelli's typewriter was broken on the floor," Luis continued. "I grabbed the man away from her and locked him up in the storage room. The *cojones* left the key in the door. Then Evelyn came down and I told her to call you guys." He pulled down his blazer in the back and still holding on to Giovanna, took a step forward. "Now my theory is this guy was trying to make off . . ."

"Let's deal with facts first," Greenhouse said. "Simona, would you please?" He gestured toward Giovanna.

I asked Giovanna to tell me her side of the story, offering to translate if she preferred to speak in the comfort of her own language. She accepted with a nod, swallowed, and clutching the front of her uniform as if the flimsy fabric might give her support, she began to talk in Italian. I translated in a whisper.

"Every night, before going back to *Signor* Critelli's home, I come down to the storage room to clean his belongings, the things that used to be in his office. It is not right for them to have dust, not respectful." She looked directly at Greenhouse, excluding the rest of us standing in that gray, fluorescent-lighted corridor. "Tonight I noticed the key was not in its place."

"Where was that?"

"Mattie kept it, but with her gone, it was kept in the mailroom, on a hook. Tonight it was not there. When I go down, I find the corridor dark, but the door at the end open. The storage room door. I keep it dark and tiptoe down. And I see him. Him!" Giovanna walked away from Luis's shielding arm and pointed at the door several times, stabbing the air with her finger. "He had the typewriter in his arms. He was going to steal *Signor* Critelli's typewriter. He is a thief. A thief." The finger continued to stab as she repeated *"Ladro, ladro, ladro."* She looked around, at me hovering on her every word, at the others waiting for more. Her hand came down and reached into her pocket. She took a step forward, closer to Greenhouse.

"I find this," she said, suddenly shifting to English. "When writing machine break on the floor, I find this." She handed him a gray envelope, the distinctive HH&H gray.

"Hey, I thought the guys had gone through his stuff real good," Raf said loudly, staring at the envelope like the rest of us.

"When Luis lock man up, I start to clean machine," Giovanna said. "Even if broken, I clean and I find in here." She quickly walked over to the typewriter still lying on the floor, and swooped up the instruction manual. "Maybe thief not only thief, but killer too. Maybe he kill *il signor* Critelli." She caught her breath and grasped her mouth with her hand. Tears welled up in her eyes. Greenhouse gave her an awkward pat on the arm. He did not look comfortable. "Miss Giovanna, we need you to come to the precinct with us to sign a statement," he said in a soft, calming voice. "Do you think you can manage?"

"I can come with you, if you like?" I offered.

"No, no," Giovanna said, hastily wiping her eyes. "Now with policemen, I am OK. I am no longer afraid. I cried of fear, you understand. Now *tutto* OK."

"Luis, we'll need you too." Greenhouse held out a hand and Luis handed him a key.

"Sure thing. I'm telling you, he's the thief we've been looking for."

"Luis, take Giovanna upstairs and wait for us. The rest, please go home or wherever." For Greenhouse I had become "the rest," and he obviously didn't care where I went, as long as I was out of his way. That made me feel really good.

We were far too curious to go far. Luis, Giovanna, Evelyn and I gathered in the mail room, next to the stairs. After only a few minutes, Raf and Greenhouse marched by holding a man in handcuffs. He looked like a boy really. Was he my thief? I didn't recognize him and he wasn't wearing a leather jacket, but he did have hightops. Not clean white though. Old, very dirty, and untied. *Dio* I hope it's him, I thought, anxious to put an end to one bad event at least.

"I know him," Evelyn said in surprise. "He works down in the studio. He's only been here four or five months." She shook her head. "He's going to lose a good job because of an old typewriter. Isn't that dumb?" She didn't wait for an answer. She waved good-bye and walked out of the entrance after the alleged thief. I heard her telling Greenhouse the boy's name. Through the glass door, I watched Greenhouse hail a cab and then get in the back seat of his double-parked car with the thief as Raf got behind the wheel. Luis and Giovanna got in the waiting cab and followed the policemen's unmarked, blue sedan.

I was left alone in the building. It was a familiar feeling, but not one that I liked. I hurried out of there and went back to the smaller dimensions of my apartment and the comforting company of television.

Chapter Twenty-three

The next morning, I waited for that elevator to come and lift me to the studio. There was no way I was going to walk up those stairs all the way to the fourth floor. I had spent the previous evening trying to find the connection between a murdered Fred and various elements like the missing perfume bottle, Giovanna finding a thief and a letter, the angry Friday phone call, a weeping, befuddled Julia, Evelyn hiding an emptied glass from me, Mattie's coke-dealing nephew, Dana getting sick and screaming, Ellen worrying about her father, Gregory being upset, and finally Bertrand being Janick's lover. I had not succeeded. Strong pangs of self-pity and a night of heavy, dreamless sleep had not improved matters any.

The shooting day started at nine o'clock, and when I walked in Scriba and his fedora were having breakfast; the assistants were checking the cameras; Johnny was sitting at his desk like a brooding hen about to hatch the perfect ad; Ellen was in the dressing area being combed, creamed and powdered. The only person missing was Bertrand, but I didn't expect him until ten. I said "hello" to everyone, grabbed myself a coffee and three of the gooiest Danish I could find, and settled myself near Ellen to sulk and quietly get fat. She looked fantastic even at that hour of the morning. I turned my chair away from her and the mirrors.

At ten-thirty, Ellen was ready for the photography session, but Bertrand hadn't shown up.

At eleven o'clock, Scriba walked into the dressing area and demanded to know where he was. I called Bertrand's apartment. There was no answer. I called the office. Reception said he wasn't there and he hadn't left any messages. I called Ann Lester. She didn't know his whereabouts, but she promised to be right over to help us. No one had Janick's Trump Tower telephone number. Bertrand had left orders not to start shooting without him so all we could do was wait. We passed the time by making Ellen try on all the dresses, just to make sure they fit. They did. When that was over we all went to the eating table and vented our frustrations. All except Ellen. I wouldn't let her eat a thing. No one's allowed to be beautiful, well-built, and able to pig out. At least not when I'm in one of my moods.

At eleven-thirty Evelyn called and asked to speak to me. Everyone stopped talking and eating at once, and I walked across that long, wooden floor, footsteps echoing against the bare walls, as if going to the electric chair.

"Call it a day, send Ellen shopping or something and get the hell over here."

"What are you talking about?" I protested. "We've got a deadline to meet. Bertrand wants to shoot in the Grand Canyon next week, and we're not even sure Ellen's right yet. We can't . . ."

"Right now we've got nothing. Just get over here. Go directly to Mr. Harland's office. We are all here waiting for you."

"Scriba and Johnny are going to have a fit. What am I going to say?" I had pushed the panic button.

"At this point, it doesn't really matter." The phone went dead.

I straightened up, took a deep breath, and walked

back into the large room, this time letting my heels dig into the floor with a resounding crack. The sound helped me feel heavy, more important, stronger.

"I'm afraid we won't be able to shoot today. It seems Bertrand isn't feeling well, and he's asked us to forget it. Johnny, please go ahead with yesterday's shots. We still want slides and contact sheets by this afternoon." I was speaking quickly. An interruption and I would have burst into tears. "Of course, we will pay for the studio and your time at the full price. Ellen, I'm sorry, but can you keep yourself busy?" I didn't give her a chance to answer. "Go to the World Trade Center, the Statue of Liberty, Bloomingdale's. Wherever you want. It's on us. Johnny, could you give me the photographs you took of that ledge on the Grand Canyon? I don't think Bertrand got a chance to see them. I'd like to send them over to him. He likes to keep busy even when he's sick." I laughed stupidly and then quickly looked down at the floor.

No one protested. Scriba did his shoulder shrug without the usual theatricality, and Johnny quietly went to his desk to produce the photographs. I hadn't fooled them.

"Tell Bertrand I hope he gets well soon. He's such a nice man," Ellen said. She smiled to reassure me and managed to bring out the tears I had been fighting. I almost ran back to the office.

Mr. Heffer, Evelyn, Wally, Ann Lester, and Mr. Harland were sitting in the living area of Mr. Harland's vast office. When Mr. Harland chooses not to preside from the authority of his eighteenth-century mahogany English desk and conducts a meeting sitting next to his fellow conferees instead, it is to be considered a great honor. From the expression on everyone's face that day, the honor wasn't very appreciated. They looked like government employees who had just flunked the urine test.

"What has happened to Bertrand?" I asked the minute I walked in.

Mr. Harland ignored me and proceeded in his calm way. "As you all know, Janick, Inc. is our most important account, and we must put all our energies behind it and meet this crisis head on."

"What crisis?" I asked, almost screaming. Evelyn grabbed my hand to stop me and offered me a cigarette to shut my mouth.

"We almost lost the account once, and I don't intend to have that happen again," Mr. Harland continued, oblivious of me. "Even though Bertrand is no longer available, we must go ahead with our plans to shoot our first ad for 'Free' next week. Bertrand, thank God, has left a very clear, detailed layout."

"Left." The word felt like a bag full of ice cubes crashing to the bottom of my stomach. Left? Left for where?

"I think Wally and I, with Scriba's help, can shoot the ad exactly the way Bertrand and Jean have envisioned," Mr. Harland said. "Simona, when do we get to see what this girl looks like in a photograph?"

"She was shot both in black and white and color, and we'll have the results this afternoon before five. Or so Johnny promised."

"What's her name, who is she?"

"Ellen Price from Omaha, Nebraska," I said proudly. After all, she was my baby.

"I want to be told the minute those slides and contact sheets get here. Everyone is to behave as if nothing has happened. Mr. Janick especially must not get a feeling that we are panicking. HH&H has reassured him that we will meet all our deadlines. Thank

213

you for your time." Mr. Harland had dismissed us and I was none the wiser.

"What happened?" I asked Evelyn and Wally once we got to the elevator.

Wally looked at Evelyn and she took the lead.

"Bertrand was picked up by the police this morning and is being questioned about Fred's death."

"Has he been charged?"

"We don't know that. All we know is that he's been with the police since nine o'clock this morning. Bertrand asked his lawyer to call Wally and fill us in, and you know the rest."

"I don't know the rest. Why is he being questioned again? What's he got to do with Fred's murder? The police knew he was in the building that Sunday, but so were a lot of other people. Why are they picking on him?"

Evelyn got a very funny, uncomfortable look on her face, and she turned to Wally for help. He stared back at her blankly.

I waited until we had reached Evelyn's office and closed the door. "I know about Bertrand and Janick."

Evelyn still hesitated.

"Bertrand is gay," I said to clinch it.

Wally muttered "Shit" under his breath.

Evelyn shifted her body in her chair. "Listen, for the moment no one knows Bertrand's gay or that he's being questioned at the precinct, so shut up about it. It'll come out soon enough when the press gets a hold of it."

"Of course we had to tell the two H's," Wally mumbled unhappily.

"What have you told the two H's?" I asked him.

"That Fred was blackmailing Bertrand over his sexual preferences."

214

"Bertrand wanted it to be a secret," Evelyn explained, "because apparently Mummy's estate lawyers would have punched the delete button if she ever found out he was gay."

"Did Bertrand tell you about being blackmailed?"

"Hell, no. Fred spelled it all out in the letter Giovanna gave the cops last night."

Wally cleared his throat and took over. "The letter shows, in strong and unequivocal terms, that Fred had been blackmailing handsome Bertie for some time."

"That's ridiculous," I said. "Fred had tons of money."

"Bertrand wasn't being blackmailed for money, my dear. Nothing of that vulgar a nature. Remember that Freddie boy liked to collect little secrets as a hobby, and it seems that Bertrand was anxious to leave our agency. Fred was kindly persuading him to stay."

"Why would he want him to stay? Fred was jealous of Bertrand's talent. You'd think he'd have wanted him to leave. The farther away, the better."

"Not if you lost the Janick account along with Bertrand," Evelyn said with half of her mouth; the other half was holding a cigarette.

"But why put it down in writing?"

"The written word has far more power than the spoken one." Wally started picking on his face nervously. "I can just picture Fred showing Bertrand the letter and gleefully watching him tremble."

"Did the letter specifically mention that Bertrand is Janick's lover?" I asked. Letter, letter, why did the word "letter" ring a bell in my mind?

Wally shook his head.

"Then how does the lawyer know about Janick and Bertrand?"

"He doesn't," Evelyn said. "I bet Bertrand is keeping his mouth shut to protect Janick. Wally has known for ages, though. He found out the same way you did. He noticed them touching once too often. And he never told me. Not until today, when the lawyer called. That's when we started piecing it together. By the way,"—Evelyn turned her blinking eyes toward him—"I love you for keeping your mouth shut. God knows it doesn't happen often."

Wally's pimples turned bright red. "I just figured it wasn't anybody's business."

"Why didn't the police find the letter right away?" I asked. "And it's funny that the letter makes no mention of the affair. Why would Fred want to spare Janick's reputation? They couldn't stand each other."

"If Janick goes, chances are the agency goes," Wally said.

"I still think someone else could have written it," I insisted. "The police can't be that stupid."

Evelyn gave me a funny look. "Just because Greenhouse has a nice ass doesn't mean his brain works. Look, they've already established that it was definitely typed on Fred's Praxis Olivetti, and we all know he typed everything, so that's nothing unusual."

"He liked people to know he had been a reporter for the *Chicago Trib* before going into advertising," Wally said, forever anxious to contribute his words. I looked at both of them doubtfully.

"Giovanna said she found the letter inside the instruction booklet," Evelyn said still trying to convincing me. "There was no reason for the police to look there for a suicide note."

"What about the thief? How does he fit in all this?"

"I don't know, Simona," Evelyn answered with some impatience. "He probably found out about the storage room key being kept on a hook for anyone to grab, and he gave it a try. I don't know. Anyway, the lawyer is getting the signature on the letter authenti-

216

cated, but dumb Bertrand already told the cops he recognized it as Fred's."

"Well, it's a distinctive signature all right." I thought of all the memos I had received signed with long, fast lines. "Illegible for one." I could just picture Fred, behind his important desk, signing with a self-aggrandizing flourish. *Dio*, I wished I could get rid of the man. I wished I could get rid of all of them.

"That's great," Wally said. "Great. If he keeps admitting things, how are we going to get him out to shoot our ad next Wednesday?"

Evelyn shook her head. "Wally, start getting used to the idea that Bertrand's not shooting any ad on Wednesday. It's going to be you, Scriba, and Mr. Harland."

"What do an innocuous copywriter, such as yours truly, and a bleached-brain like Harry Harland know about shooting an ad? We've got a model who has never posed before, assuming that we even have a model. We are putting said model half naked on a narrow, jutting ledge overlooking the Grand Canyon, which would be enough to scare a professional goat, and we've got a photographer who thinks he's the Raphael of the advertising world. Given the cast of characters and the backdrop, there is no way we are going to get a decent ad. And I forgot to mention our very own Doubting Thomas, Mr. Janick. He wants to stick his finger into everything to make sure it will evolve to his satisfaction. Believe me, without Bertrand, the whole thing is going to be a mess."

"What do you want us to do about it?" Evelyn asked.

"Clear him," Wally said, making it sound as if it were as easy as cooking pasta. He looked at me. "Ev said you wanted to solve the thing to settle some score or other, so get on with it."

"Where is Janick now?" I asked.

"In his ivory tower on Fifth Avenue," Wally said. "In his Napoleonic furor, he has threatened the Hs' with everything from the bubonic plague to nuclear annihilation if his perfume doesn't show up. I have to give credit to our silver-haired Harland. He reassured Janick without ever letting on he knew about the affair."

"Did Janick say anything about Bertrand?" I asked.

Wally pointed a fat little finger at me. "If you are wondering whether he expressed concern commensurate to your romantic expectations of their affair, I doubt it. I have a feeling Monsieur Jean Janick could easily forget his loved one, especially if that loved one happens to be rotting in a New York jail. *Ce n'est pas chic.*"

"What happened to Ann Lester down at Scriba's studio?" Evelyn asked me. "She's acting as if she's got a wet finger stuck in an electric socket."

"I don't blame her." I said. "She had the only bottle of 'Free' in the country, and it got stolen from her."

"But she swore to me no one knew she had it," Wally said.

"Fred knew and he might have told somebody," I suggested. "Besides, just because Janick is convinced the bottle was taken for espionage purposes doesn't mean that's what really happened. The whole agency knows she loves to douse herself with perfume, so she obviously must bring the stuff to the office. Some woman probably liked the scent Ann was wearing one day and proceeded to remove the bottle from her purse."

"Or someone took it to spite her," offered Evelyn. "Ann has her enemies on the upper floors. She keeps her Joan and David boots well sharpened when it comes to giving orders."

"She could also be lying," Wally added.

"I don't think so," I said. "She volunteered the information about the missing perfume quite naturally."

"Do you think there is a connection between the stolen bottle and Fred's death?" Wally asked me.

"There are a lot of question marks that need answers. You have a great way with women." Wally acknowledged the compliment with a bow. "Why don't you go upstairs, tell a few jokes, and listen to what the secretaries and the junior account people have to say about Ann and the 'Free' bottle?"

"Great idea," Wally said. He saw Evelyn's glum face. "Don't worry, my pet. I will only tell jokes, maybe a compliment or two, a surreptitious touch here and there, nothing more. It's all in the line of duty."

Evelyn laughed despite herself. "You vain jerk, I'm not glum about you. I'm glum about the whole fucking situation."

"Sure you are, sweetlips." Wally blew her a kiss and slipped out the door.

All Evelyn could do was give one of her soul-clearing sneezes.

"God, I'd like to be as optimistic as he is about Bertrand," Evelyn said once the door was closed. She settled back in her chair and blinked at me, her full lips hugging the perennial cigarette. "What are all the question marks? Maybe I can help."

"Well, for one, who took Ann's perfume and why? Does the missing perfume have anything to do with the murder? Then there's the fact that Fred's pinky ring appeared in my desk, in my Kleenex box. Who put it there and why? Wally said he saw Dana that Sunday, but she doesn't appear on the sensor chart. Was she really there? No one else saw her." At the mention of Wally, Evelyn's face had stiffened and I decided to shift gear.

"What intrigues me about Fred's death is why he took the capsules. There had to be a reason. One doesn't swallow capsules just for the fun of it."

"They could have been stuffed down his throat," Evelyn said with some relish.

"There was no sign of struggle."

"Too bad."

"Evelyn, I wanted to ask you about . . ." I hesitated, not sure how to form the question.

"Don't," she said, guessing I was after her privacy. "Let me give you a word of advice." Her grating voice cut right through the smoky haze of the small room. "Bertrand's your man. Just leave it at that."

"No." I was getting a little tired of being pushed around. "I'm sure Fred didn't limit his blackmailing to Bertrand." I paused and let that sink in for a moment. "What about Janick? Did he stay with HH&H because of Bertrand, or was he worried about what his snob Parisian family and friends would say if they knew he was a *pédè?*" Janick might have even killed Fred to help his lover. I'm sorry, Evelyn, Bertrand isn't the only possibility. Janick had the motive and, as for the means, he was there that Sunday."

"We all left several hours before Fred died," Evelyn reminded me. The cigarette haze had overpowered us, and she got up to open the door and push it back and forth to fan the smoke out. I waited until she was through to answer her.

"Yes, I know. The sensor recorded the times all of you left, except Janick. He doesn't have an employee card."

"But that's the whole point," a more sharply visible Evelyn said as she sat down behind her desk again. "Since he doesn't have a card, he can't get out of the building without an employee to open the door for him. Unless he stayed at HH&H overnight and slipped out in the morning, he couldn't have killed Fred. You aren't going to tell me Janick hid in Fred's bathroom to wait for the light of dawn and liberation?"

"He didn't have to. I got a chance to peek at the sensor readings for that Sunday, and there was one discrepancy. The sensor had Fred leaving the building at five-twenty-seven, but we know that Fred only left the building the next day, a dead man. Whoever killed him used Fred's I.D. card to get out. So you see, it could have been Janick." I was very satisfied with my sudden burst of logic.

"Or anyone else," Evelyn said with her characteristic bluntness.

"Yes, I know, Evelyn, but somehow it's so much easier to think it wasn't one of us."

There was a knock at the door, and after waiting a few seconds for the answer Evelyn did not bother to give, the door was opened gingerly by a small hand with perfectly polished *Eté d'Amour* nails. It was skimpy Jenny, all five-foot-one of her inside a bright yellow dress. Her short curls had been freshly dyed bright orange.

"Oh, great, you're both in here," Jenny said and waved her hand at the smoke. "I'm sure you know the great news about Mattie." Evelyn confirmed with a nod. "The mail room and the receptionists convinced 'Moneybags' to shell out the money for a 'Welcome Back' party after the one o'clock closing today. Everyone's invited." She started to leave after her little announcement, but Evelyn stopped her.

"Where you going with that hair?"

Jenny stepped back in the room and twirled around. "What do you think?"

"You really want to know?" Evelyn asked. I could just hear her getting her sandpaper ready.

"Even if I didn't," Jenny smiled back at her, "I'm sure you're getting ready to tell me anyway."

"It's great for Halloween."

Jenny laughed, obviously not offended. "At least

people will notice." She waved two hands in the air and started coughing. "How can you stand it in here?"

"Adds to the atmosphere of mystery. Simona seems to think Janick is our murderer. She wants it to be someone outside our little family. Who's your favorite?"

"Not Mr. Janick. Fred said he came from a real good family. And he's so elegant and everything." She pulled at her curls, lost in thought. "Why not one of the two H's?" she suggested with a guilty giggle. "Wouldn't you just love it if it were 'Moneybags'? Then maybe we could all get a raise." She walked out of the room, but a contrite Evelyn called her back again.

"Hey, Jenny, I've changed my mind. Your hair reminds me of the setting sun, and that's always a beautiful sight."

A slow grin spread on Jenny's face. "You should watch it, Evelyn. You're sounding more and more like Wally." Jenny quickly ran off with the last word.

I left Evelyn to contemplate the futility of hiding anything at HH&H, and went back to my office. Already little pieces were beginning to fit together in my head, but I needed some more facts. I decided to place a call to Greenhouse, even though the thought of his voice made my stomach do an instantly strenuous aerobic routine.

When I heard the voice my pulse rate dropped to zero. It was Raf.

"Hi, Detective Garcia. It's Simona Griffo over at HH&H. Is Detective Greenhouse around?" I did so want to hear his voice.

"No, he's busy on another floor. What's up?" Raf wasn't sounding particularly friendly.

"How's our typewriter thief?"

"Making up stories like he just happened to be there and typewriters fascinate him, but we'll break him down."

"Did his fingerprints match the ones on the spray can found in my apartment?"

"Naw, he's not your man."

Great, I thought. Not even the thief was my man. I plunged into my own made-up story, hoping it made more sense than the thief's.

"Listen, Detective Garcia, Mr. Heffer is looking for Fred Critelli's I.D. card. For security reasons you understand. He wants to make sure you have it. It would probably have been in Mr. Critelli's pockets or in his desk. Did you find it during your search?"

"Wait a sec, let me look at the list. I've got it somewhere here in my drawer. Here it is. Cartier gold pen, handkerchief, house keys on gold key chain, office elevator key, scraps of paper." There was a pause during which I heard only a light hum.

"No, I don't see no I.D. card. His wallet had some money, a couple of credit cards, driver's license, but no I.D. Sorry. But you can call me Raf," he offered as consolation. He was warming up to me.

"Thanks, Raf. I guess the I.D. must be here some place. We'll look for it. By the way, what happens to his belongings, the clothes he was wearing and stuff?"

"We keep them until the case is closed," Raf explained. "You want them back, huh? I don't blame you. That guy knew from elegance, huh? Wore great clothes. I know what I'm talking about. My uncle is a tailor, you know, he works in one of those cleaners. Fancy uptown shop. He's taught me a lot about clothes. I know good stuff when I see it, and that silk shirt he was wearing? Now that was some shirt. His initials on it, heavy silk. Gorgeous. Too bad it had a big stain on the back of his shirt. Hard to get stains off silk."

"On the back? That's an odd place for a stain. Do you know what kind of stain it was?"

"Well, it wasn't tomato or coffee. I mean, it didn't really have a color. More like he had leaned against something wet. Maybe even water. You know, water can stain silk. My uncle warned me. I got a couple of silk shirts, too." I could just picture Raf's flourishing rib cage girdled by a tight silk shirt, buttons open to reveal Mamma's baptismal gold chain. That vision made me feel right at home.

"So why'd you want to know?" Raf asked.

"In case anyone asks me the whereabouts of his personal belongings," I lied. "I'm supposed to be the go-between with the police, remember?"

"Yeah, that's right," Raf said, laughing as though he had finally realized to whom he was talking. "Sorry we didn't get a chance to talk last night, but business has gotta come first. My girlfriend Tina loved that garlic, olive oil recipe you gave me." He was now his old, friendly self. "I told Stan you must be a great cook 'cause I think he wants to take you out."

"Raf, don't joke with me."

"Who's joking? You know what Stan said after we brought in that art director of yours? You'll never guess."

"He made some nasty comment about Bertrand." I was preparing myself for the worst.

"Come on, lady, Stan's not like that."

"So what did he say."

"He said, 'Shit, now she'll never speak to me again' and he was talkin' about you, lady."

That damn, obstinate, wonderful man cared enough to say "shit." It was all the encouragement I needed.

"Well, tell your friend, Stan, that I will speak to

224

him again because Bertrand did not kill Fred, and I will prove it to him by Monday. *Ciao*, Raf."

I had gone completely *pazza*, crazy, thinking I could come up with a murderer in three days, but at the time I didn't think there was anything wrong with that. I told myself I was following my mother's advice. "Plunge into boiling water only," she always told me. I forgot she was talking about pasta.

Chapter Twenty-four

A lot of people had stayed behind to welcome Mattie. She towered over us in the middle of the conference room, a wide, happy grin spread across her face.

"I'm tellin' you now," she was saying, "it sure is great to be back. Those New York City cops are as bad as my horny husband. They kept comin' back for more even after I was all dried up." As we all laughed Mattie reached out to pull sour-faced Dana firmly under her large protective arm. They looked like fast friends. "Moneybags," Heffer strode up to them with authoritative weight and handed Dana an envelope.

"Oh, thank God," Dana cried out in a voice destined to be heard even by the Devil. "It's my new I.D. card, isn't it?" "Moneybags" muttered something back which I didn't understand. It didn't matter; I had heard enough to want to follow him to what I presumed was the "refreshment corner"—a small folding table offering a couple of bowls filled with pretzels and potato chips, several plastic bottles of Coke, and one white wine magnum, already half empty. "Moneybags" stooped and scowled over his treasure. I sidled up next to him.

"How wonderful of you to have gotten Dana her new I.D. card so quickly."

"Quickly?" "Moneybags" nearly choked. "That

damn company took more than two weeks."

"I didn't realize she had lost it so long ago. That is correct, isn't it?" I gave him my most innocent look. "She had lost it?"

"Of course she had," he snapped. "Why else would she ask for another one?"

"Hey, Mr. Heffer," Evelyn's voice called from behind him. "It's real democratic of you to foot the bill for this party." She gestured with an empty paper cup toward the small table. "This welcome shindig must have cost you all of $3.98."

He straightened up to his full, tall height. "Listen, Miss Dietz. This agency will be lucky if it lasts out the month."

"Has something else come up?" I asked.

"Either we find the missing perfume bottle by Monday or Janick, Inc. sues," he growled, confirming what Wally had told us. "And if you want a word of advice, Miss Dietz, I would leave that wine bottle alone."

"Sure, it might cost you another fifty cents," she answered, continuing to fill her cup to the brim.

"Come on, Evelyn. Stop it." I led her toward an empty corner. "You don't need this," I said gently taking the cup away from her. "Here, have a cigarette."

"Why not? They're both killers." Her hand trembled as she lit it.

"Why the sudden need to drink again?"

"Look at fat pimples over there." She lowered her head as if worried someone might catch her looking. Wally was making a perfect idiot of himself with Ann's secretary, laughing with her and running his fingers through her hair. He was carrying the line of duty a little far.

"You know he likes to make an ass of himself," I said.

227

"Did you see him with that model the other day?" Evelyn took a deep drag. "He was practically rubbing his penis against her."

"You're the one he loves, Evelyn."

"Does he? And for how long? I'm helpless without my contacts, my body looks like a deflating blimp, my face has permanent diaper rash, and if that isn't enough, I'm nine years older and I show every month." She pulled at the red cotton scarf she had wrapped around her wrinkling neck, making sure it covered as much as possible.

"You keep drinking and you'll show every minute."

Evelyn blinked at me for a moment, the red blotches of her face throbbing. Then she threw her unfinished cigarette in the wine cup I was holding and walked away. I noticed Wally watching her.

I walked up to him and asked, "Can I talk to you?"

"Looks like this is my day with the lovely ladies. I am sorry, my dear," he said to Ann's secretary with a smile, "your turn is up." He waved a pudgy hand and she left us.

"I didn't find out much," he said in a conspiratorial whisper, "except that our resident vamp, the hard-hearted Ann, is not very well liked on the upper floors, but no one admits knowing about the perfume. Nevertheless I had a very good time titillating the moronic girls."

"Evelyn and I noticed. In fact, Evelyn noticed a little too much."

Wally looked at the cup I was still holding. "She isn't . . .?"

"I'm afraid she is. I'd go find her if I were you." Wally rushed off, almost bumping into a sauntering Gregory.

"You look gloomy," I said to him. "Nervous about Ellen's slides?"

"Not at all," he said, the blush spreading over his

228

face revealing the lie. "I promised I'd wait for her here. She's still sightseeing."

"You could have gone with her," I said, wondering why the gentle Gregory I knew was such a lousy father.

"I have work to do."

"What did Fred have on you, Gregory?" I asked in a low voice.

His head whipped around. "What are you talking about?"

"It had something to do with Ellen, didn't it?"

Gregory stared at me, his jaws clamped shut and twitching. "Help me," I pleaded. "I'm trying to solve this murder. We might all lose our jobs if we don't find out who took Ann's perfume bottle, and I'm convinced whoever took the bottle also killed Fred. Don't you understand that the more I know the easier it will be to figure it all out? Please, Gregory."

Gregory slowly shook his head. "Count me out on this favor," he said and walked away. That was the second person who had turned his back on me in the space of a few minutes. My tactics were a real success.

"Miss Julia," Mattie's resounding voice called out, "what are you doing sittin' all alone in that corner? Come and join in the fun." I followed Mattie's eyes and saw Julia look up, a little startled by the sudden attention. Her large lap held a paper napkin full of pretzels. In one hand she grasped a small pot of African Violets, in the other a half-eaten pretzel. Her companion handbag was securely hanging from her arm.

"I'm quite well here, thank you. I take up so much room." She gave a short, embarrassed laugh. "It's a lovely party, Mattie, and I'm so glad you are innocent. I always did know, of course. One just does. Hate and love. It is so strong you can sniff it in the air." She wriggled her nose and stared at her plant. "Oh, yes. I almost forgot. This Saintpaulia is for you." She stretched out her arm and Mattie walked to meet it. "She wants plenty of moisture and not too much sun."

"Thank you, Miss Julia." Mattie stooped over and kissed her smooth cheek. "For this," she shook the plant, "and for the trustin'." Mattie lowered her strong voice into a grumble. "Now don't you worry about that nasty phone call. I'm sure Mr. Harland didn't mean any of those things."

"I'm sure you'll take good care of her," Julia answered, giving her plant a last wistful look.

Mattie turned away and shook her head. I followed.

"What nasty phone call were you referring to?" I asked her the minute we were beyond earshot.

Mattie gave me an assessing look.

"Come on, Mattie, I'm only trying to help. Please."

"She had one of her crazy mix-ups and Mr. Harland found out. He was fit to be tied. He called Mr. Fred and chewed him out. Said the poor woman had to go, that he had to fire her by Monday."

"Was this on the Friday before Fred died?"

"It sure was."

"How did you find out about the phone call?"

Mattie big hand patted my shoulder. "Simone, honey, like I told you, I got big ears. *And* I run the switchboard." She laughed and I looked at Julia slowly eating the pretzels on her lap. She had tried to convince me Fred would never fire her. Now I knew better.

Hunger for real food and the need to ask a few questions took me to the kitchen. Giovanna was washing the lunch dishes, the front of her black uni-

230

form completely wet. She still refused to wear an apron. No color was going to adorn her body until a year of mourning had passed.

"*Ciao,* Giovanna, how are you feeling after your confrontation with the thief?"

"I thank Luis it is finished. He was very good to me," she said, without a hint of a smile. "Simona, you look hungry," she decreed. "There is still good food left. It is a sin to waste it." She reached behind her on the counter for a large blue Rosenthal serving plate.

Two *Saltimbocca alla Romana,* surrounded by sautéed artichoke hearts, stared at me.

"Come on, Giovanna, one for me and one for you," I said, accepting the fork she also offered.

"No, I cannot. It's Friday."

"The Pope said it's okay to eat meat on Friday ages ago." Half of the veal was already in my mouth.

She shook her head. "I am not hungry, Simona. You eat." She would have rather starved than betray a Catholic tradition. The twentieth century hadn't arrived for Giovanna. Take her mourning clothes — Fred wasn't even family.

"I was wondering," I asked, after having swallowed the last of the veal and getting ready to attack the artichokes, "if you had noticed whether Fred was ever allergic?"

"The police say the same thing, and I say *il signor* Critelli was never sick. He was a very strong man."

"Oh, we all know that, Giovanna. But having an allergy isn't a sign of weakness. It's like a cold. Didn't Fred ever get colds?"

"*Il signor* Critelli," she said slowly, making it clear she did not approve of my calling him by his first name. "*Il signor* Critelli," she repeated, "never was sick." That was that. As far as she was concerned the conversation was at an end. I stopped eating.

231

"*I carciofi* are not as good as they should be," she said, misunderstanding the reason I had stopped. "There is no garlic. Mr. Harland cannot eat the garlic. He has a sick stomach." She made a sympathetic clucking sound. Mr. Harland was allowed to be weak.

"Did *il signor* Critelli tell you about the perfume campaign we are working on?" I asked her, trying a different approach.

"Stinko?" She smiled for the first time in two weeks.

"Yes, Stinko. Why does it make you smile?" I didn't think she knew what the word stinko meant.

"I smile because he wanted to give me the perfume. He said, 'Stinko is for you, Giovanna. You will no longer smell of garlic, you will smell of Stinko.'" Giovanna covered her face with a dish towel like a shy schoolgirl.

"Do you still have the bottle?" I asked.

"Oh, no, he never give to me. He give it to Miss Ann." So Fred had not kept his mouth shut about the bottle. If Giovanna knew, who else did?

"Weren't you upset?" I asked.

She shook her head. "No, there is a good reason."

"What reason?"

"He said I have no place to go, so if he give me the bottle, I wear it in his house or in the office, and he did not like the perfume. He said Miss Ann promised she would not wear the perfume in the office."

I gave her a very doubtful look. I didn't think it was a very good excuse for reneging on a gift.

"No, it's the truth," Giovanna said, wanting to convince me Fred could do no wrong. "He promise for Christmas he give me other perfume, one that does not give a tickle to his nose."

"A tickle to his nose? Stinko made his nose tickle?"

"Yes, that is what he say."

"And maybe he say it make him sneeze too?"

"Yes," Giovanna said happily. *"Starnuti. Tanti starnuti."*

"Giovanna *bella*," I said, getting up from the stool and hugging her. "That is what is called an allergy in this country."

"No," she said emphatically. "It is only a nose tickle."

I wasn't going to argue.

Mattie's party was breaking up. Most had left, but the people I was interested in were all there: Wally embracing a smiling Evelyn for the whole world to see; sharp-nosed Jenny in her optimistic yellow dress and orange hair, looking like a gaudy tropical parakeet; a forlorn Julia sinking heavily into her corner chair, her lap empty of food; taut Gregory shifting from one Nike to the other like a lightweight ready to challenge the world, his red plastic satchel slung over his shoulder ready to go; pouty Dana still clinging to Mattie's motherly arm; Giovanna, armed with a tray, ready to clean the room of all its trash. Even elegant Ann was there, the paper cup she held in her hand looking like a crystal goblet. She has that ability.

"Listen, everyone," I called out. "Can we hold a meeting first thing Monday morning in Fred's office?"

"What in heaven's name for?" Ann asked with throaty smoothness.

"We have a perfume bottle to find if we want HH&H to survive," I reminded her gently.

"And a murderer," Wally added.

"Yes, exactly," I said. "We may be able to do both Monday morning." I was really plunging into boiling water, with no fear of getting burned.

"Oh, Simona, that's so exciting," Jenny said rush-

233

ing up to me. "Did you really find out something?"

"Oh, shit," Wally shouted before I could answer. "I've got to go pick up Ellen's slides or I'll be axed even before Monday."

"God, you're right," I said. "Run. I'll set up the slide projector in Bertrand's room. Okay, everyone,' I called out, suddenly feeling very hyper. "Please, nine-thirty Monday morning, Fred's office." I walked out without waiting for answers or questions.

Chapter Twenty-five

"Have you peeked?" I asked Wally anxiously when he came back with the slides twenty minutes later.

"Nope." When I looked at him doubtfully, he raised his right hand and added "Scout's honor."

"Well, let's peek together before we show them to the H's."

"Superb idea," Wally said. "Let me get Ev and Gregory. He's drowning her in espresso. And by the way, thanks for the tip. She's going to be just fine. I'll see to that."

He really did love her.

We went to Bertrand's room and clustered around the projector waiting for the empty wall in front of us to reflect Ellen's lovely image. I was going to operate the machine and eliminate what slides we thought were weak.

"Does anyone know where Bertrand keeps his cotton gloves?" I asked. "I don't want to get any smudges on these slides." Wally started opening some drawers of Bertrand's desk. "I don't know where those damn things are," he said in frustration.

"Yes, you do," Evelyn said impatiently, fiddling with the red scarf tied at her neck. "He keeps them in the drawer just under the telephone." Much to Wally's chagrin, Evelyn was right.

With cotton gloves in hand, I started the silent movie. I showed one slide after another and no one said anything. Even when I made a mistake and one slide appeared upside down no one said anything. There just wasn't anything to say. Ellen was gorgeous, she photographed beautifully, her left profile was her weak spot, her smile was a knockout, her ass didn't look at all fat, her limp hair looked good, and she was even great upside down. She also had an advantage over Lauder's Paulina. She could laugh and still look magnificent. When the wall went white again and we had reached the end of the slides, Wally started clapping. The three of us started clapping in that darkened room, and we turned toward Gregory. He got up and flicked the lights back on. His face was a bright red.

"Don't clap at me. I've got nothing to do with this."

"You certainly did not contribute to her beauty," Wally said. "That is painfully obvious to anyone looking at your beet-red face. No, I was clapping because you had the foresight some twenty-two years ago to reach over to the lady sleeping next to you and bang the bejesus out of her to produce this lovely child we have just seen immortalized on Bertrand's grubby wall. Only a spectacular bang could have produced such beauty, don't you agree, Ev dear? Throw your damming diaphragm away, my fading beauty, and let's go for it."

"How she was produced is none of our business," Evelyn answered evenly, ignoring Wally's parenting proposal. "All I can say is I'm happy we've found her. You must be very proud of her."

Gregory didn't answer.

Evelyn stood up and patted him on the arm. "Oh, cheer up. They'll do everything to spoil her, but if she's inherited any of your stamina, she'll survive. Besides, she looks like she enjoys life."

"Which certainly can't be said about our dear illustrator," Wally added to have the last word.

While they were talking, I started running the

236

slides again. I wanted to eliminate the one showing her left profile. I looked at it carefully. She wasn't smiling and her hair was pulled back exposing her ear. There was nothing soft about the picture. She looked like a lonely, unhappy kid.

"I know one thing she inherited from Gregory," I said as I continued to stare at the slide. All three turned to look at me and then at the wall.

"See her ear? She has no lobe. Just like Gregory."

Gregory instinctively reached for his left ear to seek confirmation.

"We'll have a hell of a time putting earrings on her," I said.

Gregory continued to caress his ear and stare at Ellen's projection.

"Down with your hands," Wally said, reaching for Gregory's arm. "No use trying to hide your defects." Gregory opened up both of his arms and displayed first one ear then the other for all of us to see. For once he seemed to be enjoying himself thoroughly.

"She's right, you have practically no earlobe," Wally said. "I've never seen anything so eccentric. What in heaven's name made you notice Ellen's ear?" he asked me.

"I'm a resident alien."

"What's that got to do with anything?"

"It's got to do with the fact that when you first enter this country, they take a photograph of you, and they ask you to expose your right ear. When I asked the immigration officer why, she calmly explained that it was for identification purposes. An ear identifies you."

"Well, well," Wally said, looking very satisfied with himself. "Gregory will be your friend for life, Simona. I now clap to you." And he started applauding loudly. I wasn't quite sure what he meant by all that.

"Instead of making so much noise," Evelyn said quickly, "why don't you call Ann and Mr. Harland down to see the slides and the contact sheets. As far as we know we still have an ad to shoot."

"Well, I'll be going," Gregory said with a big smile as he slung his red satchel on his shoulder. "I'm meeting Ellen at the bus station in twenty minutes."

"You idiot, why are you taking the bus?" I asked him. "I could have called a limousine for you. In fact, I still can." I was feeling guilty about our run-in at Mattie's party.

"No, thanks, Simona. She asked me to take her home my way, you know, the humble bus."

"Well, tell her the good news and have a great weekend together," I said.

"It's not definite yet," Wally was quick to point out. "Our panic-stricken Janick has yet to pass judgment and, after that Monday ultimatum he's come up with, I don't even know if he's come to see the slides."

He had come. They walked into the room as if going to a funeral, an attitude that was only mildly out of place. A very chastened Ann came with her blond curls combed back severely, a white unadorned Adolfo knit and no perfume. Janick was polite and formal in his greeting, his anger at the agency nowhere in sight. Mr. Harland was pale despite his tan, and "Moneybags" looked his usual self—unpleasant.

I put my gloves on again and did my bit. Again no words were spoken as the slides clicked past. At the end, when Ellen appeared on the wall for the last time, with hair and black lace whirling around her, Ann let out a gasp of awe. The lights came back on, and all the faces looked considerably better. Not ecstatic, but better. I turned to watch Janick.

"Elle est charmante," he said and smiled at me. "She will be my 'Free.' If there is to be a 'Free.' " With that he looked directly at Mr. Harland, whose tan turned a perfect khaki. Ann shrank in her seat.

Janick stood up and the meeting was over.

* * *

"God, what a group," Wally groaned the instant the elevator door shut. "Give me Reagan and Nancy any day."

"How did it go?" Evelyn asked. Her head was peeking around the corner at the end of the corridor.

"Ellen's in," I said, "but if you want descriptive detail of the summit meeting, ask our copywriter. It's more up his alley." I was too tired to describe anything.

"How shall I put it?" Wally said, beaming at the thought that he had been offered center stage. He was more used to stealing it. "Miss Lester was full of remorse and was about to get herself to a nunnery, when she gave out an orgasmic moan . . ."

"Thanks," Evelyn said, putting a restraining hand on Wally's arm. "I think I've heard enough."

"Is Gregory gone?" I asked her.

"Yes, he slipped away as soon as he saw the group coming."

"I'll have to call and tell him Ellen is our girl."

"If we find a perfume bottle by Monday and get Bertrand off the hook," the vigilant Wally reminded me. "But then you are taking care of that, are you not, my sneaky Italian?"

"Yeah, what's this Monday thing?" Evelyn asked me.

"Nothing. I just have some ideas I'd like to air."

Evelyn blinked at me doubtfully. "Bertrand just called while you two were showing off the slides. I told him how great Ellen looked. He wants to meet with you right now, Wally. They haven't arrested him yet, but he's afraid they're going to keep him down at the police station again all day tomorrow. And he said to tell you 'thanks,' Simona."

"After the fiasco with Mattie, the police are being a little more prudent in their judgments," Wally said with smug conviction.

"Like hell they are," Evelyn said. "It's a simple case of Connecticut White outshining Bronx Black."

"Mattie wouldn't have said it better, my love. Let me reward you with a premium kiss." Wally leaned over to hug her.

"Wally, stop it. Bertrand's waiting," Evelyn reminded him, raising her arms for protection.

"I'm off faster than a speeding bullet." It was more like a wobbling ball. When he got to the elevator he burst into his best Doris Day imitation. "Now our secret love's no secret anymore," he sang out before the elevator mercifully swallowed him up. There was something very reassuring about Wally's outrageous personality. He never let me down.

"Well," I said, "I guess Gregory and Ellen aren't the only happy ones."

Evelyn tugged at the red scarf at her neck and pretended she hadn't heard me.

"It was nice to see Gregory smile after such a long time," I tried again.

"Yes, it was," Evelyn said quietly. "The two of them owe you a big 'thank you.' "

"I can see why Ellen does, but I'm not sure Gregory wants to thank me at all. I'm not even sure there's a friendship left. He was dead set against Ellen's becoming a model."

"I'm not talking about that. I'm talking about his ears, the fact that he has no lobes."

"I had nothing to do with that."

"You made the connection. You pointed out the one thing that he gave Ellen, the one thing that makes them similar."

"I wish it had been something more attractive than a missing earlobe. I'm sure he's gotten tired of hearing people tell him that his beautiful daughter doesn't look anything like him."

"Yes, he had gotten very tired of it." Evelyn sounded so serious that I looked at her sharply.

240

Slowly the fog started to lift and I began to understand.

"What was Ellen's mother like?" I asked.

"Not as beautiful as Ellen, but still a real looker. Gregory said that when he married her, he thought he was the luckiest man on earth. Then he found out one man wasn't enough. She played around a lot, got into the drug scene, and I don't know what else. Ellen was born in the middle of all that. Gregory sent his wife to a rehabilitation clinic. Three days after she was discharged as 'cured', she jumped from the eighth floor of an office building." Evelyn stopped and fumbled for a cigarette.

"Did Fred know any of this?"

"He made sure Gregory never forgot." She found the cigarette and lit it. "I guess ever since Ellen was born," she continued, the words coming out with the smoke, "he was never sure she was his. He paid out money for her, but he wasn't about to love her. And now, thanks to you, he can look at her ear and love her to death." Evelyn gave me a big, unexpected hug. It was my day to be thanked, but I wished all the news I had in me was going to be as good.

Chapter Twenty-six

Don't take me away, please don't, I cried silently. It was so beautiful, I couldn't let go. I turned around facing the wall, covered my naked body with the sheet despite the heat, and buried my head under three pillows. I refused to wake up, to let the piercing ring of the telephone shatter my dreamworld.

Greenhouse was kissing me gently, lips barely touching. His hands grazed my neck, my back, my arms. He was tentative, like a suspicious child with a mysterious object in front of him. His moving fingers felt like tickling feathers, but it wasn't enough for me. I couldn't feel him. I reached out to touch him. I wanted his smooth warmth. I wanted to rub him, squeeze him, glue my hands and lips everywhere, but the minute he felt my touch, he grabbed my hands and held them firmly behind my back, pulling my body and face away from his. His free hand kept up the search, never staying long in one place. My breasts tingled waiting for that hand to reach them, but he stayed away. He kept to neutral territory. I was burning with frustration, my body slippery with perspiration. I was dying to press myself hard against him, open my mouth wide for him, but he remained aloof. His hand and fingers stayed light and his body unreachable. I turned around on my back and my hips started heaving. The shame of it woke me up. I was completely wet, everywhere. I told myself it was the temperature of that early Sunday morning. What's another lie in my life? At least the phone had stopped ringing. I wasn't even sure it had rung at all.

Damn it, couldn't I have him even in a dream? That's what dreams are for — to have your pick of men, careers, clothes, apartments, whatever, for very little. At its most expensive, it was puffy eyes in the morning. After a Saturday closed up in my closet of a home making notes to convince myself I knew who had actually killed Fred, I felt I had a right to be distracted by a spicy porn home video starring all my repressed, unfulfilled wishes and wants. After a night of it, they weren't so repressed, but they were certainly unfulfilled. Greenhouse was not to be won over. I sighed loudly and decided to face the lousy day. Instead of climbing down the ladder from my loft bed, I slid, thanks to all the perspiration (sweat is more like it, it was pure animal) and slipped into the shower to clean my mind and my body. I used only hot water and burned myself to hell, a sinner seeking absolution. I know the nuns of my childhood would have approved. I was still standing under the steaming water, all desire boiled out of me, when the phone started to ring again. I ran to get it.

"I called before, but no one answered. I figured you were in the shower."

"Hhmm" was the only sound I made. It was he, the stingy one. He was in my dream and on my phone.

"Are you eating breakfast?" Greenhouse asked innocently.

"Never," I managed to say. Garrulous Simona finally at a loss for words. I was having an even harder time with him in the real world. He sounded so friendly.

"You should eat. You have nothing to worry about," he said. "You have a good figure." He said good, not great. I stupidly sucked in my stomach, as

243

if he could see me standing there, wet and naked, hair crying over my face.

"It's a gorgeous day," his nice, warm voice said. "How about meeting me in Central Park again? This time not on official business. We'll read the paper, soak in the sun, talk. It's time we got to know each other a little better."

"Oh, yes," I wanted to say. To everything. To whatever he wanted. Instead I panicked and said, "The fingerprints didn't match."

"No, they didn't. I'm sorry about that. He did admit finally that he'd been stealing around the agency. He boasted he sold the Burberry and the leather jacket that same night."

"But I wanted him to be my thief too," I said, still hoping for the pat solution, hating the threat of loose ends. Find the lover, find the thief, find the murderer, find the solution to all the pain, wrap it up tightly in a neat bundle and throw it in the Forget river.

"Let it go, Simona," his soft voice told me. "Admittedly a bad thing happened to you, but it's happened to a lot of people. It's a part of being in New York City. Maybe it's a part of being anywhere. You've got to put it behind you and move on."

If you keep talking to me, I can do it, I thought. I'll put all the bad things behind me.

"Meet me at the corner of Fifth and Sixty-fifth, park side, in an hour." And he hung up without giving me a chance to reply. It had sounded very much like an order.

By the time I got uptown, via a subway and true hell, I was a chastised woman determined to talk to him about Bertrand and Fred's real murderer, even if it meant risking his anger, his walking away from me. But then I saw him. He was leaning against the park wall, one leg bent to help support the load of the Sunday *New York Times,* the other hand holding a

244

blanket. I stopped behind a tree and enjoyed the sight of him: blue jeans, green sport shirt, hair tousled by his own hand, long, needing a haircut. I couldn't see his eyes, but I went by memory. It was almost as good. I didn't move, hesitant to spoil that wonderful moment of expectation. When the plate is before you, don't touch the food, I had been taught back home. Feast your eyes with the shapes and colors first, then take a deep breath and let the aroma seep in through your nostrils. Arouse your senses slowly. When the saliva has moistened your mouth, taste, eat, and be happy. I did just that. I teased myself with his sight. Only after he had looked at his watch for the third time, did I walk up to him, every sense wide awake.

"*Ciao.*"

He stood up and leaned forward to kiss me lightly on the lips, all ten hefty sections of the *New York Times* between us. My dream coming true in more ways than one.

"Let's sit in Sheep's Meadow," he said, decision already made. "Lots of space and no trees to block the sun." The last thing I wanted was to be roasted dry, but when he took my hand to lead me there, all I could think of was the nice warmth of his hand. Besides, from the corner of my eye, I could see clouds gathering, ready to march against us from the west.

He selected a small, empty patch of grass, with no shade in sight and with a good view of orange and blue saucers spinning through the air and kites being taken for an airy walk. On that fourteen-acre stretch of green, the diverse Manhattan population spread itself like thick jam on toast. Tall trees surrounded us and beyond them, taller buildings fenced us in. I stood by, clumsily watching Greenhouse prepare the nest. I didn't know what to do, what was expected of me. He looked so self-sufficient as he opened his red and blue blanket and smoothed it out without looking at me for help. He sat down cross-legged, looked up at the sun in worship and at the same time, pointed a spot a few inches away from him. Obedient Simona sat down where he indicated. I kept my back to the sun. I looked at him instead. It was a much more pleasant sight, though not much cooler.

"How've you been?" he asked, his eyes either crinkling into a welcoming smile or crinkling from the glare.

"Fine," I said. I was at that moment, sitting in front of him. I must have looked fine, too, because his hand reached out and held my neck, bringing my face close to his. He kissed me again. This time his lips stayed on mine a few seconds longer. No pressure though. Just gentle contact. I remembered the dream and tucked my hands under my thighs. I wasn't going to ruin those seconds by being greedy.

"What section do you want?" he asked me as he released my neck. Without waiting for an answer, he took the first section and left me the rest of the paper.

"TWA," I read out loud, looking at the blanket we were sitting on. It was easier than reading the headlines upside down. I also wanted his attention back. "Where did you get this blanket? You couldn't have stolen it."

Greenhouse didn't move, but his ears turned bright red. His silly ears were blushing, and they told me I had put my foot in my mouth one more time in my life.

"Your wife was an airline hostess?" I asked. He shook his head.

"Girlfriend?" Why not stuff myself with that foot while I was at it.

Greenhouse nodded, eyes still glued on the print.

"Frustrating," I said with fake nonchalance.

"Why?" He squinted at me.

"If she flies, she must be away a lot."

"I found it very convenient." Verb in the past tense and even then, obviously not a great passion. I felt him handcuff my ankle with his fingers. I kept looking at him, grasshoppers dancing inside me, and I smiled.

"Do all Italians smile from one side of the Atlantic to the other?" Greenhouse asked, tightening the handcuff. Just the happy ones, I said to myself.

"You should smile more often. It becomes you."

"Sometimes I need help," I admitted.

"Why did you come back?" He pushed the paper aside with his foot and moved closer. Our knees touched and both his hands held my ankles firmly. I watched a young slim man sit near us, despite the wide green space still available farther off. He turned on the radio, not bothering with earphones, and a surprising Vivaldi came our way. Even Greenhouse turned around in astonishment. In the distance we could hear the loud voices of Los Menudos, Tina Turner, and what sounded like a thousand electric guitars vying to dominate that Sunday morning air. Vivaldi whispered to victory.

"Anything's possible," I said, thinking of the music and of my life. "That's what I've always thought of America. That's why I came back."

"What did you want to make possible?" Greenhouse asked in a low voice. We were so obviously not alone, and I think we both wanted to be.

"Another chance." I didn't say at what, but it wasn't hard to guess. He let go of my ankles and lay down on his side, head propped up by his hand. He looked at the newspaper sections spread out around us. I think he was tempted to delve into the news, somebody else's news. Not mine, not his. But he didn't. His eyes came back to me, and he pulled me down. We faced each other again, this time lying down.

"Tell me about the men in your life," he asked with

247

a smile, the neon of his eyes flashing: *Trust me*. I didn't need any prompting on that account. At least not at that moment.

"An innocuous boyfriend in high school, one less so in college."

"Why less?" he interrupted.

"We discovered the big deed together," I explained. Greenhouse raised his eyebrows in mock amazement.

"Then there was one real stinker who picked me and discarded me in a month's time. After that, Italy." I stopped. So did Vivaldi. The young, slim man had turned off the radio and was preparing to join someone across the field who was waving at him in the distance. I watched him skim the grass like a dancer and embrace his friend. A figure standing behind them hurried off quickly and something in that furtive movement startled me.

"What's the matter?" Greenhouse asked.

Bertrand. The embracing men had reminded me of Bertrand. That was all, I told myself. Out loud I said, "I thought I saw someone I knew."

"Who?"

No, it wasn't the slim man or his friend. It was that other figure behind them. Just a quick blur in the distance. "I don't know. Someone moved and I had an odd feeling of familiarity. Almost like a déjà vu. It's spooky."

"The past two weeks must have been rough on you."

I turned and when I saw his worried face I knew I didn't want to think of murder anymore; I didn't want to think of Fred, or my past; just that morning, with this man sitting in front of me.

"You're nice," I said.

He was red and hot from the sun. He sat up and tossed off his green shirt. I looked at him and had to laugh to release my breath. There is nothing more breathtaking than a man in a bare chest and slacks.

The combination of dressed and undressed stretches me out flat on my back, limbs wide and waiting. To make it worse he was tanned, and his chest was covered with remarkable gray hairs. I hadn't been warned. There was no gray on his head; no light speckles in his close-shaven beard. Only on his very naked chest. And that gray, suddenly exposed in a sunny field in the middle of New York City, made him instantly vulnerable and so touchable. It glinted in the sun and looked like Tiffany silver. Just as perfect. Just as precious. I fell a little bit in love. Serious love.

"No more men?" he asked, as if nothing had happened. "Italy didn't live up to its promise as a land of torrid romance?" He had settled down again in his semi-nudity.

"Oh, yes, it did." I said, not really thinking of Italy. At that moment the USA looked full of promise. "I even married the torrid romance." I reached over and touched his back. Barely. He pretended not to notice, but the goose bumps that appeared on his chest acknowledged me. After a few seconds of my touch, his shoulder flicked me off as if my fingers were flies, but I had those bumps to keep me happy.

"What then?" he asked, still intent on getting the full story out of me.

"Meryl Streep in *Heartburn*."

"Haven't seen it or read it." He sure wasn't making it easy.

I took a deep breath and plunged. "My husband was unfaithful. After waiting five very long years to comply with Italian divorce law, I got my freedom and my green card."

Greenhouse looked at me fully, examining my face with his serious eyes. I looked back and drank him in. "I'm sorry," he said with his mouth and his eyes. For the first time in a long while, I wasn't sorry.

"How about lunch?" he asked lightly, giving me a

smile of reassurance. I was starving, but I didn't want to move if it meant he had to put his shirt back on.

"I know a wonderful place," he said, getting up.

I looked down at my crumbled skirt. I wasn't very elegantly dressed, but his blue jeans reassured me. He reached for his green shirt. The show was over.

"Green in honor of your name?" I asked.

"Damn right. My favorite color." He stood above me and picked me up by the waist. He kissed me again lightly. "That's for not smoking all morning. I can't stand a smoky mouth." I mentally gave up smoking for the rest of the day, or if he stayed in it, my life.

Lunch turned out not to be at Tavern on the Green, but right next to it, at Chez Sabrett, a homey, intimate, but airy hot dog stand brightly decorated with a red and yellow umbrella reminiscent of Roman sidewalk cafés. After I took my first bite and Greenhouse wiped the mustard off my lip with a proprietary finger, I gave the place a four-star rating. We sat on a bench and munched our hot dogs, while the clouds I had seen earlier, now almost black, marched in and took over. A few minutes later, big fat drops started pelting us with a vengeance, spattering the dust at our feet. The *New York Times* and the TWA blanket proved to be useless protection, and we ran under a tree, already completely wet. Greenhouse let go of the paper and the blanket of his past lady love and held on to me. Leaning against the huge trunk of our umbrella tree, we watched kites being hastily leashed in, picnickers scramble, and cyclists rush by. One exhausted jogger ran with his face lifted to the sky, mouth wide open, gulping down the heavy drops.

The rain stopped as quickly as it had started, and the earth gave off a delicious musty smell, both humid and warm. Just the way I felt.

"I live just a few blocks away," Greenhouse said. "Why don't we go and dry off?" His face was a perfect mask of seriousness—no twinkling invitation in his eyes. This time I didn't trust him.

We walked off toward Columbus Avenue, our feet squishing our wet shoes. A few minutes after we hit the asphalt of the street, I heard a sharp sound behind me. I quickly turned around, but all I saw were a few faces who didn't know me and didn't care.

"What's the matter?" Greenhouse asked. "Are you afraid Fred's ghost is following you or does the idea of my apartment give you the willies?"

I laughed. He might have been right. "No, of course not," I reassured him. "I guess I'm just a little edgy."

"I can take care of that." He pulled me back toward him.

I didn't get to see much of his apartment. We didn't even get to the bedroom. We started making love the minute he closed the door. He kissed me hard, pushing me against the wall, and I hit my head against a shelf. I happily felt the bump for weeks. He wasn't like my dream at all. He was just as hungry and eager as I was, and our skins became raw from the rubbing, the squeezing, and the kissing. Even our bones seemed to grind together. We made love on a rug, on a sofa, on a table, whatever surface we met up with. As soon as we came, we started over again, just as voraciously as the time before. I wouldn't let him go, afraid that if we rested we would lose each other. We reached his bed when we were near exhaustion, and after one last weak, trembling release, we peeled ourselves away. The afternoon had lightened, the clouds gone out to sea, and I watched his silvery chest heave in instant sleep. I tiptoed to the bathroom to take a shower, and the mirror showed me my red and white breasts, mottled by Greenhouse's hands and lips. Stupidly I thought of Evelyn's blotchy skin and Fred's murder reared its ugly head.

When I came out of the shower, Greenhouse was awake, lying on his back, propped up by his pillows. Behind him, alongside his bed, a wide window looked out on the city and the setting sun. Fires burned in the neighbors' windows. It is New York's golden moment, which always brings me back to the warm ocher and terra-cotta colors of Rome. It doesn't last long. Half an hour at the most and it never fails to fill me with sadness.

Greenhouse lay there naked; I had protectively wrapped myself in his towel. He made room for me on his pillow, but I didn't obey this time. I sat in an armchair at the foot of the bed and looked out at the dimming, unfamiliar skyline of the West Side of New York. Now that we had given and taken so much from each other physically, I was frightened of the emptiness that could follow. I love sex; I gulp it down like my food, but I also need the tenderness and the caring. Yes, all that romantic crap that men are so reluctant to give. I need to be part of someone's everyday life, and I didn't know how much Greenhouse wanted or was willing to let me in.

"I've wanted you since that first day at HH&H," said the dark silhouette on the bed. I'd heard that line before, but usually it came before, not after.

"You were wearing a white, slinky blouse that got stuck on your breasts whenever you moved. It was driving me crazy." He moved his body to face me. "Why are you sitting so far away?"

"I don't know you, Greenhouse, and now I'm a little scared."

Greenhouse got up and went into the other room. Outside the city had turned on its lights, and they gave the room a pale glow. As he walked away I could see his beautiful white ass shine in the dark. It

252

was a very reassuring sight, and despite the exhaustion, something stirred in me. He came back holding a notepad and a pencil in his hands. He stood up straight, almost at attention, and I couldn't help but notice his penis shaking its neat American head at me, foreskin hygienically snipped off at birth. The man was absolutely mouth-watering.

He started droning in an expressionless, official voice. "The suspect is aged thirty-nine, divorced six years ago, has one son by the name of Willie, aged twelve, who lives with his mother. Reason for divorce: need to search for self on the part of the wife, but suspect is willing to sign a sworn statement that he has been happy about his divorce for the past two years. Suspect has been seen around town with various ladies, one of them being a hostess, but until this morning, he was free of all debts toward others, and there were no liens and/or mortgages on any of his properties, said properties including his body and heart. As of this moment he is confused about the future and would like to re-examine the only promising prospect. Right now." Without giving me a chance to get away, he scooped me up, threw me on the bed, and we were at it again. Not as frenzied this time. We couldn't. We just didn't have the energy. His gentleness scared me even more.

"I wanted to see you before today," Greenhouse said into my hair, after coming in me slowly. I had tried, but he had been too tender, and all I had wanted to do was hold on to him and cry. "Even without those tits, you looked like you needed some big hugging." He squeezed me to him. "And something else, too." He pushed his pubic bone against mine to make his point.

"Why didn't you see me?"

"I couldn't. Not with the investigation going on."

253

"That's right," I said, moving in closer to his wonderful chest. " 'I don't mix my social life with my work.' Your nasty words on the phone the last time we spoke."

"It's illogical to fraternize with possible suspects." Fraternize. Nice euphemism.

"Is the investigation over then?"

"It's a little early to tell."

I sat up. "Then you don't think Bertrand killed Fred?"

"Let's just say that once we realized we had made a mistake with Mattie, we decided to proceed more cautiously."

"That sounds like something you might say to the press. Why did you let her go?"

"I believed her." He pulled me back down and settled my head on his shoulder. "I asked her to call work and let people know. I hoped spreading the news of her release might get a little action going." He looked at me with his brown, candid eyes. "Then the letter was found." Was there just a hint of mischief? Why did the word "letter" echo faintly in my head? Familiar words, familiar movements. It was getting so confusing. Greenhouse's smell and warmth didn't help any. I snuggled closer.

"Do you always botch up your cases?" I mumbled against his skin, feeling very sleepy.

"Let's just say, in Mattie's case, I was in too much of a hurry."

"Mmm, I like that." I was so warm and comfortable.

"Hey, you can't fall asleep on me." He pulled me up. "Raf said you're going to deliver a murderer tomorrow. Aren't you going to fill me in?" He flicked the light switch and the romance was over.

"No, I'm not going to fill you in." I reached for the protective towel.

"Why not?"

254

I'm just not ready to." A small question mark was beginning to nag my brain. Something didn't quite fit in with my picture of the murder. "I'm having a meeting tomorrow with all the people who were closely involved with Fred. I think by then I'll be sure." I was going to have to be.

"Ah, the great business presentation." Greenhouse got up and disappeared into the bathroom. "I have to go out now, Simona," he yelled from behind the door. "I promised Willie I'd go to a movie with him." The sound of the shower cut off any further communication.

I slowly got dressed in that unfamiliar room, the future loneliness of the evening engulfing me quickly. Greenhouse and Willie had somewhere to go without me. I didn't belong with them. How could I? We hadn't even had a normal date. God, I just wanted to be a part of someone, the half, or the third, or whatever fraction I could get of a man. That's all. It wasn't much. I looked out the window and tightened my jaws against tears.

"Have you called the meeting already?" Greenhouse asked, walking back into the room to get dressed. I couldn't turn around to look at him.

"Yes. The office gave Mattie a party and just before it broke up, I asked the people involved to meet tomorrow morning in Fred's office."

"Perfect. The scene of the crime," he said matter-of-factly. I couldn't tell whether he was making fun of me. "Did you tell them you knew who the murderer was?"

"Not in so many words, but they could have guessed."

"You can be sure the murderer did." He walked up behind me and kissed my head. "You like the view from my window?" I nodded. That's where I'm going to be in a few minutes, I thought. Outside.

"Give me a minute," I heard his voice tell me. "I

have to make one phone call and then we'll go." I heard the bedroom door close.

"Are you ready?" he asked coming back.

I practically ran to the door.

"Hey, wait a minute. What's your rush." He closed the door I had already opened and held me close to him. We swayed from side to side in the dark.

"How nice to find a lovely Italian lady in the middle of a murder case. Promise to stick around?"

I nodded my head happily and we walked out into the blinding light of the corridor.

"Are you going home?" he asked once we reached the street.

"Yes, I am."

"Don't take the subway. It's too dangerous at this hour. In fact, let me pay for a cab."

"Don't be ridiculous." I laughed, loving his caring. "I'm fine. I do this all the time." I pushed his money away. "I'll take the bus just to make you happy, all right?" A man passed us, brushing against me. I jumped back instinctively.

"You're getting to be a real New Yorker," Greenhouse said. "Are you sure you wouldn't feel better if you told me who you think murdered Fred?"

"And let the New York Police Department get all the credit? Absolutely not. Besides, the more I hold out, the more you'll come begging."

"It's a little late for that," he reminded me with a grin. I got a hurried kiss on the cheek, a brief wave, and he was off.

Chapter Twenty-seven

Fifth Avenue and my bus were waiting for me just across the park. I could see the East Side lights sparkle across the trees. The rain and the dark had cooled off the city, and the air smelled clean, of newly washed trees. I knew not to enter the park despite the inviting lights across the way, but I stood just outside its limits and peered into the shadows. It looked deserted.

"I wouldn't go in there if I was you," a rough, male voice said close to me. I turned around and gasped. It was the man who had brushed against me a few minutes before. He had the same long hair pulled back in a pigtail. I turned south and hurried away.

"Hey, I didn't scare you, did I?" he yelled after me. Well, he had. He didn't mean it, as Jenny might have said, but I couldn't help myself because his voice was hoarse and his hairdo strange; because it was the first time I had made love to Greenhouse; because the city wasn't yet home for me; because the park had become dark and deserted; because I had been alone for such a long time; because Fred had been murdered and his killer was still on the loose; because I knew who it was; because now the murderer knew it too.

Maybe Pigtail hadn't meant to frighten me, but I

was frightened. I hurried along the edge of the park as quickly and silently as I could, listening for footsteps, looking for sudden movement. No one followed.

When I reached the open space of Columbus Circle I breathed a sigh of relief. Here the buildings relented to allow a jumble of streets to cross each other haphazardly. I looked up at the statue of Cristoforo Colombo, the man who had started the whole "Go to America" fad. His back offered me no comfort as he stared south toward the Atlantic Ocean, perhaps having second thoughts himself. I started to walk along the southern perimeter of Central Park and was overpowered by the smell of a few horses, lined up along the sidewalk, still waiting patiently to parade tourists to Rockefeller Center now that darkness had decreed the park out of bounds. I stopped to pat the first nose I came up to and looked back abruptly to see if Pigtail was anywhere around. I thought I caught a movement just inside the park, behind a tree. I wasn't sure. I waited, but whatever it was did not move.

I walked up to the next horse and turned around again. Nothing. Everything was normal, the street full of people enjoying the summer night. I turned back to give the horse a reassuring pat meant for myself when a rapid scraping noise startled me. It sounded like a knife was being sharpened against a stone. I shut my eyes and held on to the horse's mane. The sound continued with a regular, steadying rhythm. The horse did not move. Well, if he wasn't frightened, I told myself, neither was I. My eyes opened and looked toward the sound. The horse driver, a young boy wearing jeans, a dirty T-shirt, and an impeccable bowler, was carefully cleaning the metal tips of his cowboy boots against the curb. I watched him until my goose bumps subsided.

"Do you want a ride?" he asked me.

"How much is it to Fifth and Ninth Street?"

"Seventeen bucks the first half hour, five every fifteen minutes after that." That meant not eating lunch for a week. I wasn't that scared.

"Thanks. I guess the bus will have to do."

"Sorry. The prices are set by all the drivers." He looked at my disappointed face. "Come on, treat yourself," he urged. "It'll do you good."

I was tempted by his shiny white carriage adorned with pink plastic flowers with a white horse to match. Fit for a bride, I thought ruefully and shook my head. It was simply too much money. Besides, an open carriage didn't offer much protection if anyone was really after me. A cab would be better, but I knew the bus was only a block away and four to five dollars cheaper. I stared at the faces passing me by, and they seemed innocent enough. Pigtail was nowhere in sight. I crossed the street, away from the park, toward the reassurance of the elegant buildings and hotels of Central Park South. The Plaza was just ahead. Nothing could go wrong near the Plaza.

A large group of people was waiting at the bus stop on Fifth Avenue. The bus had obviously not come in a long while. I was glad of the company, feeling safer in a crowd. Just as I reached the curb, the approaching headlights of the bus elicited a collective sigh of relief. I stared at those strong beams like a mesmerized rabbit and suddenly I felt very lucky. Despite the Pigtail scare, despite the pang of loneliness when Greenhouse had left me for his son, the day had been exhausting and exciting at the same time. I knew I was going to cherish it for a long time. The headlights had almost reached me and I lifted my foot, ready to step off the curb. I

259

felt a sudden, hard push from behind. I tried to scream. A flash of red crossed my eyes just before the lights hit my face and blinded me.

Chapter Twenty-eight

It was hot. Much too hot. The left side of my face felt branded, and I was wet with sweat. I tried to move, but I couldn't. My body was pinned down, bound by something heavy. Something I couldn't see in the blackness. My hands only felt a burning pain.

A corpse wound up tight for burial—that's what I am, I thought. No, it's too hot for that. The dead are cold. Morgues are cold with their gray dead freezing in metal drawers. Dark. It would be dark in there, like here. Dark and silent. No sight, no sound. I'll suffocate if I don't get some air; if I don't move away from this black void.

I tightened my stomach muscles and tried to lift myself up. My head met something hard and I quickly retreated back down.

"Are you awake, dear?" a trembling voice asked me somewhere in the not-too-far distance.

"Am I badly hurt?"

"Oh, heaven's no. Just a little bit knocked up." A short, stupid laugh. "Well, I don't think I meant that." She sounded familiar, but I couldn't quite place her. So many things I couldn't place. I closed my eyes in that darkness and letters floated down into my eyeballs; a little girl in pigtails laughed gleefully; bare feet made sharp sounds hurrying across grass. Everything so familiar and so wrong.

"You had an ugly fall," she said right next to me. No, it wasn't wrong. Fred had died. Fred had been murdered.

"Quite lucky really," the voice said. She's just above me, I thought. "Good bus driver. He swung to the other side of the street. His brakes never would have stopped him in time." She gave a big quavering sigh. Of course. I remembered her, too.

"Why is it so hot, Julia?"

"It's good for you. I've wrapped you up in all the blankets I have in the apartment. Nice and tight. Your muscles will thank me. So will your skin. A nice bath of perspiration opens up the pores." Her voice was weaving near and far. She was moving around the black space, and I wondered how she did it, not bumping into anything. But then she was on her own territory.

A loud snap. "There," she said. "I've pulled up the blinds to let the street lamps light the room a little. I don't want to startle you with too much light. You need rest."

"I can't see anything."

"Well, my dear," her voice was down, close to my ear. "It might help if you opened your eyes." I could hear Julia's breathing break up each syllable of her words. How did she move so silently, I asked myself still clinging to my blindness. She had so much weight to her.

"Now be brave and face the world," she whispered. I slowly lifted my eyelids. Julia had been right. There was not enough light to startle. I barely was able to distinguish a clutter of odd shapes surrounding the window. Tentacles of many lengths reached out in disarray. I looked up and a shadow quietly swung above my head, like a condemned man.

"It's only my fern," Julia said. "You're in the conservatory. It's the warmest room in the apartment.

262

Warm and humid. It's so good for you, dear." She passed a handkerchief over my forehead. "You're quite wet," she said with satisfaction.

"My face feels funny."

"I'm quite sure it does. By tomorrow that lovely cheek of yours will look like a squashed eggplant. It's nothing permanent."

"Did you take me to the emergency room?" I began tugging at my blankets from the inside of my cocoon.

"You don't want to go there. Nasty places, full of drug addicts, wounded criminals, terrible contamination. No, no, not if I can help it," Julia said, fueling her lungs with a deep breath. "There is nothing wrong with you that a day or two of rest won't cure. I've put a little iodine on the scratches."

"My hands hurt."

"Of course they do. And your knees, too, I'm sure. You pitched straight forward, you know?" she said with the pride of one who had seen it all. "You landed on your knees, but they didn't manage to hold you up. One side of your face got a nice imprint of the New York asphalt. At least it was Fifth Avenue." She wheezed, not having enough breath left for laughter.

How idiotic Julia was. She had seen me at the bus stop, seen my fall in all its details. Why hadn't she called out to me?

"Someone pushed me," I said.

"Did they, dear?"

I turned to look at her round, creaseless face. She was almost at my level. She must have been sitting on a low stool. Wisps of wet, red hair hugged her forehead. She didn't believe me.

"Someone pushed me," I repeated and turned away. I renewed my efforts to free myself from my woolen captors. Julia did nothing to help. "Someone pushed me from behind. Hard," I insisted.

"Perhaps that someone was anxious to board the bus in order to get a seat," Julia suggested. "It's so hard these days. No one offers anymore." Her breath felt hot against my burning cheek. "Not to pregnant women, not to the old, not even to the old and fat like myself." Julia took a deep breath and moved slightly to one side. I saw a long, vertical shadow against the wall. A bench maybe. Why doesn't she get away from my face and sit on the bench. She was gulping down the hot, humid air, leaving me breathless in the semidarkness. If only I could see the details surrounding me, I'd be all right.

"Could you turn the lights on?" I asked. She heaved herself up and moved beyond my eyesight. She wasn't silent then. Her slippers slapped the bare floor with a flat, weary sound. Her back must be turned, I thought and threw away the binding blankets with a shove of legs and arms. I was free, but the effort left my head throbbing with pain.

The ceiling suddenly glowed with purple lights. "No, no," she said in a trembling voice. "You mustn't catch cold." The slippers hurried toward me and I saw a white, disembodied hand reach across my face. I screamed and my head split open.

"Oh, dear," Julia gasped. "I am so sorry. Of course, you've had a terrible fright. Chamomile, that's what you need. A hot cup of chamomile to calm you down and keep you warm." I wanted an ice pack to squeeze my head back together. "You just lie there quietly and I'll be right back. You can talk to the plants if you wish." Her voice had moved away on silent slippers. "I find that very soothing when I'm upset." I looked up. Maybe the drooping fern would believe me.

"Don't worry about the meeting," Julia continued. "I'll tell everyone you're not feeling well."

"I'll be fine by tomorrow morning," I yelled and it made my head throb even more. What had Julia been doing at the bus stop? "Did you notice anyone else you knew at the bus stop?"

"I wasn't really looking, dear. I just happened to be walking by on my way home. I only live two blocks away. I saw you an instant before you fell. I didn't even have the time to say hello."

Could I really face that meeting? I wasn't sure I knew who had murdered Fred anymore. Greenhouse had said something that had started doubts, then the push . . . Familiar kitchen sounds interrupted my confused thoughts. I heard a drawer opening, the jingle of spoons and forks. That's what the problem was. All day I had seen or heard familiar things, without being able to recognize them.

"Are you feeling better?" Julia asked, her weight suddenly looming over me. She had no neck, I noticed. Just a round, smooth melon of a head pushed deep into her body. "You fainted after your fall. Thank heaven there was a strong man who offered to help."

The throbbing in my head stopped. Everything in my body stopped. "What strong man?"

"He wanted to take you to the hospital, didn't want to let go of you," she called out from the kitchen. "I convinced him I could take care of you quite nicely. He was very polite, but he would have looked so much nicer with a proper haircut."

"Oh, my God, did he have a pigtail?" I yelled, sitting straight up.

"There's no need to scream." Julia was right beside me again. "Yes, a pigtail. I suppose that's what you'd call it. Long hair gathered in the back in a depressing squiggle. Perhaps he was one of those pop musicians. They dress so strangely."

"He pushed me," I gasped. "He's the one who

265

pushed me." Julia, looking like a bloated ghost in the purple light, started to dance before my eyes.

"You mustn't get excited. You'll faint again." A firm hand pushed me back onto the sofa. "Really, you don't know what you are saying. He turned out to be a very nice man. Carried you all the way to the door of my building. Here, drink this." A strange, nauseating smell struck my nostrils. One thing I knew was that she wasn't offering me chamomile tea. I had been brought up on the stuff and what she was shoving under my nose didn't smell anything like it.

"No, thank you. Chamomile makes me sick," I lied.

Julia lowered herself to her stool. "I've added some nice spices to help the taste a bit. Cloves and cardomon, a little nutmeg. Drink it." She pushed the cup underneath my nose. "It will smooth everything away." She looked at me, her white skin glowing under the ghastly greenhouse lights. I half expected a black cat to appear crouched on her shoulder. I held my lips together tightly and refused to drink.

"You're quite wet again," Julia said softly, touching my forehead with pudgy, foam rubber fingers. She placed the cup on her lap. "You'll feel better after I dry you off." She reached into the sleeve of her flowered bathrobe and pulled out a long chiffon scarf, like a magician showing off a new trick. So in keeping, I thought stupidly and then stopped. That vague, familiar sensation seized me again. I stared at the scarf Julia was patting along my body. It was red. A dark red that shone eerily in the purple light of that room. As I looked at that soft heap of red nearing my face, I gasped for breath. I was on the street again, the white heat of the headlights hitting my face. Just as my face hit the asphalt, a flash of red crossed my eyes. A memory slipped neatly into place.

266

"Oh, Julia," I cried. "Why did you use Fred's letter?"

The cup with its mysterious brew crashed to the floor.

Chapter Twenty-nine

This was going to be the worst Monday of them all, I thought, as I watched people gather in Fred's office. Exactly two weeks before, Giovanna had discovered Fred's body lying dead on the plush carpet — now the luxurious office of the creative director of HH&H had become the appropriate place to bring an end to the mystery of his death.

Evelyn greeted me with an encouraging, "God, you look awful," and sat on an armchair. A subdued Wally stood guard behind her. Julia lowered herself onto the gray leather sofa next to Mattie and Dana and stared at her lap. Giovanna refused a chair "out of respect for the dead" and stood in the corner nearest the door. I doubt she had ever sat in the same room with Fred, dead or alive. Jenny sat straight up in her customary chair in front of the desk, as if poised for dictation. Ann walked in, swishing her blue silk Lauren skirt, and sank gracefully into the armchair next to Evelyn. Gregory was the last to arrive. He closed the door softly and leaned against it. With my notes in hand, I stood behind the desk next to Fred's empty chair and faced them all. I briefly explained I had tripped and fallen on the sidewalk to justify my swollen, bruised face. Thankfully no one asked questions. Fred's death was center stage.

"I've called this meeting because on Friday we were given an ultimatum," I began in a flat voice. I was

268

going to conduct this as a business meeting—no emotions showing.

"On Friday," I continued, "Mr. Janick told us that if we did not find his missing perfume bottle by today, he would sue us. We all know what that would mean to the agency."

Ann groaned and clutched the hem of her skirt.

"But that's not the only problem," I said. "Although the police released Mattie, they are now questioning Bertrand. He might be charged with Fred's murder any minute now."

"Why are they picking on Bertrand this time?" Gregory asked, putting one sneakered foot against the door as if to keep it shut. "Has anything new come up?"

"Giovanna found a letter and handed it over to the police," I said. "Apparently it held some incriminating information . . ."

"Oh, that's terrible," Jenny whispered in front of me.

". . . but I'd like to get to that later. Please let me go on." I took a deep breath and fixed my eyes on my notes. "With all of this going on, I decided I should try to find the answers to some questions that had cropped up, in hopes of discovering who the real killer was, and what had happened to the perfume bottle that Fred had given to Ann."

"I wasn't allowed to wear it in the office," Ann said, nervously folding the edge of her skirt into tiny pleats. "He was afraid someone would find out I had it. My mistake was not taking the bottle home. But I never wore it in the office, and I didn't tell anyone about it."

"You told Wally," Evelyn said.

"Well," Ann said, blushing under her Janick, Inc. *Fraîcheur d'Automne* foundation, "Wally's on the account. He's safe."

Wally lifted himself up on his toes and beamed at the room in general.

"Supposedly, no one else knew about the bottle except Giovanna," I said.

At the sound of her name, Giovanna moved toward me.

"Don't worry, I'm not accusing you of anything." I told her. "You did know about Ann having the bottle because Fred told you. You knew, Wally knew, and I think someone else knew, too."

"How?" was Ann's simple question.

"Wally is not exactly a paragon of silence," I answered.

"Wally is not the only one who could have spread the word," Evelyn quickly argued. "Fred liked the sound of his own voice too."

"True," I admitted. "And Fred was close to many of you here. Jenny kept his life in order in the office, Giovanna did the same at home. Evelyn helped him run the creative department, and Julia was a friend from way back. Dana was his protégée . . ."

"Why did someone steal my bottle?" Ann interrupted. "That's what we must find out. Why?" Her long hands fluttered across the silk of her lap. "If the scent turns up with a competitor, my career is ruined."

"It wasn't stolen for espionage purposes," I told her. "It was stolen to kill Fred Critelli."

Ann gasped. At that moment her face did not look like it had any freshness of autumn on it at all. It was more like the *Rigueurs d'Hiver.*

"How can a perfume kill someone?" Gregory asked skeptically from his post at the door.

"This particular perfume killed Fred because he happened to be allergic to it," I said. "Giovanna let that important detail slip out this past Friday. Fred's allergy gave the murderer the opportunity to offer

270

the Nozphree capsules, full of cyanide, as supposed relief."

"The murderer would have had to know about the allergy," Wally countered.

"Whoever killed Fred was on very intimate terms with him," I answered him quickly, anxious to get on with my story. "First, the murderer spilled the perfume on Fred . . ."

"How do you know that? You weren't there," Wally interrupted.

"Detective Garcia told me he had noticed a colorless stain on the back of the shirt Fred was wearing that Sunday," I explained. "But if perfume had been spilled, I wondered, how come no one smelled it?"

Mattie slapped a heavy hand on Fred's desk. "That's why it was so cold that Monday morning!"

"That's right. The murderer increased the air-conditioning to get rid of the smell."

Gregory let go of the door and took two steps into the room. "Why bother to do that?" he asked.

Wally happily opened his mouth. "Since I'm assuming Simona is trying to tell us that the murderer is one of us, and therefore an employee, I can only suppose he or she did not wish to lose a job, which we all would if 'Free' were to be discovered as the modus operandi of a murder."

"That sounds pretty plausible to me," Evelyn said, looking around to see if her colleagues agreed.

"But the cops said the Nozphree bottle only had Fred's fingerprints on it," Mattie said. She got up and walked around the room. As her weight left the middle of the sofa, Dana, momentarily unbalanced, tilted toward the heavier Julia, and their shoulders almost touched.

"How did that happen?" Mattie asked. "It would look kinda funny if the murderer wore gloves in the middle of July." As she sat down next to me in Fred's empty chair, I heard Giovanna's sharp intake of breath.

"The murderer could easily have wiped off the prints when Fred wasn't looking," Evelyn said. "And then offered the bottle perched on the palm of the hand."

"What about motive," Ann asked and looked around the room with narrowed eyes. "Who had a motive?"

"As Gregory once told me, almost everyone," I told her. "Fred liked to collect little secrets that he could use to his advantage. Fred also found it easy to make women fall in love with him."

"You can count me out, honey," Mattie snorted.

Julia smiled and two bright pink rounds highlighted her cheeks. "He had something I never encountered in any other man—an added charm, a fourth dimension. He made things exciting, vibrant." She sighed happily. "He could be happiness and misery all at the same time."

"Well, I knew better than to fall for a guy like that," Ann said. She inspected her long nails colored with 'Peau,' Janick, Inc.'s flesh-colored nail polish. "I let him know right from the beginning it was no go."

Julia turned to look at Ann. Her round, childlike face, surrounded by erratic wisps of thinning hair looked suddenly sad. "Fred liked vulnerable, pliant women," she said. "You're hardly that, are you, Ann, dear?"

"What about you, Dana?" I asked in a quiet voice.

She looked up at me quickly. The skin of her face seemed to tighten and hug her skull.

"You were in the office the Sunday Fred got killed." Her eyes widened in fear.

"Even though your I.D. number didn't show up on the sensor, you were there. Wally saw you." I took a step toward her.

272

"I lost my card," Dana said, addressing her Maud Frizon shoes. They couldn't answer back. "I'm always losing it. It's the third time."

"Oh, Dana, dear, don't worry about it so," Julia said and patted Dana's arm. She used her voice as a soothing balm. "I've lost mine countless times. 'Moneybags' just pretends he's angry. He doesn't mind at all."

"You had to see Fred that day whether you had a card or not," I continued. "Why, Dana? Why was it so urgent you see Fred? What was going to happen the next day?"

Dana's eyes let go of her shoes and slowly looked up at me. Then she looked at all the other expectant faces. She turned back to me. "You know, don't you?"

"Yes, I do, but I thought you might prefer to tell it."

"Go ahead and tell it, Dana, honey," Mattie said with a soft clap of her hands. "It's gonna come out soon enough."

Dana addressed her words to Mattie, the only smiling face in the room. "I'm expecting Fred's baby."

Giovanna whispered a *"Ges Maria"* and made the sign of the cross. I looked down at my notes and folded them.

"When I told Fred," Dana continued in a high voice that crashed against the walls of the room, "he was dead set against it. He told me," she stopped and swallowed, "he told me I was to get rid of it or he'd never see me again. He even threatened to fire me. At first I said 'yes.' I was so in love with him." She looked at Julia as she said this. Understanding Julia gave her another reassuring pat.

"He even made the appointment for me. I was to go that Monday, the Monday he was found dead. I was all set to do it and then, about two weeks before, I started getting morning sickness. Every morning it

273

got worse. My whole body got violently ill. It was like the baby was protesting, making me pay for that decision."

"The Lord speaks in many ways," Mattie said.

"I called Fred from home that Friday morning. I was so sick I couldn't come to the office. I talked to him." Dana lowered her voice to her shoes again, the words coming out in hiccups as she constantly swallowed to hold back the tears.

"I told him I couldn't go through with it, that I wanted the baby more than I wanted him. That's what I told him. He laughed. He actually laughed." She held her forehead in her hand and rubbed her fingers back and forth. Those pacing fingers reminded me of caged animals.

"I begged him not to fire me. I promised I wouldn't ask him for anything, if only he'd let me keep my job. I told him no one was going to hire a pregnant art director especially if he blackballed me. Then I got completely hysterical. He tried to calm me down. He offered to see me in the office on Sunday, after his meeting, to talk things over. I was so worried all weekend I forgot I had lost my I.D. card. I only remembered when I got here on Sunday, and I didn't dare interrupt the meeting."

"So you called the one person you had confided in," I said. "The woman who told the police a Nozphree capsule would have been bad for you. You must have asked her for the keys to the office, but Mattie probably insisted on coming in herself to open up. Maybe she wanted to reassure you with her presence. Anyway, she came, let you in, and that's when the news vendor saw her. You were going to keep the keys, let yourself out, and then return them to her the following morning."

Dana looked at Mattie. Mattie closed her eyelids slowly, once. Dana was free to speak.

"Yes, Mattie has been very good to me. She even went to jail for me. She didn't say a word to the police." Dana held her stomach with her two arms and leaned forward protectively. "I just couldn't tell them. They would have arrested me. I had the baby to think of."

"Don't you worry," Mattie said. "Mattie's got real big shoulders. It worked out okay. You still got the baby and the both of us got a job."

"What happened that night?" I asked Dana.

"After seeing Wally, I waited downstairs in my office." Dana looked across the room. "Fred liked to spend Sunday afternoon in this office, getting his work done. He said that he couldn't work at home because Giovanna was always hovering over him."

Giovanna made a small disapproving sound with her tongue.

"That's where we'd meet sometimes." Dana's eyes glazed over. "Right here. I'd pick him up, maybe do some work together, and then we'd go to my apartment."

"What about Sunday night?" I reminded her.

"After I heard the elevator going several times, I called up and got no answer. I just sat in my office in a panic thinking he had changed his mind and wasn't going to see me. I was just getting ready to go up to his office again when he called me."

"Do you remember what time he called?" I asked.

"It was a little after three-thirty. All he said was 'seven o'clock,' and I looked at my watch. That meant he wasn't going to see me until then. When he just gave me the time it usually meant someone was with him." Dana leaned back and rested her head on the back of the sofa. "How did you find out I was pregnant?"

"Bertrand made a comment about you and Fred that told me you were having an affair," I answered.

275

"Right after that, Evelyn mentioned you were missing deadlines, which was very unlike you. Then I noticed you were gaining weight and not feeling well. To top it off, you threw up in Central Park, after the police left you."

"I thought I was going to die," Dana moaned.

"To tell the truth, I wasn't clever enough to pick up on those clues by myself," I admitted. "What really put the idea in my head was a movie I watched on television, *To Each His Own.*"

"Lovely film," Julia interjected with a surprisingly firm voice. "Olivia De Havilland becomes pregnant, but the father dies in the war before he can marry her. She has the child anyway, and lives happily ever after. At least I think she did. I do remember my handkerchief was drenched in tears at the end." Julia opened her handbag and offered Dana a crumpled lace handkerchief.

No one said anything after that. Evelyn was wriggling her nose, about to sneeze, while Wally held her shoulders protectively. Gregory looked down at the gray carpet and nervously shifted from one sneakered foot to the other. Jenny sat at the edge of her chair, her minute body tautly stretched toward Dana. Ann was looking at Dana with undisguised disgust. Giovanna was still, a pious angel standing guard. Julia opened and shut her handbag repeatedly, the sound of the soft snapping like the slow ticking of a bomb. Mattie sat up straight in Fred's chair, her eyes closed. She looked like she was praying.

"I didn't kill Fred," Dana said. "You don't really think I did, do you?" She looked at her colleagues with the big moist eyes of a cow before the slaughter.

"You planted Fred's ring in my desk," I said in a flat voice. "When you saw Fred dead on the floor, you couldn't resist taking some romantic memento of your affair. You took the ring from his outstretched

276

arm and calmly let yourself out of the building with Mattie's key. When Mr. Harland spoke of cyanide poisoning and officially introduced the police, you got scared. What if they started a search and found the ring? They would connect you to the murder and once they found out you were pregnant, that would be it. Once Harland's meeting was over, you rushed upstairs and planted the ring in my Kleenex box."

Dana burst into fresh tears and covered her face with her massive black hair.

"When I walked into my office and found you there," I continued in a gentler tone, "you made up the story about no longer needing Paul Langston to justify your presence. I would never have connected the dots if you hadn't used Langston to shoot the Merry Shirts ad anyway."

"He was the best for the job," she said while wiping her nose on Julia's handkerchief. "I did take the ring," she admitted between prolonged sniffs. "But I swear to all of you I didn't kill him. He was dead when I got there, I swear." She bit into her lower lip to stop its trembling. "I thought he had died of a stroke or something."

"The police might find your story a little hard to believe," Ann crooned.

"What about Bertrand?" Dana screamed. "Why won't you believe Bertrand killed Fred? They couldn't stand each other." She turned around to face me. "Why don't you tell them about the letter. Go on," she was practically spitting the words at me. "Tell them what the letter said and then we'll see who had more reason to kill Fred."

"You tell us, Dana," Evelyn barked back at her. "Since you know so much about it, you tell us."

Dana cleared her nose with one long, hard sniff. "Fred was blackmailing him to stay with the agency. Just like he was blackmailing you, Evelyn, for drinking too much. Simona was right about Fred collecting secrets. He knew things about all of you," Dana said, waving Julia's handkerchief across the room. It had turned black with running mascara. "Anyone of you could have killed him."

"Harland told me Fred was going to fire Julia on Monday," Ann contributed with a toss of her blond coif.

"Never," Julia gasped. "He was my friend. He was not going to fire me." She snapped open her handbag. "I can prove it." She took a much folded letter from her change purse and opened it gingerly, as if afraid it might crumble to the touch. "Read it to them," she said, handing me her treasure. "You know what it says."

I took the letter and started reading the typewritten words.

"Julia — Harry Harland has just called me, demanding that I fire you because you didn't show up at the right studio to shoot the Belvino commercial. Can you believe he had the gall to use the word "demand" with me? He seems to forget I can shut his mouth whenever I want to, but he is not the reason I refuse to fire you. You and I simply go back too far. You've been a friend throughout the years — perhaps my only friend. Without you around, I know my luck would run out.

I admit I was upset with you at first, but *don't worry*. I refuse to fire you. What I will do is hire a capable assistant never to leave your side. If you have anyone you would like to fill that position, let me know ASAP."

                                                            Fred

I looked up at my silent audience. "In one of my

conversations with Julia this past week, she had mentioned a letter to me. I had completely forgotten about it until last night, at which point I accused her of having planted the letter incriminating Bertrand in Fred's typewriter for Giovanna to find. That's when she showed me this letter." I lifted the piece of paper for everyone to see. "This proves Julia would have wanted Fred very much alive."

Julia took her letter, folded, and put it back into her change purse. "His luck ran out anyway," she said with a long sigh. "It's so very sad, my dear." Julia patted Dana's knee. "He had quite made up his mind, and he was so happy. Friday night at dinner he told me all about you and the baby, and the abortion. You had just stood up to him. Not many people did that, you know. That's why he laughed. That you were willing to lose him and your job for your baby made him quite happy." Julia took a long, much needed breath. "He thought you had 'a lot of spunk.' He said he had never found a woman he couldn't command. Until you. That's what he said. And he talked about getting old. He told me he might like the idea of a Fred II being around. It was a way of fighting death, he said."

Dana gasped. "Did he really say he wanted a Fred II around?"

"Yes, yes," Julia said, patting her again. "He even mentioned marriage. Try to find some solace in that. What's done is done and there's no going back. But a happy memory can help."

"For Christ's sake, Julia," Evelyn spurted out. "If you knew all this, why didn't you tell the police? I can understand why Mattie kept her mouth shut, but not you."

"No," Julia said loudly and snapped her handbag shut. "They would have arrested Dana. And with Dana, her baby too. Fred wouldn't have wanted that

279

for either of them."

"You can't help her now," Ann said, unwrapping her thin, long legs and sitting back in her armchair. "We can't all keep it from the police."

"Dana is not the only woman in love with Fred," I stated. "Someone else has been close to him for a very long time. Maybe since Fred's Chicago days. Someone who knew everything about him, from his blackmailing schemes to his unfortunate perfume allergy. It was because of Fred's allergy to 'Free' that last May, while Mattie was on vacation and couldn't ask questions, this person took the Nozphree bottle from the first aid room and kept it handy. Murder wasn't a possibility yet. At that point she only wanted to help the man she loved, despite his affair with Dana. Maybe she had grown accustomed to his escapades, maybe Fred always told her, 'stick with me kid, you're the one I really love.'"

I stopped, my mouth suddenly dry. For a moment I felt the sharp pain of my own Roman past. I was feeling and talking about a pain familiar to thousands of women who were left in despair and anger, and who rarely struck back.

"I know Fred asked her to arrange Dana's abortion," I continued without looking at my silent audience, "because I saw the doctor's name on her office calendar, saw the same name advertised in an ice cream store. When I made the connection a few days later I did not suspect her of murder, only of loving Fred and doing his bidding. Until last night I was convinced Fred had been murdered by Dana." I finally looked up at the faces around me. "Last night Julia told me that there was not going to be an abortion, that Fred might even marry Dana."

"But Dana's just admitted she didn't know that," logical Gregory said.

"No, she didn't," I agreed. "Only Julia and the

murderer knew." I looked down at only one face.

"When did Fred tell you to cancel that abortion appointment?" I asked Jenny.

She shook her bright orange head. "What do you mean, Simona? He didn't ask me to cancel anything. Dana was going to abort." She ran small hands through her tight curls. "He insisted she abort. He told me that."

"I think Fred told you something very different the Friday before he died," I said. "I think he told you Dana wasn't going to go through with it. I think he might have even told you he was happy about it." Her head continued to shake in disbelief.

"You must love babies very much to dedicate your free time to holding them and rocking them to sleep," I went on. "But you don't love Dana's baby. Why should you? While loving Fred, you had grown too old for babies of your own. Now he was going to have a baby with someone else, and you were going to lose him for good."

"Simona, I don't think you mean any of this," Jenny said, her face still naively happy in disbelief.

"That Sunday," I continued, "you probably called Fred from a corner pay phone, after you had seen everyone leave the building. You convinced him to let you in, maybe saying you had found the missing 'Free' bottle which you had actually stolen from Ann's desk two days before. Even though Fred must have known you weren't happy about Dana keeping the baby, his blinding ego would never let him suspect that faithful little Jenny could wish him harm. He postponed Dana's appointment in your presence, but you had no way of knowing she was in the building. Actually you were very lucky, Jenny. Gregory was in the building, too. On the very same floor, working on some ads for Dana. Had he seen you, Fred might still be alive today. But Fred's good luck had run out in spite of Julia. You were in this office with him a long time, at least two and a half hours. Did you try to convince him he had no right to ruin your life? Or was there some happy reminiscing—perhaps even one last moment of love? However you passed those hours, I know that you 'accidentally' spilled perfume on Fred, offered him the two cyanide capsules that you had brought with you, made sure he was dead, and then let yourself out of the building at five-twenty-seven with Fred's I.D. card. The only hitch to your plan came when Fred fell over the empty Nozphree bottle, which had fallen on the carpet, and you did not have the physical strength and perhaps the courage to move his dead body to retrieve it."

"How can you say that?" Jenny protested, her mask of happiness beginning to crack. "I didn't say a word about Dana to the police."

"You didn't want to call attention to yourself. You wanted to keep playing the role of Fred's optimistic, bouncy secretary, making sure everyone liked you. Perhaps you even felt last-minute remorse regarding the baby, or perhaps you figured the police would find out sooner or later. You kept your mouth shut and watched. When Mattie was arrested you felt safe."

Jenny held her face with her small hands, as if to keep it from falling apart, shaking her head in denial.

"But then Mattie was released," I continued unshaken, "and you got scared. Wally had seen you with the boarder babies; I had seen the doctor's name written in your calendar and knew he wasn't just a gynocologist. You had even made the mistake of mentioning to me that you had moved to Chicago, where Fred had lived for so many years. Suddenly you must have felt very vulnerable. It was too late to point the finger at Dana without arousing some suspicion, so you dug up Fred's blackmailing letter, which he might have asked you to guard for him, and planted it in his typewriter for Giovanna to find. By sheer coincidence, one of the studio employees tried to steal the typewriter, and the letter was found even faster than you had hoped for."

"This makes a fascinating story," Wally said, reaching for his pimples, "but can you prove any of it?"

"But there's nothing to prove. Simona doesn't mean any of this," Jenny insisted.

Oh, yes, I do, I thought, not daring to voice the words for fear I might back off, deny what I knew to be the ugly truth. I turned toward Wally, eager to avoid Jenny's face. "Jenny was in Central Park yesterday . . ."

"Yes, I was." Jenny popped up from her chair and took a few bouncing steps away from me. "That doesn't make me a murderer." She looked straight at me, sharp nose first, then wide, hurting eyes. Seeing her stand in her frail high heels surrounded by solemn, staring faces, I was reminded of a sparrow among pigeons, feathers desperately fluffed to make itself look bigger, holding on to that piece of bread, all the time knowing it doesn't have a chance.

That's how she must have held on to Fred, I thought, and said, "You followed me and overheard me refuse to tell Greenhouse who the murderer was. You realized you had to act quickly if you didn't want to be discovered. Too bad you didn't know I was convinced Dana was the culprit. If you had just gone home, I would have no proof at all. But you didn't. You followed me to the bus stop and when you saw the oncoming bus, you couldn't resist. One hard push, and it would be all over."

Jenny started to laugh. Short waves of shrill sound shattered the tomblike silence of the room.

"You can't laugh this away, Jenny," I told her. "I

saw you just as I hit the sidewalk. I saw your bright, new, red shoes standing right next to my face."

She didn't stop. She stood in the middle of the room, her small body shaking in shoes half buried in the plush carpet. Black shoes this time.

The door to Fred's bathroom opened and Greenhouse stepped out. "Red high heels may not hold up in a courtroom, but the eyewitness account of a New York policeman will." Greenhouse moved to one side. Pigtail stood behind him.

At that moment, Evelyn let go of a soul-clearing sneeze.

Epilogue

Dana thinks it was 'pretty neat' of me to figure out who had killed Fred. Now that the whole agency knows she's expecting Fred's child, she walks around prouder and louder than ever. She's sweeter, though, and we're getting along better these days. I think prospective motherhood has softened her prickly skin. Giovanna has found a new home with Dana. In April, she plans to give up her job at HH&H and take care of Fred's baby full time. Giovanna still walks around the agency shrouded in black, but a radiant smile has appeared on her face.

Luis often boasts about the time he caught the thief and saved Giovanna's life and virtue. He's gained a lot of weight lately and rumor has it that he is often seen leaving the agency kitchen smacking his lips. I wonder if food is the only thing a smiling Giovanna is giving him.

Wally and Evelyn are still at it. She continues to sneeze at inappropriate moments; he continues to talk at inappropriate moments. Their relationship is out in the open now. Evelyn doesn't rasp as much, and her drinking has become only an ugly memory.

My bad memories are slowly disappearing. I wake up happier every day. I still miss Rome, especially at sunset when New York turns orange long enough for me to remember the ocher of my native city. Nostalgia lingers, but I've started to look forward. "That's where it's all at," Mattie assures me. The two H's gave me that raise I wanted to ask for that first fateful Monday morning. It isn't much, but it's enough to allow me to continue living in Manhattan. I think the H's were grateful I supplied Jenny as the murderer. A good secretary is so much easier to find than a good art director. With Fred gone, they were going to fire her anyway.

All of us offered to help raise the money for Jenny's bail, but she refused. She's started a secretarial school which has turned out to be a great success with the inmates. Jenny told Mattie she enjoys the attention she gets as a teacher, says she doesn't feel skimpy anymore. One day I'll screw up enough courage to visit her. Meanwhile, I go and cuddle some of her boarder babies on weekends. I know she'd like that.

After Bertrand was cleared of Fred's murder, he sent me a dozen long-stemmed yellow roses with a "thank you" and an "I'm sorry". The kiss in the cab and the invitation to a weekend in Connecticut have been forgotten by both of us. Bertrand has also made sure Julia's still at HH&H. Sometimes I see her new, "efficient" assistant desperately looking for her in the corridors of the agency and I laugh, because I know that Julia can appear and disappear at will with a wave of her magic wand.

Bertrand's and Janick's love for each other is still a secret. Most of the agency doesn't know, and those of us who do, pretend we don't. I suspect that includes Mummy.

I've asked Mattie about her nephew, Buddy, and she tells me he's doing fine. He finally found a job with a downtown quick-printing company, where they're teaching him how to operate copiers. Mentioning Buddy reminds me of the one question mark I haven't been able to answer. I'm not sure whom

Fred was trying to protect when he fired Buddy, but I've begun to wonder about Mr. Harland and his frequent trips. Fred's letter to Julia mentioned he could have shut Mr. Harland's mouth whenever he wanted to, and I hear you can get a great tan in Betty Ford's back yard in California.

All of HH&H is in a flurry about the big bash at the Plaza in October. The ballroom is going to be covered with photos of Ellen raising a glass of champagne to the sun climbing over the Grand Canyon. Liters of 'Free' will be sprayed into the air, and each female guest will go home with a white satin purse embroidered with a burst of colored beads spelling the perfume's name and full of Janick, Inc. cosmetics, including a half ounce of 'Free.' Scriba's photographs are gorgeous and Ellen is gorgeous. She's also very happy. She has moved in with Gregory permanently, and he goes around offering food and drink to everyone in the office like a brand new father. With Ellen at his side, Gregory has finally found the courage to venture outside of his own country. They're going to Venice for a Christmas vacation. That's the best present they could have given me.

Only the top management of the agency is going to the party, plus those who work for the Janick account, which in these days of looming deadlines is almost half the agency. My invitation is taped to my bathroom mirror, requesting me to "Celebrate 'Free' at last!" which I have every intention of doing. Scriba's studio has promised to get me that black lace and green velvet dress that Ellen danced in, which means I won't be able to smoke all night for fear of burning a hole in it. But with Greenhouse as my date that's just as well.

By the way, I finally painted my graffiti wall. The black squiggles the thief left don't match my mood anymore. Now I have a sparkling clean wall just waiting for new photographs. Maybe the first one will be a shot of Greenhouse walking through Washington Square Park in the bright light of morning. In his tuxedo.